THESE

THINGS

HAPPEN

MICHAEL EON

THESE

THINGS

HAPPEN

A NOVEL

GIRL FRIDAY BOOKS

This is a work of fiction. Names, characters, organizations, places, events, and incidents are either products of the author's imagination or are used fictitiously.

 GIRL FRIDAY BOOKS

Published by Girl Friday Books™, Seattle
www.girlfridaybooks.com

Produced by Girl Friday Productions

Cover Design: Megan Katsanevakis
Production editorial: Laura Dailey
Project management: Mari Kesselring

Image credits: cover © Danny Lyon/Environmental Protection Agency/National Archives

ISBN (paperback): 978-1-959411-16-1
ISBN (ebook): 978-1-959411-17-8

Library of Congress Control Number: 2023904965

First edition

For Kit

CHAPTER 1

With the palms of his hands on his pale cheeks, Max sat at the kitchen table and moaned in pain. It was the morning of October 30, 1995—a Monday—and my older brother had just tried to kill himself. Fortunately, the barrel of the gun had not been perpendicular to his temple—more like forty-five degrees—so though the result was gruesome, it was not fatal. A small piece of his scalp and skull lay on the floor behind his chair. The slice of skin, covered in brown hair, had curled up. It looked like a miniature sugar cone. The little fragment of skull lay concave, like a wet piece of dirty pottery. The area of exposed brain, though clearly nicked, appeared largely intact.

On the white tile floor, beneath the kitchen table, lay a half-peeled, uneaten banana. It was the only one missing from the bunch on the table. The bananas were almost perfect. Peak yellow and exquisitely ripe, the peel of each unblemished but for one thing: a handwritten notation in blue ink. Max had been writing the days of the week on his bananas for as long as I could remember. Whenever Mom returned home from the supermarket, my eldest brother, Harry, and I would dig inside the big brown bags for the cookies and chips. Not Max. He'd search for the bananas, and when he found them, he'd label each with a day of the week.

"These are mine. Keep your hands off," he'd demand every time, which was fine with Harry and me. We preferred the junk food.

Now, a banana marked "Monday" lay on the ground near his feet.

I grabbed the .22-caliber pistol off the kitchen table, flipped on the safety, and shoved it into my jacket pocket.

"No." Max reached for it. There was anguish in his voice. "It's mine." He said it matter-of-factly, as if I would actually give it to him.

"Cut it out." I stepped behind him so he couldn't reach me. I tried to remain calm, but my voice, echoing inside the small apartment, sounded shaky. I would not be giving this gun back to Max. Not that it made a difference. He was a grown man. I knew he could get another gun whenever he wanted to. But that was a problem for later.

Groaning, Max reached for his head.

"Don't touch." I pushed his hands away.

A siren wailed in the distance, making its way through the walls of Max's third-floor studio apartment, located on Ridge Boulevard in the Fort Hamilton section of Brooklyn. His kitchen countertop was littered with at least a dozen empty beer cans and one empty bottle of El Toro tequila, wearing its little red sombrero cap. Only two days before, I'd begged him to come with me to an AA meeting. He'd refused, the way he always did.

"Suicide isn't an option, Max," I said now. The words coming out of my mouth sounded surreal to me. I couldn't believe I was in the position of having to say them to anyone, let alone my brother. Max had been struggling for a long time. But I'd had no idea his desperation would make him do something like this.

Max fell toward the table, his shoulders shaking as he began to cry. I caught him with one arm and gently lowered his forehead to the table edge, then began to rub his back. Across the table lay the remainder of the bunch of bananas—a total of six—each marked by day for the rest of the week. I couldn't understand what had happened. He obviously hadn't planned on killing himself when he labeled the bananas the day before.

I held him as he sobbed and rocked in the chair. His forehead banged on the edge of the table each time he moved forward.

With one hand pressed against the wound on the top of his head, I tried to stop his rocking with the other. The siren outside grew louder and closer. "Hang on, Max. They're almost here."

The seconds felt like hours. In those moments, I thought how lucky we both were that I was even here. I hadn't planned on stopping by Max's place after my meeting. I'd simply followed an impulse. *Why?* Was the fact that I had come on this day, at this moment, due to luck? Coincidence? God?

Max was no longer rocking, and I returned to rubbing his back with my free hand. I felt helpless. Max was unwell. He'd been unwell for as long as I could remember. Existence had seemed to him miserable, pointless, or absurd. *Life is a cruel joke.* That was his motto. He'd been miserable for years, but I'd never believed he was a danger to himself. None of us had.

"I won't let you do it," I whispered into his ear.

Max lifted his head shakily. "It's my life, not yours," he whispered back, and then he leaned heavily to one side and fell off the chair.

Catching him in my arms, I lowered us both to the ground. As we waited, I sat there, dazed, my brother heavy in my arms. The wound was like a red eye staring back at me, and I had to turn away.

Lying there against my chest, Max was warm. He was

still alive. I couldn't believe how close I'd come to losing him. Though I was shocked by what he'd done, I probably shouldn't have been. All three of us Zimmer brothers had run from our family, from our shared past, in one way or another. As I'd grown older, however, the challenge had changed for me. It was no longer just about running from something. It was also about trying not to self-destruct along the way.

CHAPTER 2

It was a hazy Brooklyn morning in 1975 when our father took Max and me to Woolworth and slapped some money into our hands. I felt the force of the gift like a sting. Walter Zimmer was a big man. That summer, I was skinny and not quite five feet, and my father believably claimed to be six three. But it felt to me like he was twice my height, and at roughly 230 pounds, he was almost three times as heavy. His face reminded me of Superman's: strong and chiseled, except for his nose, which was crooked from all the fights he had gotten into as a kid. His black hair was always pushed back on the sides and on top, and he typically wore starched white or solid-colored shirts and pressed dark slacks. Nothing was ever out of place on Walter Zimmer.

"Here's two dollars for each of you," he said when the bills hit our palms.

Max and I looked at each other in disbelief. Our mom had recently taken us shopping for some school supplies. But Dad had told her that things were going well at his brokerage firm, and he was going to take us to get something special. It was only the second time in my twelve years—and Max's fourteen—that Dad had given us money to buy ourselves something.

"Make the right choice."

We nodded and took off in different directions. Max ran straight to the cap guns, Dad following. As I turned from one side of the toy aisle to the other, the choices and colors made me woozy with pleasure. I knew exactly what I was searching for: a Wolfman action figure.

"*Dan-iel!*" After what felt like only a couple of minutes, Max shouted my name from farther down the aisle, waving a cap gun. "Come on. Let's go!" he called. Dad appeared behind him, stone-faced with his arms crossed.

I eyed the shelves anxiously in search of something that looked like the monster. A few nights before, I had watched my favorite Lon Chaney Jr. film on TV again—I'd seen it several times. I could relate to him. Somehow, I sensed that there was a raging animal inside of me, too.

"Come on, Daniel!" Max shouted. Now he and Dad were in the checkout line.

With time running out, I broadened my search to any-thing monster related. Movies, books, television shows—if something was scary or gruesome, I loved it. I was especially drawn to old silent horror films. In contrast to my own life, which felt unpredictable and perilous, scary movies followed a train of logic that made a kind of sense to my young mind; watching them soothed me as nothing else could.

In the next aisle, I finally found the perfect choice: a small rubber Wolfman figurine. I yanked the monster off the rack, then rushed to the front of the store. I slapped it on the counter beside Max's cap gun and grinned at my brother in victory. He rolled his eyes.

"What the hell is that?" Removing his glasses, Dad bent to look, then turned on me. "You're not getting a doll."

"It's not a doll. It's the Wolf—"

"Put it back where you found it. *Right now.*"

Recoiling from the bite in his voice, I stumbled down the aisle to go drop the monster back on the shelf. It didn't matter to my father what I wanted. It didn't matter what any of us wanted. Max had, in the moment, simply chosen the path of least resistance. He'd do anything to gain Dad's favor. Why else would he—a teenager who loved music and who always spent his birthday and Christmas money on magazines—have chosen a cap gun over *Hit Parade* magazine?

Putting the Wolfman back on the shelf, I decided that if I couldn't get what I wanted, I wouldn't get anything. When I returned to the counter, however, Max dropped a second cap gun and box of caps in front of me and snickered. It was one of those rare times when Dad's wrath was directed at someone other than him, so, of course, he was eating the moment up.

"You're getting this," Dad announced. He pushed the gun and caps to the clerk, who let out a forceful breath but otherwise remained silent. "Put your money down."

I clenched my fist around my two dollars. I didn't want to let them go. "But I don't want a cap gun."

Max's smug grin vanished, and his eyes widened.

My father's response was immediate. "I don't give a shit what you want."

"Yeah, well I don't give a shit what *you* want, either!" I shouted. I knew better than to talk to him this way. But the words just popped out.

Dad stared at me in shock. His face turned red and contorted, and the veins in his neck popped. Every muscle in my body tensed, and I closed my eyes and shrank into myself, waiting for his backhand.

Then I heard a thunderous clap of laughter. Opening my eyes, I saw Dad bent over, slapping the counter. Max, white as a ghost, stood behind him in disbelief.

"Kids today . . ." Dad said to the clerk, almost weeping. "What boy doesn't want a gun?"

Swiftly, he grabbed the two bills I still held in one hand, threw them onto the counter, and then picked up the guns and caps and strode past us to the car.

I watched from the store entrance as Dad got into his yellowish-tan Buick LeSabre and started it. There was no doubt in my mind that his reaction at the register had been a ruse, a show for public consumption. He was livid, and I would surely be punished. As he pulled up to the curb, he scowled at me through his window and unlocked the rear doors with a click. Max slid into the back seat. I stepped onto the sidewalk in front of Woolworth's, hesitating before I followed him in. Dad threw the guns and boxes of caps onto the seat between us, hitting the yellow "Monday" banana Max had brought along as a snack.

The plastic cap gun had a gray barrel and an embossed black grip. With one finger, I traced a line from the base to the hammer and trigger and down the muzzle, then fit my finger through the trigger guard and twirled the gun in my hand. Clutching the grip, I brought the gun forward with my finger on the trigger. I looked at Dad in the rearview mirror, my eyes little more than slits.

Dad was watching me. "There you go, boy," he said as we pulled away from the curb.

I lifted my arm and pointed the muzzle directly at the back of the driver's seat. My arm shook, but my finger was stiff.

Max's eyes darted between me and the gun in my out-stretched arm. He nervously reached for his own and pointed it at the back of the driver's seat, too.

I turned back to Dad, who was still eyeing me in the rear-view mirror, then pulled my trigger and whispered, "Bang!" With smiles on our faces, Max and I brought the guns to our chests and blew imaginary smoke from the muzzles.

On the seat between us, the yellow banana lay pointed in Max's direction like a cartoon gun, unfired and uneaten.

———

That night, I lay in bed sucking on my thumb and listening to the buzzing of the battery-operated Mattel racing game that Max was playing under his comforter. Thumb-sucking had always soothed me. I didn't care one bit that I was twelve years old. The only people who saw me do it were my family, anyway.

"Not going to sleep?" I pulled my wet thumb from my mouth.

"What's the point?"

I knew what Max was saying. It was impossible for either of us to sleep until the thing that happened every night was over.

I rolled over and stared at the ceiling. It was almost nine, and Dad would be home any minute. He had gone straight to the office after dropping us at home that morning. To my shock, he hadn't bothered to punish me after I got in the LeSabre. The fact that I'd succumbed and played with the gun had apparently been enough to mollify him.

Our alarm clock ticked off the seconds, and the grandfather clock in the downstairs hallway began to chime. Even though each of the apartments in our building was split-level, it wasn't difficult to hear from our upstairs bedrooms what was happening downstairs. From the upstairs hallway landing, we could also see down into the foyer, den, and kitchen by peering through the railing spindles. We tried to keep away from our dad as much as we could, though, and usually stayed in our rooms, like we were doing now.

In his bed, Max was rocking back and forth—the neurotic ritual that soothed him while he awaited the inevitable. The rocking seemed a little strange to me, but who was I to judge?

"Any minute now," Max muttered.

"Wonder what she's going to do wrong tonight?" I asked.

I heard the igniter click on the stove downstairs. Within seconds, chicken cutlets crackled in oil, and my stomach growled. Mom had fed us boys hours before, but the smell of the late dinner she made our father every night always made me hungry again. Not that the rest of us ever got any of it.

The front door opened and slammed. The floorboards squeaked and I listened to the sounds of Dad striding into the kitchen and pulling out his chair at the table. I turned and hugged the wall, pressing the pillow against my ears and humming to myself.

But even from under my pillow, I could hear Dad's voice ringing through our bedroom door, which was slightly ajar. "What the hell is wrong with you, Arlene?"

I sank my front teeth into the permanent indentation around my right thumb and sucked hard.

Dishes clattered as Mom fumbled with them. Dad slammed his fists on the table. "Is what I want really so unreasonable?" That was our father's chief complaint in the world: *Everything I do, I do the right way. All I want in return is the same thing. Is that too much to ask?* "This is inedible! You know chicken cutlets need to be paper-thin! *Paper-thin!*"

I clamped the pillow around my head to drown out Dad's nightly lesson about how she had messed up. In his mind, mistakes were a betrayal of him, and perfection was the only option.

The doorbell rang, and Dad stomped out of the kitchen to answer it.

Max and I sat up in our beds. I stared across the room at my brother. His eyes were wide. My breath panted in time with my hammering heart.

"Who is it?" Dad barked. "Yeah, yeah. We're just fine—go back to your house."

I looked at Max. It was a neighbor, bothered by the yelling. I tensed up even more. Would the interruption make our father quiet down or only anger him further? Things could go either way.

"I hate that doorbell," Max whispered.

So did I. No good ever came from that tinny ring, especially when Dad was home. He hated people, particularly when they stuck their noses where they didn't belong. He dealt with people all day long. But for some reason, at home, he just couldn't deal with even one more.

Occasionally, someone from his work would stop by to pick up or drop off a file, and once or twice he'd given a ride to one worker or another who also lived in Brooklyn, and who'd made it to our neighborhood via the subway. But even that was something he barely tolerated, and in those cases, only he was allowed to answer the door. He fixated on the worry that some disgruntled vendor might come to the house. He also wanted to be able to stand in the doorway and determine when the exchange ended. This behavior was, I realized years later, one more manifestation of his controlling nature—and perhaps even an indication of barely controlled paranoia.

At the time, though, the rules made the rest of us nearly as paranoid as he was. Our mother became skittish, fearing how our father would react if someone dropped by. We kids weren't allowed to open the door to strangers, whether he was there or not, and the sound of the doorbell made us cringe. Our father's rule was a strange one, but we knew well not to break it.

I hopped off my bed and walked to the bedroom door.

"Don't go out there, Daniel."

But the wondering was driving me crazy. I crept down the hallway to the landing and watched my parents through the spindles.

Objectively, Walter and Arlene Zimmer were a good-looking couple. Mom had brownish-red hair that was usually pulled into a puffy bun on top of her head, brown eyes, and a nose that was larger than she wanted it to be. Her freckled cheeks were smooth, her jaw narrow, and she never left her bedroom without makeup on, as it helped mask her sad, tired eyes. With his strong features, Dad looked to me like Clark Kent, even at the end of the workday. His crisp work clothes—today, a starched white shirt and black slacks—added to the impression. My parents were only a year apart in age, but you'd never know it. At barely five feet tall, skinny as a rail, Mom could have passed as our older sister.

"This is how you do it!" Dad shouted. He was now banging his fist into a raw chicken cutlet on the island, his face contorted and red.

Mom turned away, her arms crossed and her head lowered. She looked so tired. She was always tired.

"See how thin this is?" Dad held up the cutlet. "Turn around, damn it!" Mom obeyed. "Look at this!" He pushed the meat into her face. "Can you see through it?"

Mom backed into the stove.

"Can you?"

"Yes," she whispered.

"I can't hear you!"

"Yes!" she replied, a little louder, pushing the cutlet away. The gesture was as close as she ever came to fighting back. I wondered sometimes why she let him treat her that way. It was clear to me that she was scared of him. Maybe she thought that if she stood up to him, he'd hit her too. Maybe she was even more afraid that he'd say something worse than the already terrible things he said to her.

I watched as he stormed back to the table, grabbed his plate, and dumped the thick, browned cutlets one by one into the garbage can beneath the sink. "Wasteful and inconsiderate," he grumbled.

Following some impulse, I tiptoed down the stairs and into

THESE THINGS HAPPEN   13

the hallway outside the kitchen, where I hid behind the kitchen doorframe. I was worried about Mom. I felt sorry for her.

Dad was now sitting at the kitchen table, where he was smoking a Lucky Strike and flipping through his work papers, seemingly oblivious to the effect of his outburst. I stared at Mom's solemn face through the crack in the door. I wanted to go hug her and tell her the cutlets didn't matter. Dad broke the lingering silence with a coughing fit that brought me back to reality. I couldn't go in there. I wouldn't.

The sound coming from the small black-and-white television on the counter caught my attention. "This is Bill Beutel for Eyewitness News." The image of a young woman, Karen Ann Quinlan, appeared on the television screen.

"Turn that shit off." Dad reached for the tall glass bottle on the kitchen table next to him. "I'm tired of seeing her goddamn face."

The subject of the story had been in the news for more than four months. Back in April, Karen Ann Quinlan had fallen into a coma and now she was considered brain-dead. Her parents wanted to take their hospitalized daughter off the ventilator that was keeping her alive. The local New Jersey prosecutor claimed that such a move would amount to homicide. My father was sick of the whole story and blamed the girl. She'd drugged herself into a coma, he said, so why did *he* have to hear about it every day, month after month?

He unscrewed the bottle's dark red cap and poured the brown liquid from the tall bottle into a short glass. The bottle was familiar—green glass with a yellow label, the word "Jameson" in black letters at the top. Never far away from my father, that bottle was always present: almost like a member of the family.

Mom popped the top off a pill bottle she'd picked up from the counter and fished inside it with her finger. She placed a little yellow pill on the tip of her tongue and swallowed hard.

She called these aids "Mommy's little helpers." I didn't know what they were, but she took them often. Whenever I'd ask about them, she'd only say, "Mommy's not feeling well."

Dad narrowed his eyes at her. "You and those goddamn pills. Maybe *they're* your problem, Arlene. Did you ever think of that?" He turned his gaze back to the television and pointed. "Look at her! You want to end up like that?"

Calmly, Mom walked past him to change the channel. She glared at the whiskey bottle but didn't say a word. When she turned back, she spied me in the hall and met my eye.

Dad looked over his shoulder. "Who's there? Get your ass out here."

I stepped out from behind the doorframe, my thumb in my mouth.

"What the hell do you want?" he demanded.

I shrugged.

The look on his face was one of disgust. "You're ten years old, for Christ's sake." *Wrong.* I was twelve. "Enough with the goddamn thumb, *Thumbelina.*" He turned back to his work papers. "Where's Bananas?"

"In bed," I said softly. Like a grade-school bully, Dad enjoyed calling his three sons names. In addition to being *Thumbelina*, I was also *Blowfish*. Harmless enough for a kid who'd been playing trumpet for a few years. Our older brother Harry was *Skins* because he rarely wore a shirt indoors. Max wasn't so lucky. When he wasn't *Bones*, a dig at his skinny body, he was *Bananas*, both a dig at his sometimes-weird behavior with the fruit and a hint that our father thought he was crazy.

"And Skins?"

"He's not home . . . uh, right, Mom?"

At seventeen years old, Harry was seldom at home. It had been that way ever since he got his driver's license. In a Brooklyn alive with energy—much of it good, but some of it very bad—he loved cruising the streets with his friends. He'd become a ghost, appearing and disappearing at all hours, leaving Max and me home alone whenever Mom and Dad were out. During the day, that didn't bother me much, other than the fact that I missed him. But nighttime was different. That's when all the monsters came out, Harry had once told me. The fact was, I loved movie monsters. But I didn't want to be home alone when real ones were on the prowl. I knew Harry was probably joking. But I was a kid, and back then, anything seemed possible.

Dad eyed the clock over the television before glaring at Mom. It was well past nine. "Again? He gets caught driving that car, the state's going to take away his license." When Mom didn't answer, Dad grunted, then guzzled the whiskey in the short glass before shouting, "No more car for that boy, Arlene. You hear me? Not until I say!"

Mom stood silently over the crackling pan on the stove—her second attempt at a perfect cutlet dinner. She had no control over Harry, and she knew it. I wasn't sure how Dad expected her to keep him away from his 1970 dark green AMC Gremlin. Harry had bought the used car with his own money. He didn't care about the state's 9:00 p.m. curfew for drivers eighteen and under, and though Harry loved Mom, he sure as heck didn't care about her constant pleas to be home by nine. She'd tried hiding the keys, but he always found them. She even tried grounding him, but if Dad wasn't at home to carry out the punishment, Harry just left anyway. And Dad was always in the throes of some massive project—the latest was a high-rise renovation in Manhattan—and never home. He made the declarations; he was too busy to care about the details of enforcing them.

Mom, on the other hand, missed Harry when he wasn't around. She didn't say so—I was pretty sure her little helpers wouldn't allow her to feel much, let alone talk about her emotions—but I could tell. Those two had a special connection.

Max and I might get a smile every now and then, but only Harry could make her laugh. And, like Mom, Harry loved to read. They'd trade tattered paperback horror novels and then discuss them endlessly on the front stoop. I'd watch them laugh and scare each other by repeating the most terrifying details of the stories, carrying on like a couple of kids. It was always nice to see Mom happy. I figured Harry must have reminded Mom of a younger, nicer version of Dad from before we were born.

Dad's eyes were on the pan filled with cutlets. Disapproval was written all over his face. "Forget that crap, Arlene. We're going to Abruzzi," he snapped.

Mom slapped a pair of tongs on the stove and shrugged. "It's nine thirty, Walter. They'll be closed in thirty minutes."

"Not for us they won't."

Within minutes, Mom and Dad were standing in the foyer, ready to head out to the Italian restaurant down the street. Their faces were glum, their outfits even gloomier. Mom was wearing her usual dark blouse, tucked neatly into a pair of black slacks, while Dad had thrown a black sport jacket over his work clothes. They looked like they could have been going to a funeral. There must have been a time when they'd loved being with one another. I'd seen glimpses—Mom smiling up at him and laughing her bubbly laugh—but these were few and far between, usually on holidays or when one of Dad's business deals closed. Still, they frequently went out for dinner together, though I'm not sure how much either of them really enjoyed those meals.

"No playing that trumpet, Daniel," Dad said, as if the interruption at the door had been about my horn and not his yelling. "It's bad enough the neighbors have to hear it all day long. One more complaint from anyone, and that horn's going in the garbage. Got it, Blowfish?"

Dad thought my trumpet playing was a nuisance. He

constantly complained about the noise and joked about how most musicians were poor and suicidal. Mom had been supportive when I first started. But ever since she started taking her pills, she just ignored the sound altogether. I'd hoped to one day win them over with my playing, but that hope was dwindling. I'd been playing for three years, and nothing about their attitudes had changed.

Harry and Max, thankfully, never made fun of me. They recognized how much I loved playing that horn, how it took me away from the life we all hated. Harry had even told me once that he believed it would be my ticket out of the family business. I hoped that was true. No way was I ever going to work for Dad. I was going to go wherever my trumpet took me—Manhattan, Chicago, New Orleans. It didn't matter where I ended up, as long as it wasn't here.

I nodded and shoved the mouthpiece from my dented, gold-plated Conn trumpet into my pajama pocket. It was my lucky charm, like a steel-coated rabbit's foot. When I wasn't sucking my thumb or playing my horn, I was using it to keep my lips in shape. It takes a lot of practice to form one's lips into a trumpet mouthpiece to produce the proper sound. I pictured it as the way a person might blow their lips into the soft belly of a newborn.

"As a matter of fact," Dad said, "no playing that thing for a week."

I swallowed hard and didn't even blink.

"Did you think I forgot about this morning?" he snapped.

Keeping my eyes cold and emotionless, I shook my head.

Dad started down the front steps without Mom, who was still standing at the front door as Max appeared at my side. "Stay in your room. And no fighting," she called back to us. "We'll be at Abruzzi. The number's on the fridge."

The door slammed shut, and I caught Max's eye. We shook our heads in unison. There they went, without us. Yes, it was late. Yes, we'd already eaten, hours before. And no, we didn't want to spend more time with our father. But the way they constantly left us home alone still stung. We hardly ever ate together as a family, not even on Sundays. Dad said that he and Mom had *earned* the right to some time off from us kids. That made no sense to me, because he was never around anyway and when he was, he avoided us. Mom's mealtime ritual for us was simply to drop plates of food—usually lukewarm, pre-cooked chicken from a grocery store deli—onto the table and then go to the kitchen counter, where she'd eat her own dinner while watching TV. We'd have killed for some home-cooked chicken cutlets, no matter how thick they were.

With a smirk, I shot past Max into the den and leaped onto the sofa, a plush orange behemoth with four large segments and a longer lounge section tacked onto the end. That lounge was the prize among us kids, and Max scowled as I claimed it. He threw himself onto the other end of the sofa. Our den was a disaster of colors. The television set was built into a wooden cabinet that was painted a putrid green. Between the television and sofa stood a fluorescent-yellow coffee table. Atop a matching side table stood a tangerine phone.

I clicked the remote and found a documentary about the Jersey Devil, a creature with two legs, a goat's hooves, bat wings, a horse's head, and burning red eyes that legend said lived in the swamps and marshlands of the South Jersey Pine Barrens. The narrator's voice was creepy and ominous. "There are strange happenings in these parts . . ."

Nestling under a crocheted afghan, I gawked at the screen, hanging on every single word. Max fussed with his *Hit Parade* magazine, ignoring the TV.

When the phone rang, I was absentmindedly pushing the cold steel of my trumpet mouthpiece against my lips.

"Get that," Max ordered. "It might be for Dad!"

I ignored him, fluttering my lips into the small cavern of the mouthpiece. I couldn't have cared less about the phone; I was witnessing a television re-creation of Jane Leeds giving birth to the Jersey Devil.

"Answer it, Daniel! It's right next to you!"

I turned toward the other end of the sofa and stared blankly at Max. His buckteeth and long nose reminded me of Goofy. "You do it!"

Max crawled across the sofa until he was next to me. "Pick it up!" he yelled.

Pulling the mouthpiece from my lips, I took a huge breath, filling my lungs to capacity. Mom had told me that as a toddler I would hold my breath when I was hurt or frustrated, sometimes until I turned blue and passed out. Trying it now seemed like a good way to get a rise out of Max.

"Stop it." Max looked alarmed.

I turned my head, cheeks full, and smiled without letting any air escape.

"You can stop now, you dumb Blowfish!"

I glared at him. I'd only been teasing. But now that I was angry, I would follow through to prove a point.

"Fine. Kill yourself. See if I care."

I struggled to keep the air locked inside me, using my hands to seal off my mouth and nose. This seemed much harder than when I'd done it as a small child. I could feel the world around me growing slightly fuzzy. My grip on the mouthpiece loosened, and it rolled out of my hand and fell to the floor.

"You're turning blue, you idiot!" Max shouted.

I closed my eyes and felt my arms and legs go limp. When I opened them again, Max was standing over me with a pencil in his fist.

"Stop it, or I'll pop you!"

Everything slowed. I watched Max's mouth move in slow

motion, like a cartoon, but heard nothing. The "No. 2" etched into the side of the pencil floated over me until Max's arm came down hard.

"Ow!" I coughed and gasped, my eyes flooding with tears. The pencil stood upright, its yellow shaft buried three-quarters of an inch into my knee. I rocked back and forth, holding my leg, as blood seeped through the afghan.

"Oh my God," Max groaned, white and shaking. He grabbed the phone and called Abruzzi.

———

Mom stared blankly ahead in the hospital waiting room while I leaned, puffy eyed and dizzy, against her arm, my thumb in my mouth. Max sat across from us, holding his stomach and gawking at the six inches of pencil sticking out of my knee and the small hole in my *Six Million Dollar Man* cotton pajamas.

"I was just trying to help," Max pleaded with Mom. "He was turning blue!"

My mother rolled her eyes. The absurdity would have been undeniable to anyone outside our family, yet none of it seemed that odd to me. Stabbing his brother with a pencil to "pop" him like a balloon when he was holding his breath is exactly the sort of thing that would make perfect sense to Max.

I scanned Mom's face. Her mouth was a hard line, her lips cracked, her eyes tired and dark. She looked to me like a zombie. She turned her eyes to the ceiling and exhaled. "*Please,* give me the strength," she whispered. Then she closed her eyes and lowered her head.

"Are you talking to God?" I asked.

She curled her lip and nodded.

"Are you still mad at Him?"

I knew she had been angry with God for some time. Mom was still a teenager when her mother died of cancer. Her father died a year later from what Mom said was a broken heart. She'd told us they were just so in love, he'd been unable to go on without her.

She turned to me. "Yes, honey. You could say that."

"I'm sorry for what happened, Mom." I sucked hard on my thumb, inhaling the scent of her expensive floral perfume. My leg throbbed where the pencil stuck out of it.

She smiled faintly, then eyed Max, who was gazing off in the other direction, oblivious to the conversation. "I think your brother is the one who needs to apologize."

"I was talking about your parents."

She tilted her head and smiled. "You're a sweet boy, Daniel."

I returned her smile and went back to my thumb. In that moment, it didn't matter how much my leg hurt. My mom had smiled.

My mom had smiled *at me*.

CHAPTER 3

The Alcoholics Anonymous member at the front of the room spoke, but I was so distracted by thoughts about Max, I didn't hear a word of what the man said to the group. My girlfriend, seated next to me, jabbed my side with her bony elbow. A year younger than me at thirty-one years old, Jill Woburn had a small frame and baby-faced features—big eyes, full lips, and a small nose—that made her appear far younger. But in the halls of AA, where she had 600 days of sobriety to my 303 days—I'd started with a New Year's resolution—she was my senior.

Leaning in, Jill whispered with her wide mouth, "Pay attention, Daniel." I could hear the disapproval in her voice. Though she knew very well what Max had done, she seemed to have forgotten. She was focused on the meeting. I couldn't fault her for that, exactly. But was it so unreasonable to expect a little compassion from her in this moment?

I gave her a scowl, which she didn't notice. Jill's attention was fixed on Dale B.—people at AA sometimes used last initials to distinguish between members with the same first name—who was seated at the front of the room.

Sensing me staring at her, she turned toward me. *"What?"* she said in exasperation.

What? was right. *What,* I wondered, *am I still doing with Jill?* It had been two months since she'd moved in with me, seven months since we'd started dating, and ten months since we had run into each other for the first time since 1976. As kids, we had experienced together what was—then and still— the most tragic event of either of our lives. That very night, she and her family had left town.

Eighteen years later, on the morning of the last Saturday in 1994, I had been loitering beneath the yellow awning of a small market across the street from the Alcoholics Anonymous clubhouse. It was in that moment that I'd seen Jill again, standing with a group of people outside the tall door of the two-story redbrick building—the Old Park Slope Caton on the south side of Prospect Park. Even though we'd only known each other for a month when we were kids, I recognized her instantly. And she'd known me, too.

"Oh my God. I can't believe my eyes." She'd crossed the street and stepped onto the icy sidewalk before me. Her brown eyes blinked at me from above her cute button nose. The dual tone of her bold undercut—long, blond, slicked-back bangs over short brunette sides—gave the illusion of depth to her fine hair.

The sight of Jill alarmed me, and my first thought was that it might be better if I bolted in the other direction. I couldn't understand, given the circumstances under which we'd last seen each other, why she'd want anything to do with me, but her smile seemed to harbor no ill will. That was strange. I figured she had every reason to hate me. I told myself that maybe, for some people, time healed more than I'd understood it did. After all, it had been eighteen years. I hoped that it was true that she wasn't holding a grudge.

Walking into the AA meeting would certainly be easier if she didn't hate me.

"This is so weird. You look exactly the same," she said, examining me, "only older."

I smiled and returned the compliment, then asked how life was going for her.

"Fantastic," she said, and she looked like she meant it. "How 'bout you?"

"I'm all right." But I wasn't. I'd stood in this exact spot three mornings in a row, unable to muster the courage to cross the street and walk inside.

We caught up in the way people do. She asked what I'd been up to. I told her I was a realtor with my own business.

"Wow. Good for you. I'm a musician," she told me. "I play trumpet with the Jazz at Lincoln Center Orchestra."

I stared at her. Jill Woburn—from my own school, who'd played behind me in school band—now played the trumpet professionally? "Are you serious?"

She smiled big, exposing an expanse of large teeth. "Yep."

I had to fight back the urge to inform her that that had been *my* dream, that playing trumpet for a living was supposed to have been *my* career. "Very cool. Good for you."

She tilted her head. "You live around here?"

"Uh . . ." The fact was, I didn't. I'd walked four miles in the freezing cold from Bay Ridge, which had its own morning meeting at the Lutheran church near my apartment, for fear of being seen by someone I knew.

I looked beyond her at the crowd of a dozen or so men and women, young and old, who were chatting and laughing across the street. Church bells rang, and we watched them shuffle inside. My pulse was racing, and I took a deep breath. Did I really want to go in there? Yes, I'd finally reached the point where I knew that I'd been defeated by alcohol. But how could it help me to listen to a bunch of drunks carry on about their own defeats?

"Come on," Jill said, following my gaze. "This is a great meeting."

"How much . . . time do you have?" I wasn't sure about the language yet.

"Eleven months, tomorrow." I could tell by the tone of her voice that she felt proud. "First meeting?"

"Is it that obvious?"

She laughed. "If you're here for AA, and you're standing over here, well—" She bumped her shoulder into mine, then hopped backward off the curb. "Come on. Let's go." She grasped my hand and gently pulled me across the street. I was dragging my feet, but Jill was insistent, and I could practically feel some inexplicable force pushing me from behind. *Fuck.* I was really doing this.

When I stepped inside the building, I was greeted by an elderly man who smiled and extended his hand. He had a round face and a pointy, dipped nose that reminded me of a barn owl.

"Welcome. My name is Tony G." He tipped his plaid ivy cap, a gentlemanly custom from a time gone by. When he raised his hat, I could see the crew cut beneath it.

I extended my hand, hesitating, and Jill introduced us. The large room behind Tony was filled with dozens of people.

"First time?" asked Tony.

I nodded, wondering what happened to things being "anonymous." I'd imagined that the phrase meant I could slip in and out of a meeting unnoticed, like a ghost.

With a genuine smile, he said, "Glad you're finally here." He glanced out the doorway in the direction of the yellow awning and nodded once. "I seen you across the street." He winked. "We've all been there."

His voice was gentle, his words reassuring. As much as I

wanted this conversation to end, I suddenly felt at ease. It was nice to feel understood.

"Let's grab our seats." Jill put her hand on my shoulder before stepping in front of Tony and leading the way.

Tony and I followed her into the crowded room, where everyone was now seated. We stopped behind the last row of metal chairs. At the front of the room, behind a long white table, a middle-aged man sat facing the group. The table was covered with literature—AA books and pamphlets standing upright on racks and scattered in piles.

I whispered to Tony, "I can't believe how crowded—" But when I turned to look at him, he was gone.

"Good morning. My name is Owen, and I *am* an alcoholic," said the man behind the table.

"Hi, Owen!" shouted the seated members in unison.

As Owen welcomed people to the Old Park Slope Caton Saturday morning meeting of Alcoholics Anonymous, I took the empty aisle seat next to Jill and scanned the mostly attentive crowd. Some of the people looked miserable. But most of them, I thought, looked happy. Or at the very least, content.

When Owen asked if there was anyone present who was new, returning, or visiting from out of town, I saw from the corner of my eye that Jill was peering at me. I pretended not to notice. Next, Owen introduced a moment of silence that he said would be followed by the Serenity Prayer.

He closed his eyes and dropped his head. A good fifteen seconds of quiet followed. Though the silence felt uncomfortable to me, it didn't appear to bother anyone else. Then the entire group recited together: "God, grant me the serenity to accept the things I cannot change, courage to change the things I can, and wisdom to know the difference."

Slouching deeper into my chair with every speaker, I listened as one person after another shared their difficult experience with alcoholism and, in some cases, shared their strength and hope. They were speaking a language I didn't understand, a language echoed by the placards covered in AA slogans that dotted the walls: *First Things First. Keep It Simple. Live and Let Live. Easy Does It.* There were so many. *One Day at a Time.* Now *that*, I thought, was one I could wrap my mind around. But in my case it was more like *One Minute at a Time.*

A middle-aged man in the seat in front of me raised his hand. "Hey everybody . . . my name is Dale. I'm a grateful recovering alcoholic."

"Hi, Dale!" the room greeted him enthusiastically.

Dale's massive frame swallowed the back of his metal chair. His large earlobes seemed almost to dangle, and his big head sat atop a thick neck layered on the back with deep wrinkles, reminding me of a shar-pei. His dark hair, cut short, was graying.

"Grateful to be here today," Dale went on. "Love what I've been hearing."

Goose bumps covered my crossed arms. I was frozen in place, captivated by his words and voice, which was deep and gravelly and seemed familiar, though I couldn't place it.

"'Happy, joyous, and free,'" said Dale, scratching the back of his neck. "Years ago, that's what the program said I'd become. And I'll be darned if that promise hasn't come true, over and over again." He leaned back and folded his hands behind his head. "Don't leave until the miracle happens for you, too."

The entire crowd was looking at Dale. They appeared to be taking in every word.

"I didn't know it back when I started," Dale continued, "but I needed a new way of thinking . . . a new set of ideas. How could I have known that I couldn't fix a broken mind with broken ideas? Hell, I didn't even know yet that *I* was broken. It was you people who told me so. You showed me by sharing your own experiences. When I came into these rooms, I didn't want to learn to think differently. I just wanted to stop drinking. I

wanted off that merry-go-round of hell. I just got sick and tired
of feeling sick and tired . . ."

Sick and tired of feeling sick and tired. Those words caught
my attention. That was it, exactly. That's why I was there, too.

"Self-loathing, hate, remorse, regret . . . every morning.
Blaming everyone and everything for all my problems in life.
'Hell, if you had my life, you'd drink too.' That's what I told my-
self. It's what we all tell ourselves, isn't it?"

Dale leaned forward and chuckled. The sound was rich
and full, almost like music. He lifted his head and scanned the
faces in front of him. His bulbous nose pointed my way as he
turned toward my row.

"What a line of crap that was," Dale said, now matter-of-
fact. "Here's the truth: My problems were of my own making. I
was in a prison of isolation, anger, and self-centered fear. I was
always afraid: either of losing something I already had, or of
not getting something I wanted. I was an example of self-will
run riot, just like it says in the Big Book." I'd done enough research to know that he was referencing the recovery text used
by Alcoholics Anonymous.

Dale paused, then said in an earnest voice, "The Twelve
Steps of Alcoholics Anonymous saved my life. They gave me a
spiritual toolbox . . . showed me how to deal with the *hundreds*
of resentments I'd carried inside all my life . . . showed me how
to deal with life on life's terms. Not my terms. *Life's* terms."

I couldn't understand the expressions of solidarity on
the faces surrounding me. They were connecting with Dale's
words in what appeared to be some form of strange magic.
Could what he said be true for me, too? It didn't seem likely.
Resentment sounded like something that was unreasonable.
But the things I felt angry about were things I had every reason
to feel angry about. Trying not to feel that way seemed inau-
thentic, and I saw no sense in trying to get better by acting
fake.

"And I'll finish with this," Dale said, and then he chuckled again. "*Maybe* I'll finish." The others in the room laughed, but I was too on guard for that. "You want to know what the definition of insanity is?" He paused for effect. "Joining a twelve-step program and not doing the Twelve Steps. *That's* insanity." He leaned back in his chair again, this time reclining so far that I had to sit back in mine to make room. "Thanks for listening."

After Dale was done sharing, the meeting ended, and the group morphed back into the jovial, jabbering crowd that I'd watched outside that morning. Everyone seemed to know everyone else, and I was overcome with a sense of loneliness. Maybe this group wasn't for me after all. I didn't feel like I fit in. I considered the possibility that I wasn't as bad off as the rest of them. I couldn't deny that I identified with being powerless over alcohol. But was I powerless over life itself?

I really wasn't sure. And I had no idea whether I would come back.

———

Jill jabbed her elbow into my ribs again, jarring me from my stupor. "Hello? Anybody home?" She probably hadn't intended to poke me so roughly. But she also wasn't as charming and tender as she'd been when we first started dating. I wasn't sure whose fault that was: hers or mine. It *felt* to me like Jill was the problem. I wanted more compassion and understanding from her than I felt I received. But I also had a sneaking sense that I was no prize myself. Going to meetings was helping me to keep from drinking. But life was in many ways just as difficult as it had been before I started attending AA, and I felt that strain in my moods. And in my relationship. "Meeting's over."

The room was empty.

"Sorry." I rubbed my eyes. The memory of that first AA meeting haunted me, and my thoughts often returned to it when I should have been paying attention to the meeting I was in. Living life on life's terms—accepting people, places, and things as they were, not as I wanted them to be—was proving to be a daunting challenge, as was trusting in God. In fact, I didn't trust in God—or even believe in God—at all. Still, I kept coming back to this meeting every day. Other members of the program insisted that it was about progress, not perfection. They said that this was a hard, but not impossible, concept for perfectionists to grasp. The irony, they often pointed out, was that most alcoholics were perfectionists. That was what our dad had demanded of his family: perfection. No doubt that was part of what haunted my brother.

"Thinking about Max?" Jill's tone was finally sympathetic.

I nodded.

"Come on. Let's go to the hospital."

Desperate to grab a smoke outside, I followed her toward the exit. A brisk wind greeted us as we approached the open door.

Still standing in the doorway, Jill spun back around and looked at me. "Oh my God. What is *she* doing here?"

I peered over her shoulder and immediately stiffened. There on the sidewalk, under the glowing light of a flickering streetlamp, her blond hair glinting, stood Brie Olsson. Brie had been my childhood best friend.

She was also my ex-fiancée.

CHAPTER 4

On the television screen, next to a large tree shining under the full moon, a man lay facedown on the ground. His lifeless body was fully clothed, except for his muddy bare feet. A black cane, adorned with a silver handle shaped like a wolf's head, lay next to him.

I peered at Brie Olsson out of the corner of my eye. She had pretty green eyes and a pointed nose, and her long blond hair reached all the way down to her waist. Brie and I had been best friends for seven years—ever since kindergarten. Because we lived in the same row of homes on Carroll Street, just a few doors apart, we were always hanging out together. Like lots of people, Brie had been born with asthma. But it seemed to me that she struggled more frequently with her breathing than other kids with asthma did. This was especially true when she got excited or exhausted, so we usually stayed indoors playing board games like Monopoly and Life, drawing in sketchbooks my mom bought us, or watching television.

It was the night of Halloween, and WPIX was having a Friday night monster movie marathon. We were sitting at my kitchen table—my leg extended, my sutured knee covered with gauze and wrapped in surgical tape—watching the television on the counter. While other kids were already out trick-or-treating, we were homebound: me, because of my injured leg; Brie, because she'd been having trouble with her breathing that day. We didn't mind too much. Harry and Max were both out with friends, and my mom had turned off the porch light to keep the trick-or-treaters away—something she might have done even if I hadn't been injured. My dad hated the holiday, and she was probably happy to have an excuse to skip it this year.

She had bought bags of candy at the store just for Brie and me, and we were snacking on Snickers and Reese's Peanut Butter Cups while we watched the movie dressed in our Halloween costumes. Brie was, I thought, a beautiful princess in a white dress that her mom had sewn and a cheap plastic silver tiara. I was, of course, covered in fake gray fur. My plastic fangs sat on the table beside us.

Brie stared at the screen, her mouth agape, her eyes wide. A box of colored pencils and crayons stood upright on the table, and construction paper was strewn all around us.

"I love this movie." She blinked and swallowed. "Everything's so scary and dark. The whole idea of monsters living among us." She opened her eyes even wider and watched the exchange between Larry Talbot and Gwen Conliffe inside the antique store. Gwen was reciting the old poem about how even a good man could still become a wolf man.

We looked at each other and recited the rest of the poem together with Gwen, then laughed. I had attempted to make mine an especially spooky laugh, but it came off crazed instead. The pain pills I'd been taking for my knee had me loopy. For the past day, I'd been floating around the house in a daze. It was a peaceful feeling that I'd fallen in love with immediately. Almost nothing bothered me anymore. Nothing, except for the terrible news Mom had given me earlier that day—that the real reason Mr. and Mrs. Olsson were in Manhattan for a long weekend was *not* because they were visiting friends and seeing shows, as Brie had told me, but because they were looking for a new home on the Upper East Side, near the children's hospital that specialized in asthma.

I was upset that Brie hadn't told me the truth. The thought of her moving overwhelmed me, even if it was just across the East River. But I didn't know how to bring it up, and I didn't want to ruin Halloween. And anyway, the pain pills made it easy for me to push my feelings away. My mother's little pills suddenly made more sense to me than they ever had before.

"Wolfman is my favorite monster." I made a black scrawl across my paper. "Dracula is fine with sucking blood and being a vampire, and Frankenstein doesn't even know what the heck he is and couldn't care less. But Wolfman . . . he's a regular guy who got bit by a werewolf because he was trying to save some girl. Next thing he knows, he's turning into a monster. And he hates that monster. *Hates* it."

I knew what it meant to hate a monster. I lived with a real one. But I was powerfully drawn to monsters in films. Unlike my father, they couldn't help what they were. And I appreciated that they tried to resist their monstrousness.

I turned back to the television screen. "I wish *he* was my father," I said, pointing at the Wolfman's alter ego, Larry Talbot. "I'd take a guy who hated the monster he became over a guy who didn't any day of the week." I'd never talked to Brie like this before. The pills had apparently loosened my tongue.

Brie glanced up at me. "You think your dad's a monster . . . like Dracula?"

I turned to her. "He's not a vampire. He's more like Frankenstein." I returned to my drawing, scribbling in black. "A *real* monster."

I could feel her stare on the side of my face.

"Why? Because he yells?" Brie looked at me. I could see

that she was genuinely trying to make sense of what I was saying. "I mean, all dads get angry and shout—"

"Ha! You have *no* idea. Nobody does." I'd spoken more harshly than I intended, but I didn't apologize.

After a moment, Brie appeared to reach some kind of decision. "I think you watch too many monster movies. Have you ever tried talking to your dad?"

I gave her a disappointed look. "I think you live in a dream world." I watched Larry Talbot transform into the Wolfman. "I can't *talk* to my father. Nobody can." I made a scoffing noise. "You make it sound so easy. Most things *aren't* easy, ya know."

She threw her pencil on the table. "You don't have to tell *me* that."

I suddenly felt queasy. At least I didn't have to struggle to breathe, like Brie did.

She glared at me. "Maybe you're the monster. Ever think of that?"

I tried to apologize, but she wasn't having it.

"And anyway, I didn't say talking to your dad would be easy. I just think there's always something a person can do. I think the way I do because I have to. It's called having hope."

Her words hit me hard. I hated myself for what I'd said.

For several minutes, Brie sat in silence, drawing feverishly. My eyes wandered back to the screen, where Larry Talbot sat anguishing over what he'd done to one of his victims. He hated himself, too.

When the phone rang seconds later, Mom yelled from down the hall for Brie to take the call.

Brie jumped up and pulled the lime-green receiver off the wall. She untangled the long cord and disappeared around the corner. "Hi, Mom!"

I strained to listen, not to the conversation, but to her tone, hoping she'd be happier when she returned. When she appeared in the doorway minutes later, her lips were pursed. She sat back down and returned to her drawing, still silent.

"Are your parents having a nice time . . . with their friends?" I picked at the bandage on my knee.

She eyed me suspiciously but ignored my question.

"How long did you say they were going to be gone?"

"Too long." She kept her eyes on her drawing.

"Come on, Brie," I pleaded. "You're probably right, okay? It's just hard to see an answer to my problems sometimes." I cracked my knuckles and tried to focus on the television. "Things with my family . . . they're complicated."

She nudged my foot beneath the table. "The pastor at our church always says we only need to do the next right thing, one thing at a time." I noticed, as I had so many times before, the small gold cross hanging from a thin chain around her neck. "And God decides the rest according to His will."

Ugh. God's will. Brie was just about my favorite person. But it seemed I had inherited my mother's problems with God, and I tried not to talk about religion or spiritual things with her.

She turned to the television and pointed at the Wolfman on the screen. "You can be like him and drive yourself crazy. Or you can try to be happy." She picked through the pencils scattered across the table. "I'd rather be happy."

I watched her, unsure of what to think. Were her parents moving to New York because that was the next right thing for their daughter? I supposed it was, and it really wasn't fair for me to be angry about them doing that. But what about me? What was the next right thing to do about having a mean and bossy father? Or about losing a best friend who was moving away? Did God care about any of *that*? Did God even care about *me*? It sure didn't seem so.

None of what Brie was saying made any sense to me, and I didn't think it was because of the pain pills.

———

That night, I lay in bed with my ear against the wall while Brie wheezed and gasped for air in the guest bedroom. When I came into the hallway to check on her, my mom was already running down the hallway in her nightgown.

I followed her to the guest room but stopped at the door. Stunned, I watched as my mother calmed Brie, then delivered a shot of Adrenalin that Brie's mom had left for emergencies.

To my amazement, I noticed that I was praying to Brie's God under my breath, asking Him to help her.

"She needs to rest now, Daniel." Mom sounded relieved. She stood and wiped her hands on her nightgown. "You can go back to bed."

I hugged my mother tightly, my cheek resting against her chest. She wrapped her arms around my shoulders and kissed my head. I felt so comfortable in her embrace, and I didn't want it to end. When Mom turned to move, I squeezed her even tighter.

"I love you, Mom."

Mom reached behind her back to unlock my small grip and gently pulled away. "Back to bed," she said. She flipped off the light switch and walked out of the room.

I sat down in the love seat across from the daybed. Brie coughed. "You okay?" I whispered.

"Yeah." She looked exhausted. She wiped her eyes with a fist. "My chest hurts."

"I'm sorry. I'd give you a lung if I could."

I thought it was a dumb thing to say as soon as I said it, but Brie smiled. "Thanks, but you need your lungs for Juilliard." Brie knew my dream was to go to New York to study music and then play in the New York Philharmonic.

I shook my head. "I just want you to get better." It was bad enough that her asthma kept her from doing typical things like playing kickball in the street or running around the block—just being a normal kid—I couldn't even imagine what it must be like to struggle to breathe.

The next evening, I was sitting on the lounge doing Mad Libs next to Brie. She was drawing in her sketchpad. WABC-TV's *Eyewitness News* played in the background.

A photograph of a girl appeared on the TV screen. "Man, not her again." Max jumped up to change the channel.

"Don't. I want to watch." The pain pill turned sideways in my throat, and I made a face before taking another gulp of water. "You sound just like Dad."

Max scowled and slouched back into the sofa.

The anchorman had just begun his report. "Joseph and Julia Quinlan, parents of twenty-one-year-old Karen Ann Quinlan of Roxbury, filed a lawsuit earlier this month in the New Jersey Superior Court. The Quinlans have requested that the respirator and feeding tube keeping Miss Quinlan alive be disconnected and that their daughter be allowed to die with grace and dignity."

Brie and I stared at the television. After months of endless news reports, the image of the young woman on the screen—a portrait taken three years earlier, when she was eighteen—was familiar to us. In the photograph her long brown hair was straight and parted down the middle, her cheeks pale, her smooth lips pressed tight. Her empty eyes, sad and searching, gazed into the distance. Her expression reminded me of Mom's.

The story restated details we already knew. Karen Ann Quinlan had been comatose since leaving a birthday party in Byram Township on April 15. The anchor Bill Beutel cleared his throat and went on: "Miss Quinlan had eaten virtually nothing for two days, drank several gin and tonics, and consumed Valium that night, according to eyewitnesses. Friends later found her in bed, unresponsive and not breathing. Now, the Quinlans are suing for their daughter's right to die without life support. Miss Quinlan suffered irreversible brain damage that will leave her permanently unconscious and in a vegetative state."

I flipped over my Mad Libs and scribbled a word on the back cover.

"She's a *vegetable*," Max pronounced.

Brie drew in a sharp breath at Max's crude statement and dropped her colored pencil on the sketchpad.

"Don't call her that," I said. It was the same word Dad occasionally used to describe Mom. "How do you like it when Dad calls you *Bananas*?"

Max persisted. "How can you stick up for a drug addict?"

"We don't know anything about her, Max."

"We know she couldn't handle life. She was weak, and that's why she did drugs. That's what Dad says." The look on my face must have showed I was unconvinced, because he tried a different tack. "Anyway, if her parents win that court case and they turn the machines off, they'll be killing her, won't they?"

I shrugged and turned to Brie. She seemed to have answers to everything, even if I didn't always agree with them.

Brie cleared her throat. "I think that's their point, Max. They don't want her to be kept alive with machines. They want her to die naturally, on God's time, not anyone else's. People shouldn't play God."

"But what about what *she* wants?" asked Max.

"She doesn't know what she wants," said Harry, who was just walking into the room. "She's not in there anymore." His head was hanging upside down, and he was drying his long, bushy hair with a bath towel. Only his jeans separated his bare feet from his bare chest, which was smooth and hairless.

He'd recently grown a lot, and he towered over most of his friends.

He pulled the towel off his hair and lifted his head. "I agree with Brie. Just because the doctors can keep her alive doesn't mean they should."

Brie smiled at Harry. She'd been a fixture at our house for years and was over so often that Max and Harry treated her like a little sister—for better and for worse.

"That's right," Brie said. "People shouldn't play God."

Max sat forward. "Well, Dad says only weak people believe in God, anyway."

Harry crossed his arms and stared Max down. He knew how religious the Olssons were, including Brie. "Dad doesn't know everything."

The pain pill suddenly kicked in and my lips turned upward in a huge smile. I *loved* Harry.

Max turned to Brie. Harry's reminder about Dad seemed to have caused him to reassess whose side he was on. "Sorry. I just meant that I'm not a believer . . . in God. That's all." I knew how he felt. I was just glad he was the one who'd said it and not me.

"It's okay," Brie said quietly. "Everyone has their own beliefs and reasons for them. I only know that my faith makes me feel safe, and feeling safe helps me to be strong. And I definitely need strength." She closed her sketchbook and stood up from the table. "Thanks, Harry." She turned to me. "I'm going to go lie down for a bit."

"Check you out . . ." I said, the words begging the familiar response.

Brie summoned the strength to humor me. "On the side that's flip . . . p . . . t." The strange saying was our little thing, our little dance. My dad frequently used a CB radio to communicate with workers at various job sites, and one day I'd heard two truckers end their exchange with the phrase "Catch you on the flip side." I thought it was so cool that I decided to re-place my standard goodbye of "Check ya out" with this catch-ier phrase. At some point, I combined and rearranged the two into a more playful version: "Check you out . . . on the side that's flipped." But it was only after either Brie or I—we could never remember who—began to draw out the pronunciation of "flipped" that the joke took its full form and stuck.

Brie turned away, her soft footsteps fading down the hall toward the guest room.

"That girl may be onto something," Harry said, watching her go. "I guess if you're going to believe in something, you might as well believe as hard as you can and not ever let any-one tell you different."

He turned to see what Max and I thought of his theory, but Max was staring into space. Harry and I exchanged glances, wondering whether Max understood what Harry had just said, but it wasn't clear if he had even heard. He looked like he was miles away, in his own headspace.

"That's going to leave some scar," said Harry, pointing to my bandaged knee. He turned to leave, but before he could go, I reached for my Mad Libs and looked at the word I'd scribbled on the back cover. "Wait, Harry . . . what's Valium? I know it's a drug, but what's it for?"

Keeping one hand on the doorframe, Harry turned back into the room. "People use it to take the edge off."

I thought about the broadcaster's somber tone. "What's so bad about that?"

"Who said it was bad?"

"That girl . . . in the coma—"

"Oh." Harry shrugged. "She took too many, and she took 'em with booze." He turned and walked out of the room, then poked his head back around the corner. "You know what Valium is. Mom takes it." And he was gone.

Huh? I gazed after him, trying to understand what he meant.

Max poked me and gawked, his buckteeth front and center. "Her little yellow pills . . . duh. Why do you think she's a zombie half the time?" It was as if he'd never left the conversation.

"Why would she need—?"

But then I stopped myself. I didn't need to ask the question. I already knew the answer: It was the same reason I'd been enjoying the pain pills. My mom didn't want to feel any pain. Maybe Karen Ann hadn't wanted to, either.

After all, who would?

———

Dad stood awkwardly behind the new tiki bar in our "rec room," the space formerly referred to as our living room, a cigarette dangling from his mouth. He was visibly uncomfortable in the presence of the Olssons, who had returned that morning from Manhattan. His short-sleeved shirt had too many open buttons, and his chest hair protruded. Mom had long ago quit asking him to button up.

Mrs. Olsson hugged Mom. "Thanks again for taking care of my baby."

"Oh, it was my pleasure, Inge. She gave me a good scare, but she's fine. And such a sweetheart."

"It sounds like you were a pro. Brie said it was like you'd done it a thousand times."

Mom's face fell a little. "I had to take care of my mom when she was ill." Her gaze wandered beyond Dad to the antique picture frame sitting on one of the mirrored bar shelves. It held a black-and-white wedding photo of her parents, one of the few pictures she had of them.

"I love what you've done with this room." Mr. Olsson gestured at the bar and the sitting area with the new forty-two-inch rear-projection TV. The tiki bar was made of real bamboo knotted together with twine. A thatched roof of fake palm leaves hung from hefty bamboo columns. On the wall behind the bar, dozens of colorful liquor bottles sat on rows of mirrored shelves, and four bamboo stools were tucked neatly under the counter.

"Bringing the outside in," Mr. Olsson continued. "Who would have thought?" He pulled out one of the barstools and sat on it. "Planning some big parties?"

Dad motioned to Mom. "Whatever she wants."

"If it was up to him, I suppose we wouldn't need a bar at all. He doesn't like entertaining." Mom laughed, as though she were joking. She wasn't. Dad wasn't interested in other people, especially if he couldn't talk business with them. I knew that he was only here right now to show off his new tiki bar.

From across the room, I stared at my father in fascination. I knew very well how much he hated guests. But as he raised and lowered the cigarette in his hand, he appeared almost relaxed.

Brie pushed my shoulder. "Why are you staring at him?"

"I've never seen him smoke so much before," I whispered. Smoke drifted from Dad's nose and mouth as he blew out fat, gray rings.

"The smoke rings are actually kind of pretty, don't you think?" Brie whispered back.

Her words startled me. Even the thought of Brie smoking frightened me. "Don't *you* ever do that." I gave her a stern look.

"I can barely breathe as it is, silly." She nudged me. "Don't *you* ever do that either."

Still gazing at my father, I cringed. "Yuck." But the truth was, I was mesmerized by the smoke. I wondered what it felt like to breathe it in.

Brie nudged me again, harder. "If you think it's so yucky, quit staring at him."

I turned back to her. "Please don't move away." The words just came out.

Brie stared at me open-mouthed.

"I've known all weekend. Mom told me."

Her cheeks grew bright red. "I'm sorry I didn't tell you, Daniel. I was trying to find a way—"

"So, it's really happening then?" I watched Dad throw down a shot of Jameson. "I don't know what I'll do without you here." I couldn't even remember a time when I hadn't had the bright spot of Brie in my life. Once she was gone, what would I have left?

Brie sighed. "It's not too far. Everything will be fine." I could tell that she was trying to soothe me. But I wasn't sure if she believed it.

"You don't know that." I could feel anger swelling inside of me. I'd taken my last pain pill earlier that morning and it had worn off hours before. I was used to feeling frightened at home, and over the past few days I'd been sad between the moments of numbness. It had been so great to feel nothing for a while. I wanted that nothingness back.

Across the room, Dad fabricated one stiff smile after another as the adults talked. Between bored glances out the window, he downed shot after shot. Soon the bottle was half-empty.

Brie's mother slipped off her bamboo barstool. "Come along, sweetie. It's time to go."

Brie and I smiled at each other, but as soon as she'd left, the smile fell from my lips. I was always happy when I spent time with Brie, and I was always sad when she went away. What would happen to me now?

Dad lit a new cigarette, then emptied Mr. Olsson's half-empty beer bottle into the sink and wiped down the varnished bamboo of the bar top. When he glanced up, he noticed I was staring at him from across the room. I looked away.

"What are you looking at?" he demanded.

"Nothing."

"You've been staring at me all afternoon."

"Sorry."

"Get over here," he ordered.

I did as I was told. As I stood in front of him, my nostrils burned from the stream of smoke he blew at me. Standing beside him with a dish towel in her hand, Mom sighed.

"What is it?" He waved his lit cigarette at my face. "Is this what you've been looking at all day?"

Mom stood with her arms limp by her sides. With my eyes, I pleaded for her support, but she put her hands in her pockets and turned away. I knew she probably couldn't do anything to stop him. But I wished she would have at least tried.

"Ready to be a man?" Dad held out the cigarette. "Take a puff."

"I don't want it." I turned my head away and thought of Brie. She'd be so angry with me if I did it.

"Yes, you do." He flipped the butt around and pushed the filter toward my lips. "Go on."

My heart was pounding. I tried to turn away, but he grabbed my chin between his big fingers and pulled me back.

"You think you're real tough, don't you? Saying no to your dad? Well, let's see how big a man you are." He pushed the filter against my lips.

I pressed them tightly together.

"Open your goddamn mouth!" Dad squeezed my chin hard until my lips puckered. Then he shoved the butt into my mouth. "Suck it in, boy."

My lips closed around the cigarette, and I inhaled lightly. A stream of smoke slithered down my esophagus, filling my lungs. Dad let go of my chin and pulled the cigarette from my mouth. Instinctively, I held my breath. A blast of energy struck me. It began above my eyes and rushed backward over the crown of my head to the base of my neck, briefly numbing my entire body. After a moment the feeling dissipated, and I only felt light-headed. But for a moment, feelings of release and escape had united. A smile crept across my face.

"Breathe!" Dad shouted into my face. I suddenly felt sick. I released the breath I had been holding and coughed, my eyes watering. I could feel my throat burning.

At the sight of my tears, my dad gave a smirk. "I knew you couldn't handle it." He took a long drag on the cigarette and turned away.

For several minutes, I watched him organize the bar, putting things precisely the way he wanted them. Eventually, I walked over and stood next to him, waiting. It wasn't that I wanted to impress him; I just had to feel that feeling again.

He looked up. "What the hell do you want?"

Grinning devilishly, I nodded at the cigarette in his hand. "Another puff."

CHAPTER 5

I followed Jill outside the AA clubhouse into the unusually cold fall night. It was just after nine and Seventeenth Street was quiet.

"Hey Brie." I stepped past Jill and tried to ignore the feeling of her eyes boring into my back. "How are you? It's been a while." I hadn't seen Brie in the five years since she'd called off our engagement, and the sight of her now startled me. It wasn't just the surprise of seeing her. The contrast of her red lipstick and green eyeshadow against her pale face was stark. She looked worn out, and her body swam in the white-and-green-checkered overcoat she was wearing. As the brisk wind howled, she pulled the lapels up around her thin neck and long blond hair to shield her ears. My heart ached as it hit me that she was obviously struggling with her health.

"I'm well," she said, though she must have known I could see that wasn't true. "I came because I heard about Max." I must have given her a confused look, because she added, "I called your mom to see where you were. How are *you*?"

That made sense. Jill and I had taken my mom to lunch in the neighborhood for her birthday earlier that year. To my horror, Jill had pointed out the Old Park Slope Caton to her just before our burgers had arrived, saying it was our regular AA clubhouse and the place where we'd reconnected.

"Uh . . . I'm doing all right," I said now to Brie. "I still can't believe he did it."

"But he's in stable condition?"

I told her he was in intensive care over at Maimonides Medical Center in Borough Park, then asked, "How'd you hear?"

"I work as a contractor for South Beach now, and one of my friends at the hospital called me." I was no stranger to most of the branches of South Beach Psychiatric Center in Brooklyn. Since college, Max had received counseling at more than one of their half dozen facilities in the borough.

"You're not teaching anymore?" I was surprised to hear it. Brie loved children and had been one of the most beloved elementary school teachers at the Bayview School in Bay Ridge after we graduated from Hofstra.

"Mental health counselor," she said. "Children and adolescents, mostly. Got my master's at CUNY three years ago."

"Wow. Good for you. So, what, you deal with people like Max—but younger?"

Her eyes wandered behind me to the symbol on the clubhouse door of a triangle inside a circle. It was one of AA's logos. The triangle represents the three cornerstones of the program—unity, service, recovery—while the circle represents the world of AA.

Her eyes locked on mine, and she offered me a sympathetic smile. "Addiction is my specialty."

An awkward silence followed. My addiction had been the cause of our demise. In fact, Brie had understood I was an addict before I did.

I felt someone's hand clutch mine, and Jill stepped up next to me.

"Oh, shit. Sorry, Jill." I felt my whole body flush red from embarrassment. "Brie . . . this is Jill Woburn."

"Hi, Jill. Nice to meet you." Brie extended her hand and introduced herself.

Jill feigned a half smile. "I know who you are."

Although she'd only seen Brie in photos, Jill knew all about her. She knew that Brie and I had lived next door to one another and were best friends as kids. She knew that we'd attended Hofstra University together, had lived together for years, and were even engaged at one point. I'd never held myself back from talking about Brie. I didn't see the point of it—she'd been a big part of my life, after all. But my talking about her had only annoyed the hell out of Jill. That was probably one of the reasons why I did it.

Brie asked in a friendly voice, "Are you guys together?"

I nodded and looked away, while Jill nudged in closer, her grip tightening around mine. "We sure are."

"Good for you." Brie smiled. I searched her face, hoping for jealousy, but found only authenticity. She was truly happy for us.

"We're heading over to the hospital now," I said. "Wanna come along?"

Jill dug her fingernails into my palm. When I wrenched my hand away, she gave me an innocent look, as if I was the one acting ridiculous.

A stiff breeze engulfed us. I could see that Brie's eyes were watering from the cold, and that her breathing was becoming labored. When she fished inside her handbag, I guessed that she was reaching for her inhaler.

Instinctively, I grasped Brie's arm. "Come with me." I led her to the steel entrance door of the AA clubhouse, which was still unlocked.

"Where are you going?" Jill's voice was high, almost a yelp.

"I'll be right back." I answered without turning around.

Brie and I walked inside and sat down on the metal folding chairs in the last row. The door to the kitchen at the far end of the room was still open, and the light was on inside. Water ran from the faucet. Whoever had kitchen duty was still cleaning up.

Brie glanced at the posters on the walls and continued to fish around in her handbag. "Is this your home group?"

She knew the lingo. I wasn't surprised. "Yeah."

She pulled out a gray albuterol inhaler, popped off the red cap, and placed the mouthpiece to her lips. She pushed down on the canister and inhaled the fine mist, then paused a few seconds while holding her breath. Keeping her eyes closed, she repeated the process two more times. Within seconds, she was taking deep breaths again. A little color returned to her pale cheeks. Her profile—that combination of green eyes and a pointed nose that I loved, framed by long, flowing blond hair— hadn't changed much since I saw her last.

Staring forward, she said, "It's getting worse." She'd spent much of her youth receiving treatment at the best children's hospital on the East Coast, trying to get relief, but nothing had helped. "Don't ever take for granted how easy breathing is for you," she always used to say after a bad episode. The doctors had been managing her symptoms fairly well back when she and I were together, and she'd sometimes enjoyed long periods between more serious spells. Now I worried that this was no longer the case.

I turned to her and felt the pack of Marlboro Lights jostle inside my coat pocket. My stomach knotted. When we had been together, I'd managed to curb my smoking dramatically, but I was never able to quit completely, and I'd often tried to hide it from her—though she was never fooled. She would be so disappointed if she knew I still smoked—now, more than ever. Whenever we'd argued about it, I'd blamed PTSD and an affinity for self-destruction. Brie had always said that my self-destructive behaviors were caused by my inability, or un-willingness, to reconcile my past with my present. It didn't matter to me which reason was true. Either way, I'd never felt able to live up to her standards. Tonight was no different, and I could feel my failure all the way down to my bones.

"What are you guys still doing here?" Tony G. appeared outside the kitchen and flipped the row of light switches. His brow was wrinkled, his eyes tired.

"Hey Tony." I waved.

He stopped at the end of the row and squinted. "Where's Jill?"

Fuck. "Uh . . . she's outside. This is my friend Brie."

"Well, how do you do, Miss Brie." Tony tipped his cap.

Brie smiled, and Tony headed for the door.

"We'll be right behind you, Tony."

Tony jingled his keys, a reminder that he still needed to lock up. The steel door slammed shut behind him.

"Feeling better?" I asked.

Brie took a deep breath to show that she was. As she dropped the inhaler in her bag, she glanced at my left arm. Her face pinked up further, with pleasure, I thought. "You *still* wear that?"

I spun the silver ID bracelet around my wrist with my right pointer finger. "Of course. I feel naked without it." It hadn't left my wrist since the day she had given it to me when we were kids, except for those times when I'd had to take it off to add more links.

We walked slowly to the exit. Affixed to the inside of the steel door was a twelve-by-twelve-inch picture frame with a timeworn photocopy of a prescription from the pad of R. H. Smith, MD, Second National Building, Akron, Ohio. The typed prescription dated "Feb 1937" was for "alcoholics" and num-bered on three lines: "1. Trust God, 2. Clean house, 3. Help others." The phrase "always remember it" was handwritten above the physician's signature: "Dr. Bob." Along with Bill W., Dr. Bob was one of the two founders of AA.

"That's the program in a nutshell," I said.

Brie smiled a smile that told me she knew it was. "How many days?"

I wasn't sure how to answer. I wanted to tell her that I was doing great, that sobriety was a dream come true. But the truth was, sobriety was almost impossible for me. Each of the 303 days under my belt had been a struggle: not just a struggle to not drink, but a struggle to live my life.

I was, as they say in those halls, stark-raving sober . . . a dry drunk. And despite my days of sobriety, I knew it. I'd long been resistant to the spiritual principles of the program, and I was paying only lip service, doing the bare minimum: not drinking and going to meetings. But even with those changes, my personality and my problems remained the same. I was still impatient, controlling, hateful, angry. My father was still alive, Max was still a burden, and my girlfriend was, to put it in the most positive light possible, not the "right" one.

I wanted to tell Brie how much I missed her, how sorry I was, how much I still loved her . . . but saying any of those things wouldn't matter. She'd heard it all from me before and would never fall for those lines again.

I saw her now, searching my face for some indication of whether I had really changed, as if it wasn't enough that I'd taken her inside, warmed her up, and helped her catch her breath. And the fact was, it *wasn't* enough. Doing those things didn't mean I was well. I'd do those things for her no matter what my condition. But true sobriety, beyond the outward motions, would have meant that I could be there for her in even more meaningful ways. And true sobriety was something I still didn't have.

"Just today," I answered with a wink. The line was cliché, I know, but it was true. When it came to sobriety, the addict had only a daily reprieve. I had learned this both in the halls of AA and from my own experiences.

I pushed open the front door, and Tony came limping back through.

"Sorry to keep you, Tony."

"Not a problem." Tony pulled a collection of keys from his pocket.

Brie pulled her lapels up to cover her neck. "Please tell Max I'm thinking of him."

I asked if she wanted to come with me. It was, after all, only a five-minute cab ride to Maimonides. But Brie said she needed to be going. I stepped off the curb and raised my arm to flag a yellow cab.

When one pulled up, I opened the rear door. For a moment, Brie and I stood face to face, and then she smiled and slid inside. I closed the door and knocked on the window. Brie pushed a button, and the window slowly lowered.

"Yeah?" She looked at me questioningly.

"I've missed you."

"I've missed you, too," she said. And then the window rose again, and the taxi drove off.

Covered in goose bumps, I stood on the curb and stared until the taxi was out of sight, a smile on my face. Brie missed me?

A firm finger poked me in the shoulder, and I jumped.

"You said Jill was out here waiting for you?" asked Tony G.

"Shit." I scanned the nearby sidewalk. "Yeah."

"Well, I haven't seen her," he said with a shrug, and then he turned away.

CHAPTER 6

It was eleven in the morning on February 28, 1976, which also happened to be my thirteenth birthday. There were only two days left of midwinter recess, and it was the Olssons' moving day. Brie would probably be arriving at her new home right about now. I, on the other hand, was still sitting on my bed, half-heartedly practicing the trumpet and still wearing my pajamas. It was hard to feel anything that resembled motivation. With my return to school after the holidays approaching, worries about returning without Brie loomed large. All I wanted to do was climb back into bed and pull the covers over my head.

"Hey bud," said Harry, walking into my room. Now eighteen, Harry had recently grown a full beard and mustache to go with his long, bushy hair. "Happy birthday!"

I pulled my lips off the mouthpiece of my trumpet. "Thanks, Harry."

He sat on the foot of my bed and handed me a shoddily wrapped package. It was long and narrow, shorter and slimmer than the wrapped boxes that were stacked on the kitchen table—birthday presents from my parents, but really from my mom, that I had refused to open in an act of rebellion. The only thing I wanted was for Brie to stay in Brooklyn. If I couldn't have that, I told my mom, I didn't want a birthday party, presents, or a cake, either. She'd reluctantly agreed to cancel the party. My dad hadn't even noticed. This was something different, though. This was a gift from Harry, the big brother I idolized. I had to open it.

I hesitantly removed the tape from each corner, and the wrinkled newspaper fell away to expose a dark plastic figurine glistening beneath cellophane. I turned it over, unable to contain my excitement. It was the newly released Mego Wolfman action figure. His face and chest were covered in fur, and he wore a moss-green vest, gray pants, and black boots.

"Wow! His eyes and hands even glow in the dark!" I pulled the figure from the box. It was the best gift anyone had ever given me, but I didn't know how to say so. I hoped Harry could see it on my face.

He stood there, smiling. "I knew you'd love it."

From downstairs, I heard our mom calling me, shouting something about the kitchen.

"What?" I yelled back, annoyed at the interruption.

"Daniel Zimmer, you come here right now!" *That*, I heard.

"Ugh." I flung the trumpet onto my comforter and, with my Wolfman in hand, followed Harry out the door. Before he turned away, I wrapped my arms around his waist and hugged him hard.

"Don't mention it, kid," he said and headed for his room.

I trudged down the hallway, stopping short as I peered around the corner at the kitchen table and the stacked boxes, probably plastic models of ships, tanks, and airplanes. In the center of the table sat a frosted chocolate cake with thirteen candles burning tall.

"But Mom, I told you I didn't want—"

Then I looked and saw that someone was sitting just on the other side of the presents.

Brie. It was Brie. Her eyes sparkled in the light of the birthday candles.

"I—I thought you left." I stood up straighter, mouth open. "Your family's not moving anymore?"

"No, they are, Daniel," Mom said quickly. "Brie just stopped by for a minute. It's a surprise. Brie wanted to be here for at least the start of your party. Wasn't that nice?"

My smile disappeared.

"Where is everybody?" Brie looked around the room as if she was just realizing the others should be there by now.

I looked at my mother.

Mom sighed. "He canceled the party when he found out you were leaving today, Brie." I threw my mother a look, begging her to help me out of this situation, but she just shrugged as if to say, *What do you want me to do about it?* and walked out of the kitchen, leaving me to explain myself.

"You never told me you did that." Brie sat at the table in front of a present that hadn't been there before—a small square box wrapped in gold paper.

I shrugged. "You're the only one I wanted here anyway."

Brie made a small sound of disapproval. "I told you not to feel sorry for yourself, Daniel. *I'm* the one leaving everyone I know." She gave me a stern look. "I'm the one who has to live next to a hospital."

"I know, I know." I stared into the burning candles as they dripped wax onto the cake.

"I'm only going to Manhattan," she said, but her voice sounded sad. She nodded at the candles. "Make a wish."

Manhattan might as well have been the moon. I closed my eyes tightly and cursed God for taking my best friend away, then blew out all thirteen candles in one huge breath.

"So, what'd you wish for?"

"That you get better and move back to Brooklyn fast." It was a lie. I hadn't wished for anything. I wasn't about to let myself wish for something that would probably never come true. I didn't believe in granted wishes anymore, anyway.

Brie gave me a suspicious look, then slapped her present down on the table in front of me. "Open it."

I removed the gold foil paper, revealing a small black box. Beneath the box cover and the small piece of soft cotton underneath it lay a silver ID bracelet with my name engraved in block letters. I lifted the shiny bracelet out of the box and unlatched it. Linked ovals connected the smooth nameplate to the latch on both sides.

Brie reached across the table to latch it onto my wrist. "Turn it over," she said.

I rolled the nameplate over. On the underside were the words *From Brie*, engraved in cursive.

"It's real silver," she said. "Sterling."

I told her that I would wear it always.

"I'm glad you like it." Brie smiled and stood. "I need to go."

"Wait! Check it out." I slid the Wolfman figurine across the table. "Harry gave it to me. Isn't it cool?"

Brie rubbed her finger against Wolfman's vest and nodded. "I'm sorry," she said. "Mom's waiting."

"But aren't you going to stay for cake?" My mind raced. I was frantic for any excuse to keep her there. "Don't you want to open all these other presents with me?"

"I'm sorry, Daniel. I can't. She said I could only stay for ten minutes." Brie picked up her shoulder bag, which had been on the chair beside her.

"Can I just play you one last song on my trumpet?" I reached in the pocket of my pajama pants for my mouthpiece. Then I ran toward the steps that led upstairs, going to grab my trumpet. "Just a quick one."

But when I turned around, Brie was already at the front door, her bag draped across her body. "We'll talk on the phone, write letters, and see each other again soon. I promise."

I wiped at my eyes, afraid she could see the tears I could feel rising in them. "Check you out . . ." I said helplessly.

"On the side that's flip . . . p . . . t." I looked down and stared at the bracelet on my wrist. When I looked up, Brie was gone, and Mom was standing in the kitchen doorway. She smiled and gave me an understanding nod.

"So, what did Brie get you?" she asked.

I lifted my wrist and dangled the bracelet, while my eyes scanned the table for my Wolfman. I reached over the model boxes, then looked under the table and on the chairs for the only other gift that mattered. It took me several minutes to figure out what must have happened. I looked at my mother in shock.

"It's gone, Mom."

She stared at me, not understanding. I couldn't believe it myself. But there was no other explanation.

"Brie took my Wolfman!"

CHAPTER 7

I followed Tony G. around the corner onto Church Avenue, where we were passed by a group of adults dressed in costume—a lion, a witch, and yes, a wardrobe. We were slammed by a sudden gust.

"Damn, it's fucking cold," I said.

Tony pulled his plaid wool ivy cap down over his ears, turned his back to the wind, and lit a half-smoked cigar he pulled from a pocket. "Why ain't you taking a cab?" he asked. "Don't you live way the hell out in Bay Ridge?"

I told him I was going to Borough Park to visit my brother.

"You don't sound too excited." Tony pulled up his jacket sleeve, exposing a worn cloth-banded wristwatch. "It's half past nine already."

I explained that he was at Maimonides. "Intensive care unit. He tried to blow his head off this morning."

Tony stopped walking and looked over at me, cigar dangling from his mouth. "Jesus."

I nodded. "He's got . . . issues." We started walking again.

"Didn't know that. Sorry to hear it. *Really*." He gave me

a sympathetic look, as if he finally understood something about me.

"Yeah." I looked away uncomfortably. "Well, that's got nothing to do with my drinking."

Tony gave me another look.

"What? It *doesn't*," I said.

Tony looked like he had a different opinion on the matter, but I still hadn't bought into the AA assertion that *everything* had to do with my drinking.

"Is he one of us?"

I shrugged. "I mean, he's definitely a problem drinker." The fact was, Max had been drinking ever since he moved back home after his first year of college. But he'd always struggled with his mental health, and I wasn't sure which issue was more of a problem for him.

"He ever go to meetings?"

"He came once or twice when I first started," I answered. "But he could never get past Step Two." In truth, I had my own problem with believing that some Higher Power could restore my sanity, but I wasn't going to be the one to bring that up.

"Ah . . ." Tony said. "Which part?"

"Well, I'm pretty sure he wouldn't argue with the insanity part of it. He can't feel exactly sane to have done what he did."

"So, it's the God part. Hmm. And how about you?"

I shrugged.

"Do you believe?" Tony persisted.

"Look," I said. "My brothers and I were raised to rely on nobody but ourselves. And certainly not some all-powerful bearded guy in the sky."

"Yes, but you know what they say—our dilemma is our lack of power. We can't stop drinking on our own, and we can't face or accept life on our own. We need God's help."

I made a little sound of irritation before I could stop

myself. I'd heard all this before, way too many times. My reaction generally depended on my mood, or my "spiritual condition," as it was called in AA. Mine usually ranged somewhere between disgust and indifference. The fact was, I did believe that there was some creative and intelligent force underlying the universe. But I didn't view that force as being in any way personal to me.

Tony could see my ambivalence. Not that I was trying very hard to hide it. "You know, you don't have to believe in a bearded anything. In AA, you just need to believe in a power greater than yourself."

"Yeah, then why does the book use the term 'God' ten thousand times?"

"It's '*God, as you understand Him.*'"

I told him I understood. That I knew that my behavior, when I was drinking, was insane. I actually did believe that there was a greater power out there—what Brie had called God. Believing wasn't the issue. "Step Two is not my problem," I said.

Tony nodded and took a drag from the shrinking cigar. "So, Step Three is." Tony was right. He had been one step ahead of me. No way was I going to give my will and life over to that power. What would become of me then?

Another burst of cold hit our faces like an iceberg.

"Tony, we're not talking about me here. We're talking about my brother. And if there's one thing I know about him, it's that he's an atheist. And there's no room for a complete nonbeliever in this program."

Tony gave me a look that told me how wrong he thought I was. "Not so."

I shook my head and kept quiet. We walked several blocks in silence until we arrived at the intersection of Church and Thirty-Sixth Street. Suddenly I felt a burning urge to get away.

"Look, Tony. I appreciate what you're trying to do. It's just that it's complicated. No one could understand what my brothers and I went through—"

Tony snorted. "Terminally unique," he said. I'd heard the term more than once and knew what he was implying: that I imagined Max's—and my—reasons for drinking were special. Unlike anyone else's.

I clenched my fist, wanting to punch him in his smug nose. "Whatever."

"'Whatever' is exactly right. Whatever *His* will is shall be done. Not mine. Not yours. *His.* Once I got that through my thick skull—that my way only causes me heartache—I was off to a better life."

The idea that *God's will—not mine—shall be done* was one of the underlying principles of the twelve-step program—and one I'd been told I would need to accept and practice if I were ever to remain sober. But I remained unconvinced. Where did accepting such an idea leave my will? And even if I did come to accept it, how did embracing the idea work, practically speaking? As a being with free will, what was I supposed to do with my *self*? It made no sense to me. But I didn't want to think about myself right now. I was worried about my brother.

"But Max is fucking crazy, Tony," I said. "There's something wrong with his brain. He's on four different meds, and I don't think any of them are working. He doesn't even know what the hell *his way* is!"

That wasn't all. I was sure something had happened to Max at Hofstra during his sophomore year that had changed him irreversibly. It happened the year before I started college there. When Max returned from school in May 1981, he was just different. It was as if his brain's limbic system had been zapped. He'd withdrawn entirely into himself, his earlier visible anxieties replaced by a numbness of indifference and isolation. After that, he lived at home and finished his degree at Brooklyn College—a twenty-minute bus ride from Carroll

Street. Following graduation, he began working for Dad. Twelve years later, at thirty-four years old, he was *still* working for Dad. But he seemed to desperately want out . . . not just of that situation, but of life.

Tony lightly tapped my chest with his finger. "All I'm saying is, stay out of your own way and God will do the rest. That's all you . . . I mean, *your brother* has to know."

I took a deep breath and looked up the street. Tony's words triggered a flood of memories, mostly of fighting with Brie over this very same issue: faith. I had both envied and laughed at her unshakable belief in this concept—*let go and let God do the rest*—an idea that was simultaneously inspiring and loathsome to me. Ironically, this very same idea confronted me daily in AA. But I couldn't take any more of it now.

I stepped off the curb. "I'm going to take Thirty-Sixth, Tony. I'll see you later."

"Hey . . ." Tony clutched my wrist as the cigar dangled from his mouth. "What's the deal with this Brie?"

I blurted the truth out without thinking. "She was the love of my life. My reason for living. And I screwed it up. There was nothing in this world I cared about more, nothing I wouldn't do for her. But there was also one thing I *couldn't* do for her and that was stop drinking. That's the fucking disease for you, huh, Tony?"

"Yeah, it is." Tony let go of my arm and stepped off the curb. "Is she okay? She didn't look too well."

I told him about her asthma.

"That sucks." Tony looked up Thirty-Sixth Street. "She needs you, maybe. But you also need to do right by Jill."

It made me uncomfortable how much he could see. I thanked him and told him I'd see him the next day.

Tony placed both hands on my shoulders. "Ask Dale to be your sponsor, will ya? I can see he's got eyes on you."

"Dale B.?" He was definitely one of the better speakers in

the group. But his enthusiasm had always intimidated me a little.

"He's the best there is."

I started to protest, but before I could speak, Tony tipped his cap and continued down Church Avenue, leaving only the acrid stink of cigar breath in my nostrils.

CHAPTER 8

It was a quiet Sunday morning for Brooklyn. The neighborhood children were still inside their houses. The May heat was bearable, but the stench of garbage rose from the dented metal cans lining the sidewalks and floated through the open windows of the den. The stink contrasted starkly with the beauty of the red maple tree that had recently been planted in front of our building on Carroll Street. Our street ran through six blocks of Carroll Gardens. We lived on the block between Henry Street and Hicks Street, which was also known as the Bronx-Queens Expressway, in one of the identical brick buildings that lined both sides of the street, each with its own five-step stoop.

The news from WCBS streamed through the small transistor radio on the kitchen table. A chartered school bus carrying the Yuba City High School a cappella choir had fallen twenty feet from an elevated freeway off-ramp in California two days earlier, landing on its roof and killing twenty-eight kids and one teacher. The national news called the tragedy "the worst bus crash in US history" and ran the story throughout the weekend.

I couldn't stop watching. At thirteen, I was drawn to all things gruesome—a natural extension, I supposed, of my love of monsters. I read and watched anything morbid. I needed to understand how some people could do terrible things to innocent people and why bad things happened to good people. It hadn't taken me long in life to decide that there were only two types of people in the world: those who were victims and those who were not. I suppose I imagined that understanding the factors that determined others' fates could help me shape my own.

I reached across the table and turned the dial on the small black radio. A jazz version of the 1969 hit "Spinning Wheel" by Blood, Sweat & Tears crackled through the tiny speaker. The gyrating swing of the trumpet as it rolled between high and low octaves was the coolest thing I'd ever heard. I turned up the volume as a new song began: a soft, slow piano melody. I closed my eyes and leaned my head back. The sultry sound of brass honked its way into the tune—a single free-flowing trumpet, expertly played. Together, the trumpet and piano created a beautifully sad sound. I listened until the song ended and the disc jockey broke in. The artist was Miles Davis. The song, "Blue in Green," had been released in 1959. I smiled and dreamed of playing in the New York Philharmonic orchestra. I'd gotten very good since the beginning of the school year. Having challenged each of the five boys in front of me, by the end of seventh grade I'd climbed from sixth chair trumpet (out of eleven) all the way to first chair. I even made it into the junior high school paper, which published an article about my ascent. Mom seemed pleased. Dad suggested it must have been a slow news day.

It was too early in the day for me to play my trumpet, so I was sitting at the kitchen table reading S. E. Hinton's *Rumble Fish*. Max was in the den eating his "Sunday" banana and reading *Hit Parade*. Dad had gone to check on a building in

Manhattan, Harry was MIA as usual, and Mom was in the shower. So, when the doorbell rang, only Max and I were downstairs.

At first, I'd simply waited for the person to go away. But when it rang a second time, I stood up and walked to the door. Through the opaque sidelight, I could see the shadow of a large man. I took a step back and peered up the stairs. The water was running. There were still rules in our family about when not to open the door, and these included when Mom was upstairs. I had been lectured on these rules countless times. I took a deep breath, stood on my tiptoes, and squinted through the peep-hole. A giant eye glared back, startling me.

"Who is it?" I asked, then immediately covered my mouth, wishing I hadn't spoken.

A grunt and a mumble came from the other side of the door. Upstairs, the water had only just stopped running, yet, inexplicably, I reached for the deadbolt and began to turn it. I watched helplessly as my hands moved of their own accord.

"What the hell are you doing?" Max whispered.

I turned to the door of the den, where he'd just appeared, but it was too late. The door was open, and a stranger stood in front of me. My eyes traveled slowly up the man's enormous body, pausing on his big nose and brooding, determined eyes, which gazed past me into our foyer.

"Where are your parents?" he said.

I couldn't speak. Max came closer, clutched my wrist, and pulled me behind the open door.

"Is your dad home?" The man's voice was low and rough, not husky, but gruff. Distinct.

Taking my place at the door, Max shook his head.

"Max! What are you doing?" Mom shouted. Her shrill voice jolted me out of my stupor. She stood at the top of the steps with a towel wrapped around her, the wall blocking her view of the door.

She took a step down and tilted her head, glancing at the open front door. "Close the door!" she screamed and darted back into her bedroom, slamming the door and locking it behind her, leaving Max to face the large man alone.

"Tell your father I'm ready," the man ordered, stepping off the landing. "Tell him Benny is . . . *ready*." Max nodded as the man made his way down the stoop to the sidewalk. As I pushed the door shut, the phone began to ring. Max locked the door behind Benny and shook his head at me in disbelief. I stood on my tiptoes again to peer through the distorted lens of the peephole, but the man was gone.

I crept hesitantly up the stairs. "He's gone, Mom," I called through her locked bedroom door. "The front door is locked."

I heard her crying into the phone on the other side of the door, and my heart sank. No, no, she assured our father, she was fine. It was only that Max had opened the front door. The man was gone now. No, there was no reason for him to come home.

But of course, our father would. I sat on the top step, my hands between my knees, trembling. Max sat down next to me.

"Don't worry about it. I got this one," he said. I could hear the fear in his voice. But it was clear that his mind was made up. I didn't know what to say. We sat on the top step in silence, waiting for Mom to come out of her room and sit by us. She never did. She was probably so busy trying to pull herself together, she hadn't yet thought about us.

Dad's car screeched outside a little while later. The deadbolt turned, and the front door flew open. I jumped up and retreated to an empty corner of the foyer.

"Max!" He slammed the door shut behind him. "Get your butt over here!"

His heavy feet pounded the hallway, vibrating up the staircase to the top step, where Max sat waiting, alone. As Dad's massive frame rushed toward him, Max crumbled into a fetal position. Instantly, Dad was pummeling him, blows raining down in rapid succession as he shouted something about rapists and murderers, drowning out Mom's cries for him to stop.

Suddenly Harry appeared at the bottom of the staircase, open-mouthed, his eyes cold and empty. I didn't know where he'd come from or how much he'd seen.

"Stop it, you motherfucker!" It was a guttural roar, something I'd never heard come out of Harry.

Dad swung around in midblow to stare at his oldest son.

Harry's jaw was clenched, his body shaking. "Don't you lay another hand on him."

"Who the hell do you think you are?" Dad's voice was like the growl of an animal. "How dare you talk to me that way in my own house—"

"Your *house*?" Harry shouted. "You mean, your prison! You think you own us. You're our goddamn *father* . . ." He looked at Mom, who was now at the top of the stairs and staring, wide-eyed. "Her *husband*. You're supposed to protect us!" Harry's voice cracked. He looked like he might cry. "You're supposed to *love* us. And you don't. You *don't*."

Dad's face was frozen. He didn't deny Harry's claim. Perhaps he was too stunned to speak. He stared at Harry before falling to the step below Max's feet and dropping his head in his hands. Harry ran out the front door. Mom stood, stunned. And Max lay across the steps like a wounded dog that had been beaten by its owner.

———

The next morning, Max and I sat across from each other at the kitchen table, eating our breakfast in silence. A cartoon played in black-and-white on the small television, but neither of us was watching. The rising sun crept over the borough and seeped through the kitchen window.

"Why'd you do it, Max? Why'd you take it for me?" I'd wanted to ask him the night before, but directly after the beating, he had locked himself in our bedroom and hadn't come out until this morning. I hadn't seen Harry either—not since he bolted from the foyer after screaming at Dad.

When it was all over and Mom had joined me in the foyer, while Dad was still on the steps, I'd told her about the man named Benny and about how he'd said he was *ready*. I had wanted to tell her too that *I* had been the one who opened the door, but I couldn't. After that, I'd watched as she went over and whispered about Benny to my father, who then picked up his coat and went out. He came back within a couple of hours, looking somber. But though I lay awake on the den sofa for hours, I never heard Harry return.

Max stopped chewing and leaned forward. "Why'd *you* do it?"

I knew what he meant. It was a good question—but one I didn't have an answer for.

I shrugged helplessly. "Are you bruised?" I said. Shockingly, his face looked fine. But I knew his body had to be hurting.

"What do you think?"

I looked down at my bowl. I really wanted to say I was sorry but couldn't find the words. I was still in shock from the day before.

As I was trying to think of something to say, I noticed the clock. It was approaching 6:45 a.m.

"Aren't you going to be late for school?" I asked. Max was finishing his freshman year at John Jay High School—a year he often referred to as being the worst of his life. He complained of being constantly bullied for his small size and idiosyncrasies—like bringing an ink-labeled banana for lunch every day, sitting alone, and sometimes zoning out—peculiarities he didn't bother to conceal. By his own admission, Max had no friends and hated pretty much everybody.

"Fuck school." He pushed himself away from the table and took his cereal bowl to the sink. But then he picked up his notebook and headed for the door.

"Hey," I said as he was turning the deadbolt to the front door. "Let's go to the record store when I get home."

Max looked over his shoulder and half-smiled. As the door swung open, the Woburn twins appeared on the stoop. Both of them were grinning with their unusually large eyes and mouths. This was their usual expression. They reminded me of a pair of largemouth bass.

"Coming," I called to the twins.

The Woburns had moved into the Olssons' townhome a few doors down. Frankie and Jill Woburn were twelve-year-old fraternal twins. They were in the sixth grade—a year behind me at Junior High School 142. Since they were new to the area and school, I'd agreed to walk with them the four blocks down Henry Street each morning and afternoon. I didn't mind at first, but once I got to know Frankie, I regretted it. Jill was sweet, however, and she played trumpet like me—she was third chair in the band—and the school year was almost over, so I hadn't bothered to cut the cord.

I hadn't heard from Brie since the Woburns moved in two months earlier. Before that, we'd spoken by phone once, but she got off the phone before I could muster the courage to ask her about Harry's gift. When I called her again in mid-March, she never called back, which annoyed me. I then wrote to her and asked if she had my Wolfman, but she didn't even mention it in the short reply it took her a long time to send back. She'd only said, "Sorry this reply is so late, I've been super busy. I hope you have a great summer." And that, apparently, was that.

Most of the streets in our neighborhood appeared at an angle on a map, as if someone had put their hand on an ordinary perpendicular grid and spun it a half turn so it looked mildly off-kilter. The Woburn twins and I jumped down our stoop onto Carroll Street, which ran roughly northwest to southeast, and headed to the corner of Henry Street, which ran toward our school. The four blocks to the school were short, and the walk usually took about five minutes. Both Carroll and Henry were already filled with cars that morning as families set off in different directions, to work and school. The stench of rotted food and other trash floated over the sidewalk as we started to make our way down Henry.

"Eww." Jill plugged her nose as we passed one particularly ripe garbage container. I didn't understand why people couldn't seem to secure the lids tight on their trash cans.

"Smells like you after dance class!" Frankie laughed at his sister.

Jill nudged me and smiled. "Smells like Frankie all the time . . . jerk!"

Frankie pushed his sister off the curb to our left just as a black Chevy Vega sped by. The car swerved, its horn blaring as its driver cursed out the window.

"I'm telling Mom you cussed," he said to his sister, though it was obvious she hadn't. He seemed oblivious to Jill's close call. Drivers regularly sped in the Carroll Gardens area, and incidents like this were all too common in our neighborhood, even near a school zone.

"Go ahead . . . *jerk*!" Visibly shaken, Jill hurried back onto the sidewalk.

I rolled my eyes. It seemed like we went through the same scene, or something like it, every morning. "Can't you guys be nice to one another?" I grumbled. "You're *twins* for God's sake."

Up ahead of us on Henry, my friend Ivan Stooger and his younger brother, Teddy, emerged from their home on the corner of the first cross street, Summit, and jumped down their stoop. I didn't bother to call ahead for Ivan to wait, since he refused to walk with the Woburns. He said that he wouldn't be their "babysitter," which is what he called me.

"Oh, I'm a jerk, am I?" Frankie said to his sister. "Well then how's this for being a jerk?" He turned to me. "Guess what, Daniel? Jill's in love with you!" He laughed again.

Jill gasped. I shook my head. I had never seen any sign that Jill liked me in that way. Seeing his sister's face turn red, Frankie hooted even louder.

"That's it," snapped Jill. "You're gonna get it." She reached for Frankie's shirt. Pulling hard, she dragged him all the way to the ground. But Frankie bounced right up again, swinging.

"That's enough!" I wrapped my arms around Frankie. "You going to leave her alone if I let you go?"

Frankie nodded half-heartedly.

I loosened my grip until he was able to escape. Sure enough, he lunged at Jill, and I pushed him away.

"Go up there and walk with Teddy," I ordered.

"Why? You wanna be alone with your girlfriend?"

"Go. *Now!*" I pushed him again, harder this time. By now, we'd covered another full block.

Frankie glared at the two of us, then rushed up the sidewalk toward the next intersection, at Woodhull Street, calling after Teddy and Ivan, who were already one block beyond that at Rapelye Street, ready to cross to the school. His calls were drowned out by the sound of a car horn blowing somewhere farther up the street.

As Frankie crossed Woodhull and ran toward the Stoogers, Jill and I instinctively picked up our pace. A yellow El Camino sped down Henry on our left, and I yelled for Frankie. "Watch out!"

The El Camino was going way too fast for a school zone. From the direction of Rapelye, a car horn still blared. The Stoogers were now standing on the far side of the crosswalk, by the school, staring in the direction of the commotion. Frankie reached the curb and began to step into the crosswalk at Rapelye just as the El Camino started to turn right. Jill clutched at my arm. I saw it, too: Frankie had no idea a car was headed right for him.

"Frankie!" I screamed at the top of my lungs. "*Stop!*"

The Stoogers had turned their attention to Frankie, who had indeed suddenly stopped, not at the curb, as I'd hollered for him to do, but in the middle of the crosswalk, just in front of the El Camino.

Jill and I were now a half block away. I yelled again, but it was too late. The El Camino and another car—a smaller, darker one, coming too fast down Rapelye to the right—from the direction of all the honking—slammed into each other at the intersection. The smaller car ricocheted off the El Camino and tumbled toward Jill and me. Pulling her with me, I dove into the street as the car skipped the curb, skidded along the sidewalk, and struck a blue mailbox, where it finally came to a stop, its engine smoking.

Shakily, Jill and I climbed to our feet a few yards away from where the car lay crumpled. I scanned the scene for Frankie, who had seemingly vanished in the commotion. Passing vehicles slowed to rubberneck. Pedestrians gathered, men shouting and women sobbing. Residents in the apartments on each corner peered out their windows. In the intersection at Henry and Rapelye, the El Camino lay still, its front end crushed.

"Where's Frankie?" Teddy Stooger yelled from the middle of Henry Street.

I turned to him. His face was pale as he stumbled toward us.

"Frankie!" Jill ran toward the crosswalk where her brother had been standing. Before I could even think, Teddy had lunged at her. They fell to the ground, Jill screaming as he held her tightly. I looked around desperately. There was no sign of Frankie.

Ivan had made his way over to us, and he stepped closer to the wreckage of the small car. "Daniel," he whispered. "Isn't that your brother's Gremlin?"

The smaller car was indeed a Gremlin, and dark green. Behind the shattered windshield, the driver's body lay motionless, a Yankees cap over his face. I strained to peer through the splintered glass but saw no movement. *Please, God, let it not be Harry.* There were lots of Gremlins in the neighborhood, after all. There was a chance it wasn't Harry. I had to believe it wasn't.

Jill screamed for her brother, while Ivan stood beside me, stunned. Sirens sounded in the distance.

The Gremlin was still smoking. The sirens grew louder. I stared at the body in the front seat.

A crowd had assembled by now and was milling aimlessly around. Women clutched their purses across their chests, and men crossed their arms and mumbled solemn words. A local traffic cop had appeared to prevent the crowd from crossing the street and approaching the wreckage. Another officer whisked Jill and Teddy away from the scene.

Inside the Gremlin, the driver's body shifted behind the cracked glass. The Yankees cap fell from his face. My mouth fell open and I turned toward Ivan, but he was no longer standing next to me.

Dodging fragments of safety glass, I carefully approached the blown-out driver's window and peered inside. "Harry?" His face was lacerated, and his body was so drenched with blood I couldn't tell how many places it was coming from. "Wake up, Harry." I gently poked his shoulder, and then jumped back as his motionless body slumped forward. My heart skipped a beat, and I leaned in close again. The Yankees cap had fallen onto his lap, and I noticed an open bottle of whiskey on the floor at his feet: green glass with a dark red cap. I poked him one more time. "Harry, wake up!" He didn't move. Without thinking, I grabbed the Yankees cap and pulled away.

I stumbled around the wreckage to the rear of the car, where I saw a trail of blood. A few feet away, Frankie lay flat and lifeless on the concrete, arms outstretched, a puddle of blood growing around him. His face, already the pale color of the dead, shone in the morning sunlight.

I felt light-headed and nauseated. *Oh, Harry . . . what did you do?* I backed away, hugging the Yankees cap to my chest. Paramedics swarmed the wreckage and then I, too, was whisked from the scene.

As I was pulled away, I couldn't stop looking at the body behind me, and an emptiness consumed me as the realization set in: Frankie was gone.

Even worse, my eldest brother—my hero—was gone, too.

———

The next morning, I lay in bed feeling numb.

The previous day, nobody had wanted to talk about what had happened. Dad and Max had pretty much kept to themselves. Mom cried all day and night, the sound of her sobs reaching me in my room.

The only one who had anything to say to me about Harry was Brie, who had called. Her comforting voice had thawed me while I stood frozen by the kitchen telephone.

"I'm so, so sorry, Daniel." Her voice trembled. "My parents told me about—" I heard her take a deep breath. "Were you there?"

Images and sounds from that morning—cars torn apart as easily as if they were plastic models, mangled metal and glass everywhere, people screaming and crying, and the blood and the bodies—had overwhelmed me all day. I started to sob.

Calmly, on the other end of the line, Brie began to pray: "Our Father, who art in heaven, hallowed be Thy name. Thy kingdom come, Thy will be done, on Earth as it is in heaven."

Her words might as well have been in a foreign language, so little did they mean to me, and my resentment toward her for abandoning me resurfaced.

"Stop. What are you doing? I don't pray anymore."

"That doesn't matter. It'll work just the same," she told me. "That's what Pastor Kircher—"

"Sorry, Brie, but I gotta go." I slammed the receiver against its base on the wall. I didn't need Brie's God. All I wanted was Harry back. *Please, God, let it not be Harry,* I'd prayed. Well, that would be the last prayer I ever made.

In those first few days, the phone never stopped ringing. Most calls went to the answering machine, but once in a while Mom would pick up; the conversations were always brief. Every couple of hours, I'd wander down the hallway in my socks to check on her. She was always in the same position: slouched over the kitchen table, her head resting in her crossed arms, sobbing. Sometimes I saw her slide two little yellow pills into her mouth.

Once, after I'd gone to check on her, I walked through our den and found my father sitting on the sofa wearing a white T-shirt and boxers. It was strange to see him home on a weekday. His head hung limp, his chin touching his chest and his eyes closed. On the end table next to him sat two bottles of Jameson—one empty, one half-full. I didn't think he'd slept since he woke up the day before, and I knew he hadn't gone to work. The strangest thing was that I hadn't heard my father say a word since we'd left the hospital, over twenty-four hours earlier. I couldn't remember the last time I'd seen him when he wasn't talking on the phone, reading the paper, watching the news, or doing work.

Dad lifted his head, and I froze. His silence frightened me

as much as his fits of rage did. At least when he was raging, I could gauge what he was thinking.

He reached for the half-full whiskey bottle, opened his eyes, and chugged. As he placed the bottle on the table, he stared at me and nodded once.

"You okay?" His voice was low and as calm as I'd ever heard it. He'd never asked if I was all right before.

"Yeah. You?" My gaze drifted to the whiskey bottles.

Seeing where I was looking, he shrugged. "Makes it easier." He scratched his unshaven chin. "Everything's going to be okay, Daniel," he said stiffly. It almost sounded like he was trying to convince himself. "Life will go on, just like it did when my father died. It may not be the way you want it, and you'll never forget, but life, that asshole, always goes on."

I nodded, my face expressionless, and turned away. *Makes it easier?* I'd always wondered what liquor tasted like. Now I also wondered what it felt like.

There was one thing I did know: everything would not be okay.

———

The kitchen light was still on when I went to the bathroom later that night. Even though I hadn't eaten much in almost two days, my stomach was churning, making it impossible for me to fall asleep. I couldn't help but think how it was all my fault. Harry must have been on his way home when the accident happened, but where had he slept that night? The only thing I knew for sure was that Harry would still be alive if I hadn't unlocked the front door. Just like Frankie would still be alive if I'd put up with his immaturity and left him alone. And on top of all those other horrible things, I'd hung up on Brie— the person whose support I needed most.

On the way back to my room, I saw that Dad was no

longer in the den, but there was an open bottle of whiskey on the end table. Looking over my shoulder, I crept to the bottle, bent over it, and took a whiff. It smelled sweet. Lifting the bottle with both hands, I tilted it into my mouth and took a gulp. I gagged, but not before swallowing the slug of liquor. I knew even while I was doing it that it was stupid. Whiskey had helped kill Harry. But I needed something to make things easier, as my dad had said the whiskey did. On one hand, my actions made no sense. On the other, they made all the sense in the world.

I sprinted to the kitchen sink, my throat burning, and stuck my head under the faucet, drinking until the fire went out. Wiping my mouth, I turned and saw Mom sound asleep at the table, her arms outstretched and her shoulders still. What would her life be like now without Harry? And mine?

Mom's body shifted position on the table and her arm hit her medicine bottle, which fell to the ground, spilling little yellow pills everywhere. Still sound asleep, she didn't budge. I dropped slowly to the floor and tracked down every pill, replaced them in the bottle, and tightened the cap. When I rose, Mom was awake and looking at me.

I placed the pill bottle on the table next to her. "Don't worry. I'm going to take care of you now, Mom."

She gave me a weak smile and brushed my curls off my forehead. "We need to take care of your father, too."

I stared at her. I wondered if she'd noticed what I had: how much he was drinking. "Dad doesn't need us."

Mom tilted her head. "Of course he does. Everybody needs others. And your father's had a hard life. Did you know that when your father was a boy, his father beat him for just about anything, including using too much toilet paper? Toilet paper! Your grandad said he was being wasteful and inconsiderate." She looked at me. "Sound familiar?"

Eyes wide, I nodded.

She tapped a finger on my chest. "Everyone's got hurt inside. Just because we don't see it doesn't mean it's not there."

I knew what Mom was trying to say, but it was still hard to imagine someone yelling at Dad. He never spoke a word about his father, and Grandad had died years before we were born. None of that mattered to me.

"He could change if he really wanted to, Mom."

She grasped my hands and lowered herself to the floor to kneel in front of me. "Some people show their love by hugging and talking to each other about things. Other people show it by putting food on the table and a roof over your head."

I wasn't sure I believed that. But I appreciated the effort she was making. I wrapped my arms around her neck and hugged her tightly.

"I'm so sorry, Mom." My eyelids were heavy.

She patted my back and then pulled herself away. She looked like she was going to cry again. "Go on back to bed."

Still feeling light-headed and sweaty, I walked to the doorway, then stopped as a question occurred to me. Did she know it was all my fault?

"Mom?" I turned back. "I was the one who—"

Before I could get the rest of my confession out—about opening the front door, about Frankie, about all of it—she raised her finger to her mouth. "Shh . . . go back to bed," she said. "Try to get some rest."

But I didn't feel like I would ever rest again.

CHAPTER 9

I stood between the pair of automatic doors at the entrance to the Maimonides Medical Center emergency room and warmed up inside the tunnel of hot wind blowing down from above. Through the glass, I saw dozens of patients sitting in plastic chairs, waiting to be seen.

A custodian who was wiping the glass doors gave me directions to intensive care. When I exited the elevator and turned the corner, I saw my parents and Jill standing at the end of the hallway, looking into a room through a window.

Dad's fake, frozen smile could not conceal his disgust at the sight of what was on the other side of the glass. Mom, facing the glass, never turned to me.

"Hey." I nodded once at my dad as I approached.

"What took you so long?" Jill's voice had an edge to it.

"I was looking for you," I said, telling myself that wasn't completely false. I had helped Brie, I had talked with Tony, and then I had walked here—and I might have encountered Jill anywhere along the way.

She rolled her eyes.

Standing behind my mother, I grasped her shoulders and

squeezed. "He's going to be fine, Mom." Max lay sleeping in the hospital bed on the other side of the glass, the top of his head wrapped in gauze.

"I know," she replied in a monotone. She looked completely numb.

In contrast, my dad was thoroughly agitated. "This shit's gotta stop," he said. "The kid's got issues. He's killing me, and he's gonna kill the business if something happens to me." He spit yellow into his white handkerchief and stuffed it back into his pocket. "A goddamn embarrassment. Not to mention what it's doing to your mother." He turned to Mom, but she was clearly too jacked up on Xanax or whatever sedative she was on to express how she felt.

Jill clasped my hand. "I told them he's got to be put in an institution or something. It's the only way to keep him from—"

"He's *not* going in any institution." I pulled my hand away.

"Damn right he's not," echoed Dad. "Bad enough he's got to take those damn pills. He just needs to buckle down, get it together, once and for—"

"Enough, Dad," I said. I knew Max needed help and not criticism. But Max had long mistrusted psychiatric hospitals. We'd both avoided them ever since we were kids—and we had our reasons. I was sure sending him to one would only make things worse. But our dad's attitude was sure to make him worse, too. "It's not a matter of willpower or character. His mind is sick. You know this. Christ, how many times have the doctors told us about his condition?"

"Seems to me he needs constant supervision," said Jill.

I glared at her. *Stay out of this, Jill.* I hated myself for being this way with her. It hadn't started out that way. But over time, we seemed more and more to be bringing out the worst in each other. I couldn't stand myself like this. And I also couldn't seem to stop acting this way.

Dad erupted into a coughing spell, then hacked another

loogie into his handkerchief, which he quickly concealed and stuffed back into his jacket pocket. He looked terrible. "Come on, Arlene. Let's go." He gently pulled Mom away from the glass.

Mom finally turned to me. "You must take care of your brother." Her voice was as stiff as her body, but the words were sincere.

"Don't worry, Mom. I will. I'm moving him into my place when he gets out of here." The thought had just occurred to me, but it felt right.

Jill gaped. We had been living together for a couple of months now. But the place was mine, so as far as I was concerned, the decision to move Max in was, too. As I watched my parents plod down the hallway in the direction of the elevators, I told Jill so.

She glared at me. "There's something wrong with you . . . you know that?"

I waved her away, and she marched off like the twelve-year-old girl I'd known decades earlier. Once she was gone, I put my head to the glass and stared at Max. Part of me didn't know if I wanted him to ever wake up from his slumber. I imagined he was happier asleep than awake. He was also a responsibility I didn't particularly want. But I felt obligated to take care of him.

I knew my parents weren't going to do it.

The following morning, I went to visit Jill at work in Manhattan. We hadn't spoken since our trip to the hospital the night before. She was asleep, or faking it, when I got home, and she was already gone when I'd woken up. She didn't even leave a note. It was increasingly clear to me that we didn't belong together. But I also didn't want to be the kind of person who treated people the way I was treating her. I had to make things right.

I slipped quietly through the heavy entrance door of Alice Tully Hall and took a seat behind the soundboard in the rear of the auditorium, which was nearly empty, except for the performers. The 1,086-seat concert hall in the Juilliard Building of the Lincoln Center for the Performing Arts was home to the Jazz at Lincoln Center Orchestra, which comprised on any given night ten to twenty musicians. The orchestra included a variety of woodwind and brass instruments and would be performing a five-song set list of jazz standards the following Saturday night. Among the brass instruments—the trumpets, baritones, and trombones—was a lone female performer: Jill Woburn.

As they waited for bandleader Wynton Marsalis, the orchestra warmed up with the tranquil rhythm of a familiar song, "El Cóndor Pasa." Though the song was made famous in 1970 by Simon & Garfunkel, this was actually the original Andean folk melody from which Paul Simon had crafted the hit song. The soft rhythm of woodwinds danced with the soothing zampoña—a traditional Andean panpipe. The music was beautiful but sad. It reminded me of playing taps on the trumpet when I was a kid.

Jill's hair was pulled back in a ponytail, accentuating her large eyes. I noticed my trumpet case, its brown leather tattered with age, near her on the stage floor next to the curtain. The case housed the silver Bach Stradivarius that I'd given to Jill a month before, on our six-month anniversary of dating. That trumpet had once been my prized possession, an astounding act of generosity from my parents at the beginning of high school. Now it was just a painful reminder of all I'd failed to achieve. Jill had thought it an extravagant gift. I'd been only too glad to be free of it.

The small orchestra transitioned into another warm-up piece—a jazz version of the 1972 hit "Superstition" by Stevie Wonder. A single saxophone glided from one dense pitch to another as if ascending a spectacular, curving road into the heavens before giving way to the accelerating rap of a snare drum and the iconic bass beat of this soul wonder.

Jill deserved that Bach Stradivarius, I told myself. But seeing her in practice that day, my stomach soured. It wasn't the first time I'd seen her play—far from it. But everything hit differently today. *To thine own self be true*—that's what the program demanded. Who was I kidding? That was my dream Jill was living! I could feel my heart racing in panic and regret. Why on earth had I given Jill my horn?

I closed my eyes. It was too late to get my trumpet back now. It was too late to fix anything I'd ruined. The truth was, I was consumed by guilt. I had no business dating Jill Woburn. I had been the cause of her brother's death, yet she'd never said a word about it, had never blamed me for ordering Frankie to run ahead, not even once. She'd never said a word about Harry's part in the accident, either. Over the months we'd been together, I'd tried to tell myself that either meant she forgave me or she hadn't ever blamed me for my family's role in her family's tragedy. Still, not talking about it hadn't felt right. And yet I hadn't been able to force myself to do it.

I pulled my headphones over my ears and pressed play on my Discman. The comforting tones of Alice in Chains drowned out the orchestra. I closed my eyes and escaped into the upbeat melody of the song "I Stay Away," my head filled with dreams of moving on from my dysfunctional relationship, and of a return to a time when music had both soothed and saved me.

CHAPTER 10

I threw open the front door and ran down the hallway and up the stairs to my bedroom. It was a sunny Saturday morning in June, eighth grade had just let out for summer, and I was in a rock 'n' roll state of mind. An older boy down the street had been blasting the new Ramones album out his apartment window, and my adrenaline was still surging from hearing it for the first time.

I walked over to my turntable and lifted the plastic cover. Sitting on the edge of my bed, I scanned my meager collection of soft rock records: Elton John's *Captain Fantastic and the Brown Dirt Cowboy*, Billy Joel's *Piano Man*, Rod Stewart's *A Night on the Town*, and a few Beatles albums. Then, of course, there was my collection of records by trumpet players Maynard Ferguson and Chuck Mangione—all great, but not exactly what I was feeling at the moment. The Ramones had broken something loose inside me.

I fell backward onto my bed and stared up into the bright light of the ceiling fixture, not allowing myself to blink. Mesmerized by the glare of the bulb, I let my mind wander until my attention was caught by the loud music coming from the bedroom next door. Until a year ago, the room had been Harry's. Now it was Max's, just like the bloodstained Yankees cap that never left Max's head.

I went and stood in his doorway. Max sat on the bed, reading the liner notes on a record sleeve. A dozen album covers were spread across the rug. He glanced up at me. I waited for him to tell me to get lost, but he only lowered his head. I took that as a very rare invitation.

I walked in and fell to my knees, picking up one album cover after another. They were all colored with flashy, edgy artwork: Queen's *A Day at the Races*, Led Zeppelin's *Physical Graffiti*, Blue Öyster Cult's *Secret Treaties*. Max had been playing this music for a while. But after hearing the Ramones that afternoon, the covers somehow appeared different to me. It was as if I'd been given a secret to decode. Could the music really sound as cool as these sleeves looked? The speakers resting on the shelf behind Max's bed thumped with the bass and then fell silent.

I asked if he had the Ramones.

Max pulled a record from its sleeve, placed it on the turntable, and threw me the empty album cover. "This was Harry's," he said. "He loved them."

I held the cover tight against my chest and closed my eyes.

"I miss him, too," said Max.

I opened my eyes, but Max was already focused on the music again. "It's their first album," he said as the notes began to come out of the speakers. The song began with a three-chord pattern that continued through the entire song, backed by a steady drumbeat, an occasional cymbal crash, and the memorable chant that begins "Blitzkrieg Bop." A raw and catchy wall of sound resonated through the speakers. Max's head bobbed up and down in sync.

I slowly moved forward and back, my head nodding along with Max's.

"That's right," he said. "You want it louder?"

My entire body was bending forward and back, accelerating with the rhythm of the song. My eyes answered him, and Max raised the volume until my ears began to ring. Something was happening inside of me that I didn't understand. I was growing angrier and yet, in a strange way, freer with each verse of the song.

When "Blitzkrieg Bop" ended abruptly, Max plucked the tonearm off the vinyl. As he turned around, a broad grin on his long face, it hit me: We had found a way to connect. And we had found another way out . . . of ourselves. That path was made up of fast and heavy, head-banging, rage-releasing rock 'n' roll.

We were on the way home from Mom's salon later that afternoon, sporting our new haircuts and listening to the Yankees game on WFAN 660 AM. Dad had demanded our hair be cut short, and Mom had finally given in. With my body dangling out the window of Mom's station wagon, I ran my fingers along my hairline, feeling the breeze on my head. My long, unruly curls were gone, and I was not happy.

"Yankees rule!" I shouted antagonistically at a portly middle-aged man on a nearby stoop as we drove past.

The man tore his Mets cap from his head, eyes bulging. "You're in the wrong borough, kid!"

Our neighborhood of Carroll Gardens, like most of Brooklyn, was brimming with New York Mets fans. But, three months into the 1977 MLB season, it was the Yankees—in first place in the American League East—who were the talk of the town. Born a Brooklyn Dodgers fan, Dad felt betrayed by their move to Los Angeles and had since become a die-hard Yankees fan. I was one, too.

"You're gonna get your butt kicked one day." Max pushed back on the sides of his short, straight hair—no longer feathered—out of habit.

"It's not my fault you're not allowed to be a Mets fan. Take it up with Dad."

Max shook his head. "I don't want to be a Mets fan anymore." He glanced down at Harry's Yankees cap, which lay on his lap. "I'm a Yankees fan, through and through. I'm just not stupid enough to wear a Yankees cap while driving through Mets territory."

Mom pulled into an empty spot in front of our townhome. "You can be whatever you want to be, honey," she said to Max, who was sitting beside her in the front passenger seat.

Max rolled his eyes up in the direction of his short bangs and smirked. "Sure, Mom. Whatever you say."

Within minutes, I was on the lounge chair in the den, soaking in the cool air from the window air conditioner humming behind me. My eyes darted from the screen to the sports page of the *Daily News*, which lay open on my lap. I scanned the star-studded lineup: Mickey Rivers, Lou Piniella, Reggie Jackson, Willie Randolph, Graig Nettles, Bucky Dent, and the team captain—and my favorite player of all time—Thurman Munson.

Max sat in the corner of the sofa, staring at the television. A pair of headphones extended from the jack on the side of the portable Sony AM/FM Cassette-Corder on his lap.

I shouted to Mom, who was in the kitchen. "When's Dad coming home? There's only three innings left." It was the biggest game of the season.

"He's working," Max responded, spraying bits of potato chip with each word. "He'll be on the phone the rest of the game, yelling about work, anyway."

But I wasn't listening. "Check it out!" I shrieked, pointing at the television screen.

Red Sox designated hitter Jim Rice had swung, and the Fenway Park crowd was going wild as the ball sailed high toward right field before dropping fast into the shallow dead zone behind first base. Reggie Jackson, playing deep in right field, jogged casually in to grab the ball. Rice sprinted to second for a double.

"Are you freaking kidding me!" I slapped my hands to my face. "Reggie just turned a single into a double because he's lazy!"

Yankees manager Billy Martin dashed to the mound and snatched the ball from Yankees pitcher Mike Torrez, gesturing to reliever Sparky Lyle. At the same time, Yankee outfielder Paul Blair ran from the dugout toward right field to replace Jackson, who jogged toward the dugout with his hands held out in a gesture of disbelief. When Jackson leaped down the steps, Martin, who was back in the dugout, rushed toward him. The two men got into a shouting match, veins bulged in both foreheads and tendons taut in their necks.

Max's eyes were glued to the set. Just then the front door opened and slammed.

"Dad, you're missing it!" I shouted. "Billy and Reggie are beating each other up!"

But he had no interest in baseball or me. He was already yelling at Mom in the kitchen—something about his dress shirts and the dry cleaners closing early on Saturdays. I turned to Max, who lay with his eyes closed, the headphones blasting music into his ears.

"You *forgot*? I swear, I'm going to flush every one of those goddamn pills—"

"Don't you dare!" Mom shrieked.

A struggle ensued, and I watched as Dad backed off and then charged toward her again, his hand in the air.

"Don't hit her!" I shouted from the kitchen doorway, clutching the frame to steady my trembling body.

From the corner of my eye, I could see Max. He was still on the sofa, staring at me, his headphones off. Mom and Dad froze, then turned to me, eyebrows lifted and heads tilted in confusion. Dad slowly turned and placed both his palms on the island countertop. Mom stepped out from behind him.

"What are you talking about?" Dad shook his head. "I would never hit your mother." His words sounded sincere. Maybe he was only reaching for her pills. Or perhaps for the cupboard where he kept the Jameson. But at the time, I didn't believe him. I'd never seen him strike her, so it was possible he was telling the truth. With Max and me, it was another story. He yelled at us more than he beat us, though the screaming was so horrible it might as well have been physical abuse.

"You're a bully and I'm sick of it!" The words just popped out of me.

Dad's eyes became slits, and he moved toward me. "Don't you dare disrespect me, or I'll—"

Suddenly, a voice from behind me cut in. "Or you'll what?" I turned and saw that Max was now standing there beside me, his entire body shaking.

Dad froze.

"Or you'll *what*?" Max screamed. It was the sound of a lifetime of pent-up anger.

All four of us stood in stunned silence. Finally, Max dropped the Yankees cap on the sofa, grabbed the handle of the cassette player, and said to me, "Let's get out of here."

I followed Max out the door. We walked thirty minutes in silence to Fifth Avenue, and we never once looked back.

———

When we stepped inside Fifth Avenue Record Shop, my eyes shot open wide. Five rows of records ran forty feet back to the other end of the building. I felt as if I was adrift in a beautiful sea.

"Here, hold this." Max pulled the headphone cord from the jack and handed me the cassette player. He dug into his pocket and pulled out a few record reviews—small pieces of white paper with tiny black print cut from *Hit Parade*. "Follow me."

Max took off, almost jogging down the center aisle, and I followed him to the section labeled "I through J." He flipped through the shrink-wrapped albums, then finally came to an abrupt stop. His face relaxed into a grin. "Found it!" He lifted the record from the bin. When I started to turn away, he stopped me. "Wait! It's for you." There was an urgency in his tone that I only heard when he talked about music.

"What is this? Is it rock?" My eyes lit up as I gazed at the cover's dramatic gothic imagery: a stone monument adorned with eagle wings, cobras, and a skull with glowing yellow eyes. At the base of the structure, in front of a tall, painted door, was the featureless shape of a woman wearing high heels and sitting on the ground. Stone columns and battered walls towered over her, while the dark shadow of another figure approached from the black sea in the distance. The album title, *Sin After Sin*, appeared beneath the horizontal crown molding, the band's logo in gothic script above it. It was the coolest artwork I'd ever seen.

"They're a new heavy metal band out of England," Max said. He told me that hardly anyone in the States knew about Judas Priest. He'd read about the creepy artwork and figured I'd like it. "You've exhausted everything I have that's hard and heavy," he explained. "These guys take things to another level. Angrier. Heavier."

I flipped the album over to examine the back, a painted rocky landscape surrounded by water, the stone mausoleum in the distance, the dark figure standing in a ray of light projecting through the center of the monument. It was menacing.

When I looked up, Max was already at the other end of the store, waving something small in his hand. I returned the album carefully to its slot in the bin and ran over to join him. He'd found the cassette tape so I could play it on his Cassette-Corder.

I paid the cashier and ran outside. The anticipation was killing me. I sat on the curb and ripped the shrink wrap off the cassette box, pulled the card out of its slot, and closely studied the track names: "Sin After Sin," "Diamonds and Rust," and "Dissident Aggressor." So cool.

When Max stepped outside, he immediately pulled off the headphones hung around his neck and handed them to me with the portable player. I pressed the eject button and popped the new cassette into the cradle. Headphones on, I pressed play and closed my eyes.

A single distorted guitar. A chugging riff. Powerhouse drums. Prowling bass. Snarling vocals. All wound together in perfect rhythm; it was beautiful. A guitar solo began. The drums beat a tympanic swing. I stomped my feet uncontrollably on the street, totally consumed by the music. The relief was glorious.

A second guitar. Soaring vocals. The bass was cruising now. Then the tympanic rhythm returned. Treacherous chords. The cymbal crashed. There was an abrupt pace change, before a single guitar shrilled, tearing straight into the depths of my gut. The guitars soared, as spectacular as they were effortless. The voice growled, raw and exquisite. Glorious mayhem. My eyes still closed, I rocked back and forth as the song crescendoed to a climactic ending.

"Max! Oh my God—you have to hear this!"

Exactly one month later, the Palladium was hosting the 1977 *Sin After Sin* tour, featuring Judas Priest. The Palladium was grander than a club but not quite an arena. Built in downtown Manhattan in 1927, it had at various times been an opera house, a musical theater, and a movie theater; now it was a concert hall with a reputation for showcasing the best up-and-coming acts in rock 'n' roll. Its three thousand seats felt almost intimate.

Max and I stood in the center of the first row of the balcony, with a clear view of the stage. I scanned the crowd with awe—long hair everywhere, boys made up like girls and girls dressed as boys. A crystal chandelier the size of a small car hung from the ceiling in front of us. When I looked over at Max, he was staring into space. "What's the matter? Aren't you excited?"

"Yeah, I guess." He scanned the crowd, then eyed the exit.

"What is it?"

"I don't like crowds." He wiped his perspiring brow. Max had always been a nervous kid, but he seemed more and more high-strung these days, and I'd definitely noticed that he had been avoiding large groups. In fact, I'd been surprised that he wanted to go to the concert at all.

"Forget about them. We're about to see Judas Priest live!" I plunked down in my seat and watched Max work his way through a variety of nervous tics, from crossing and uncrossing his arms to rubbing the back of his neck. He was now sixteen, but still barely taller and heavier than me and very self-conscious about his size. Our short hair didn't do us any favors, either. Neither of us looked like we belonged at this show, but we did, as much as anybody else.

The lights went out.

"Priest! Priest!" the crowd chanted as "Diamonds and Rust" blared from amplifiers stacked in the dark. The stage ignited, the crowd screamed, and the band soared into "Victim of Changes." As lights refracted in every direction from the crystal chandelier, the sound bombarded us, shaking the entire auditorium. Song after song, the crowd leaped around, head-banging, and I couldn't help but join in. It was the first time I'd tried it. The experience felt electric, magnetic, wicked. When the house lights finally came on, I clung to my padded metal seat, unable to move.

"Let's go," Max yelled over the crowd noise.

"I'll meet you out front. Gotta go to the bathroom."

There was a long line in the men's room, and the group inside was noisy, until a man in a bleach-stained Motorhead concert T-shirt at the far end of the room began to sing "Dreamer Deceiver," the ethereal ballad we'd all just heard.

"Fuck, yeah!" yelled a biker behind me, while the bathroom crowd shouted and howled.

On and on he sang, until finally, a space opened up at the far right of the trough urinal. I relieved myself into the frothy, dark yellow pool not far from the spot where the singing man was belting out the song's final words. As I was zipping up, another man, wearing a black leather jacket draped with silver chains, approached. With a syringe clasped in his mouth, he tightened a big rubber band around the singing man's bicep.

As I stood there, stunned, the second man plunged the needle into the singer's inner elbow. He then slid down the wall one white tile at a time, kicked my foot, and smiled up at me. "Home, sweet home," he said. A third man was already slumped on the floor next to him, drooling and mumbling; his eyes had rolled back as though he'd melted.

Whiskey was one thing, but this was something entirely different. I couldn't look away.

I heard my name called behind me and turned around. Max stood at the bathroom entrance, waving me out. We joined the massive stream of concertgoers overflowing into the street. When we got to the middle of the cordoned-off street, he turned to me.

"What were those guys doing back there?" he asked.

I just looked at him. He knew what they were doing.

"Just stay away from needles." His voice was stern. It seemed as if he'd officially become the older brother I'd yearned for since Harry's death.

I nodded, and he stepped past me, singing the words to "Dreamer Deceiver" as I followed him down the street.

"I love that song," I said. "What do you think it's about? I think the 'dreamer' is drugs . . . the way he—it—takes us by the hand and up we go . . . don't you?"

Max looked up into the dark sky. "No. I think the 'dreamer' is Death. I think the guy commits suicide and Death takes all his pain away."

As we walked home in silence, I considered the two possibilities. One minute, I'd think my interpretation was right; the next, I believed Max's. Either way, the same thought kept playing over in my head: It probably didn't matter which one the dreamer was—drugs or suicide. Because either way, the "dreamer" was still a "deceiver."

Still, I couldn't get the song, or the image of the melting man, out of my head.

———

At home later that night, after everyone was asleep, I sat cross-legged in front of the forty-two-inch rec room television playing the brand-new Atari 2600 console that Max had convinced Mom to buy earlier that summer. The house was quiet. But although the day's events had drained me, I was still wired from the excitement.

During a break in my game, I put the controller down and

began to wander. The tile floor chilled me as I padded around, lost in thought. I thought about the concert, and I thought about Max, and Harry. I thought about Brie. I felt bored and unsettled. I felt stuck.

My skinny knees burned from having been bent too long while I played. I shook out my legs and glanced up at the tikis carved into the wooden bar.

"Hello." I raised a hand to them.

The wooden carvings smiled back in silence, their eyes seeming to glow in the light from the bar.

I limped toward the under-counter refrigerator to get something to drink. Catching sight of the dozens of bottles lining the mirrored shelves behind the bar, I paused and scanned them, one at a time—all different shapes, sizes, and colors. I saw them almost every day, but they'd never been anything more to me than bottles collecting dust. Without thinking, I reached for the half-empty bottle of vodka, twisted off the cap, and poured the clear liquor into a tall plastic cup.

I lifted it and sniffed, expecting to smell the sweetness I had inhaled a year earlier when I had taken that gulp of Dad's whiskey. But this liquid was different. Almost odorless. It looked innocent enough. Maybe it would help me to feel less sad, or less stuck. Dad's whiskey always seemed to mellow him out, at least until he'd drunk too much.

I took a large gulp from the cup and choked. Then I swallowed another. As the liquid made its way down my esophagus, my eyes watered, and my nose burned. Just as I had done a year before, I tilted my face beneath the faucet to chug a cold stream of water. When I finally lifted my head, water dripped from my lips. The fire in my belly smoldered. Then the burn mellowed, and the acrid taste became sweet.

I held the half-filled plastic cup of vodka under the faucet of the copper bar sink and filled it with water to dilute it.

Lifting it to my lips, I drank until it was empty. When I was done, I felt weightless. Unattached and free.

Once the liquid was gone, I poured another cupful of vodka and sat on the bamboo barstool to drink it. The first cupful had gone down easy, and my mind begged for a bit more. Between sips, I held up two fingers in the air as though I were smoking a cigarette. Every type of liquor imaginable lined the mirrored shelves behind the bar, and my eyes roamed from one bottle to another. I wondered how each one would taste—and how each of them would make me feel.

I suddenly became dizzy, and my head throbbed as I leaned into the bamboo bar for balance. What had felt beautiful a moment before was turning on me.

I stumbled off my barstool, made my way to the front door, and stepped outside, where I vomited into the street. When I was done, I raised my head and wiped my mouth with my sleeve. The golden hue of the city lights made me feel warm in the cooler night air. I closed my eyes and smiled. I was home, sweet home.

Just like the melting man.

CHAPTER 11

No longer in the ICU, Max was now propped up in the hospital bed of a single room on the sixth floor of Maimonides Medical Center. It had been four days, and the top of his head was still bandaged. His eyes were closed and the television on the wall was muted, the rerun of a Mets game playing on the screen. As I entered, I placed the small Panasonic CD player I was carrying on top of the dresser.

Max turned slowly and tried to force a smile. His face was swollen, his eyes slits. "Don't suppose you brought me a drink?"

I didn't laugh. "The pain meds aren't enough?"

"Is anything ever enough?" He turned his head the other way.

Point taken. I doubted there was enough alcohol in the world to soothe Max. The same had been true for me. I'd learned in AA that any description of the addict can be condensed to three words: *inability to moderate*. Meaning, an addict could never be satisfied by a small amount.

I had long hoped that scientists would discover a "moderation" gene or missing neural pathway—or whatever biological defect accounted for this cursed disease—and then devise some way to repair things. But even if the nature side of things could be addressed, would that be enough? What about the element of nurture: all the damage done by external influences and circumstances in the addict's environment? That would need to be fixed, too. That, I had come to find, was the promise of AA: once the character defects caused by the "nurture" piece were treated, the "nature" piece would be rendered irrelevant. It was a tremendous promise. An achievable one, too, I'd been told, provided that a person trusted not in themselves but in a Higher Power that would restore them to sanity by aligning their will with Its will. A simple program for complicated people. And still, I couldn't bring myself to do it.

"But, Max . . . ," I began, approaching his bed.

"I'm tired, Daniel." Max was now staring out the window.

"You and me both. But we're gonna get through this. Together." I was saying the words, even as I wasn't sure I believed them. We were brothers. But neither of us had ever been able to help the other much.

He looked up at me. "Don't kid yourself. We're all on our own in this." He let out a long breath. "It shouldn't be this hard to just live."

"So, after thirty-four years, you're just going to give up?"

Max gave me a funny look. "I *gave* up. That's what the other morning was about, dummy. And so what? It's no different than what Grandpa Gabe did."

I just stared at him. "Grandpa Gabe had a heart attack."

"Uh-uh." Max picked up the small plastic box of orange juice from the table over his bed. He poked the thin straw into the sealed foil top and sipped. "Mom lied."

I slumped in the faux leather hospital chair. "How do you know?"

Max looked up at the ceiling. "Harry told me."

I snorted. "Jesus, Max. You almost had me there."

"I mean, before he died."

"Well, why didn't he tell me?" I'd always felt I was the one who was closest with Harry.

Max shrugged. "He was drunk and it just came out. Then he made me swear. Said Mom would be pissed if anyone else knew."

"I wonder why Mom told him?"

He shrugged again. "Who else did she have?"

Good point. I leaned forward in my chair. "Why would a recently widowed father leave his two young children behind?"

"Contrary to what you may think . . ." He paused and sipped the last of the juice from the box. "Life might not feel worth living for everyone, no matter who they have in their life. Or maybe *because* of who they have in their life."

I stood and paced while Max fiddled with the television remote control attached to the bedside. His eyes had welled up, and I could see that he was trying to hide that from me. "I will *never* find peace while he's still alive." He said it quietly, as if he was speaking to himself and not to me.

Deep down, I felt the same way, although I didn't want to admit it. The program of Alcoholics Anonymous had promised that if I did the work, I would find peace, regardless of everything else, including Dad. I had doubted that promise when I first heard it, and I still did.

Outside the window, the sky was cloudy and a drizzle fell. I hated seeing Max like this. I tried to think of some way to distract him from his dark thoughts.

"Hey, you'll never guess who I saw last night, coming out of a meeting," I said at last, coming back to sit by him.

He didn't answer.

"Brie. Can you believe it?" I could feel a smile rising to my face, despite everything. "She looked the same."

"That's nice." Max picked at a thread on the hospital blanket.

I could see that it was the wrong direction to take in

changing the subject. Max didn't need to hear about my life right now. "She only stopped by to ask about you," I insisted. "She knows I'm with Jill."

Max finally looked at me with some interest. "I've never asked, but don't you think it's strange that a girl could date the brother of the guy who killed her twin?" Max had a way of putting things bluntly.

Turning uncomfortably in the chair, I gazed at the muted television screen—the Mets were losing, of course.

"I don't think she blames me for what Harry did. She probably just doesn't want to talk about it." I wanted to believe this was true. "I mean, who would?"

Max looked at me more intently. "Are you even sure she knows it was Harry in the Gremlin that day?"

I looked at him helplessly. It was possible that she didn't know. Jill's parents had taken her away from the neighborhood that very night, and they hadn't returned. I had no idea, really, how much the Woburns knew about what had happened. I only had my assumptions—assumptions that, I realized now, conveniently let me off the hook. I didn't want to think about the possibility that Jill didn't know Harry was to blame. Because if that was true, I would have been a real jerk to have stayed silent all this time.

I ran my fingers through my hair. "Why're you bringing this shit up now?"

Max shrugged. Perhaps because he saw the panic in my face, he mercifully changed the subject. "So, Brie knows you're sober now . . . that's good."

"Trust me . . . that ship sailed." Of course I wanted to get back together with Brie. But she'd never have me. Not again, not ever. I was sure of it. We'd been through way too much. "Besides, she's got her own life. And I've got you to take care of."

Max rolled his eyes. "No one can help me, Daniel. Not even you."

I leaned forward in my seat. All this talk of the past had given me an idea. "No, seriously. You should just stop working for Dad. It can't be good for you to get treated like shit every day by your own father."

"No kidding, but what the fuck else am I going to do? I can't do anything else."

I didn't believe that. Max struggled to navigate the world, that was true. But as Dad's glorified gofer, he managed to deal with the people he was forced to interact with every day. Dad had somehow convinced him he couldn't do more than that. But I wasn't buying it.

"Come work with me."

Max shook his head, but I kept pushing. "Fuck the old man. He doesn't deserve you." He remained resistant, but I got him to promise he'd think about it.

On my way out, I hit the play button on the CD player. The Ramones' classic "Blitzkrieg Bop" exploded through the small speakers: a burst of joy and *hey ho let's go* excitement.

Behind me, I heard Max let out a laugh—a real one. "Nice!" he shouted over the music as I left.

"See you later!" I called back, glad that he was still around.

———

Jill and I sat facing a modern glass desk in the psychiatrist's office on the fourth floor of the Counseling and Mental Health Center at Maimonides Medical Center. The psychiatrist assigned to Max's case, Valerie Rainier, was in the hallway saying goodbye to another couple. Her credentials were impressive. A diploma from Tufts University School of Medicine hung on the wall above her desk chair. Her medical licenses from the American Board of Psychiatry and the American Psychiatric Association hung on either side of the diploma.

Facing the desk, I whispered to Jill, "Don't speak. Just

listen." She had insisted on coming along. Against my better judgment, I'd acquiesced. I still wasn't sure why. Perhaps it had something to do with the way I'd been treating her. I knew I was being unkind. But we kept pushing each other's buttons, and I didn't know how to stop.

With her lips tight, she nodded. I couldn't remember the last time she hadn't commented on something I said. I appreciated that she was trying.

Dr. Rainier walked in, closed the door behind her, and sat across from us at her desk. Awkwardly, we exchanged pleasantries. Then the doctor leaned forward and clasped her hands.

"I'll get right to the point," she said. "When your brother was admitted four days ago, the attending physician determined he met the emergency standard for mental illness admission. Two days ago, I examined Max and confirmed that assessment. Your brother will be held here involuntarily for observation and treatment. If, within fifteen days, I determine that he is no longer a danger to himself, then under certain conditions he will be allowed to leave."

Her words stunned me. I'd expected that they would want to keep Max, but I hadn't anticipated that they would actually force him to stay. A childhood memory floated at the edges of my mind, and I shook it away, not wanting to remember. "You can't keep him here," I said.

The doctor's voice was gentle but firm. "Under the law, we can, for as long as necessary."

"Maybe he just needs to change his medication? You should talk to his psychiatrist . . . Dr. Tanner . . . Mel Tanner in—"

She frowned. "Max hasn't been under the care of a psychiatrist in over two years. His medication hasn't been refilled in over a year."

"What?" I turned to Jill, who was trying to conceal a small smile that said she wasn't surprised. But *I* was surprised.

"When he's recovered from his injury," continued the

doctor, "he'll be moved from the sixth floor to inpatient psychiatric services here on the fourth floor."

"Listen," I pleaded, "Max just needs to get back on his medication, the proper type and dosage, and he'll be fine. I've already told him he's coming to live with me for a while when he gets out—"

Jill opened her mouth to protest, but seeing the look I gave her, she stopped herself.

Dr. Rainier looked at me with what I thought was pity. "Your brother wants to kill himself, Mr. Zimmer. He told me that, in no uncertain terms. He is intent on it."

I nodded. "Yeah, because he's not taking his meds. You just said so yourself. Once—"

The doctor leaned forward and spoke bluntly. "Mr. Zimmer, he'll be evaluated again next week. Until then, there's nothing more I can do for you. My office will be in touch." She stood, walked past me to the door, and opened it.

Jill jumped up and thanked the doctor.

I pinned a fake smile on my face, echoed her words, and took Jill's arm, pushing her out the office door in front of me. As we walked toward the bank of elevators, I was still gripping her arm, doing my best to contain my anger.

"Ow . . . You're hurting me!" she said. I let her go, feeling my face flush.

"Sorry."

When we got outside, I walked quickly toward the parking lot. Jill called my name from behind me. Unable to keep up, she shouted, "Daniel! What are you *doing*?"

I spun on her and pointed back at the building, toward what I imagined was the fourth-floor psychiatric unit. "What I'm doing," I said, "is trying to save my brother. You have no idea what can happen in a place like this. *No idea*."

Jill's face turned white. "Daniel—"

But I wanted no part of whatever she had to say. I felt eaten up inside. Eaten up by worry about Max and eaten up by guilt over Jill's and my shared past. It was unfair to her, I knew, but Jill was the last person I wanted to talk to in that moment.

Her pleading eyes were shining with tears as she reached her hand out to me, but I pretended not to see it.

"I gotta go," I mumbled, and then I turned away and took off into the crowd.

"Wait up," she yelled after me, but I was moving too fast, and I maneuvered in and out of the throng until I lost her.

CHAPTER 12

Max and I rode down the paths of a crowded Prospect Park, just off Flatbush Avenue. The summer of 1977 was the hottest summer of my life. The air was thick with moisture, and my body was drenched in sweat. The sun was still hovering in the late afternoon sky, a glowing orange ball that reflected off the small red crabapples dangling from the trees. The fiery light burst through a crevice between two overlapping clouds, illuminating their edges and stopping me in my tracks.

We'd talked our mom into letting us ride to the park so we could hang out at Prospect Lake and cool off in the heat. But there were too many people at the lake for Max to feel comfortable, so we decided to ride around the neighborhood before heading home.

After a while, Max and I reached Winthrop Street, and then, almost as if we'd agreed ahead of time, we rode another five blocks until we reached the embossed metal sign announcing the Kingsboro Psychiatric Center. Known to the surrounding neighborhoods as "the Flatbush Insane Asylum," the hospital took up two full blocks on Winthrop. Its well-groomed lawns were vast and crossed with intersecting sidewalks. In the middle of it all sat a ten-story central building. On both sides of the square building, massive stone gargoyles leaned over the gutter from the roof.

"Boys—the park only," Mom had told us when we left the house. "You don't need to see or hear what's going on over at the asylum. Do you understand?"

We said we did. I knew my mom's concerns about the asylum masked a bigger fear. A serial killer had been targeting victims in New York. When the murders first began a year earlier, she'd moved our curfew from ten o'clock to nine thirty. This had seemed unreasonable to Max and me, since Son of Sam seemed to be interested mainly in eighteen- to twenty-year-old women and usually only struck late at night. But our mom had insisted, telling us we were lucky she was letting us go out at all. We hadn't argued with her after that.

Streetlights ticked on in front of the asylum, and a church bell tolled seven times. We stared at the old buildings as we walked our bikes down Winthrop. It was no coincidence that Max and I had both wanted to make our way there, despite our mom's words; we were still drawn to things that we found dark and scary. And what could feel darker and scarier to a couple of young boys than the combination of mental confusion and confinement?

The buildings were like fortresses of red brick, with tinted windows and black pitched roofs, all surrounded by a thick iron fence that rose to six feet. I'd heard somewhere that the wards—which had large, arched windows and stretched five stories tall—could hold two thousand patients. That number, I figured, didn't include the countless ghosts of those rumored to have haunted its halls for more than one hundred years.

Max and I sat down on the sidewalk and stared at the hospital through the iron fence. The sun was descending in the distance, and the darkening asylum appeared almost peaceful. The church bell chimed. It was half past the hour.

As we were watching, a light came on in a top-floor room and suddenly Max and I heard people shouting. It looked like several people were running around a room, searching for something. One of them, looking alarmed, came to the window and peered up toward the roof.

Max and I looked up at the roof, too. And that's when we saw him: an old man with straggly hair, dressed in a long, sleeveless white gown, standing near the edge. He raised one arm, his palm facing us. Before we understood what was happening, he stepped off the building and fell.

The old man's gown rippled in the air, and then he hit the ground. A deafening sound—like a sack of stones hitting concrete—echoed in the asylum courtyard.

Horrified, Max and I backed away from the fence, but we couldn't stop looking at the body, surrounded by a pool of blood. Hospital workers rushed outside and gathered around it. One of the attendants swore. Two of them pulled a white sheet over the corpse and lifted it onto a gurney. The other men stood around, smoking and chatting, as easily as if they were on a regular work break.

"It's like it happens all the time," I whispered.

"If I had to live in a place like that," said Max, "I'd kill myself, too. No question about it."

———

When we got home that evening, Max followed me into my bedroom and slammed the door. He looked pale. "I don't want to be alone right now," he said. I didn't blame him. I didn't want to be alone, either.

Max settled himself on my bed and grabbed the thick

binder I kept on my nightstand. He opened it to the first page—a clear plastic sheet protector with a newspaper clipping inside. Dated Friday, July 30, 1976, the *Daily News* headline read: "Chatting in a Car, Girl Met by Death." He looked at me and shifted his position on the bed. "What is this?"

"That's the very first time he struck," I said, "exactly one year ago today."

He flipped through my dozens of newspaper clippings about the Son of Sam murders. I had originally collected them as research for a class project on current events, but out of sheer curiosity, I never stopped. For months, the killer had been terrorizing New York City—shooting young people in parked cars with a .44-caliber Bulldog revolver without warning or reason. There'd been eight shootings and five deaths as he moved between the Bronx and Queens.

"I think *he's* insane," said Max. "Don't you?"

"More like evil."

Max returned his attention to the clippings. After a while he asked, "What does he mean by 'Tell me Jim, what will you have for July twenty-ninth?'"

I told him that was a quote from a letter the killer had sent to the journalist Jimmy Breslin at the *Daily News* two months before.

"But that was yesterday, and nothing happened." Max looked up. "Maybe he's done."

I didn't know what else "July twenty-ninth" could be about. But I doubted Son of Sam was finished.

———

Max poked at my sleeping body, then began shaking me with both hands.

"Quit it," I complained, too tired to move.

"Wake up!"

I rolled over and peered at the alarm clock. It was 7:00 a.m. "Why?"

"It happened! Another shooting! Right here in Brooklyn . . . Bath Beach!"

I bolted up in bed. "Brooklyn?" A thousand cops had been patrolling the Bronx and Queens since July 29. And now Son of Sam had struck in Brooklyn, the borough to the west, for the very first time. Clever. The cops couldn't watch everywhere at once.

Max pointed toward the window. "See for yourself."

I rolled over and peeked through the blinds. The sidewalk in front of our building bustled with people, all visibly upset and angry.

We ran downstairs and turned on the news. After a while, the anchor introduced a reporter who was down at the Kings County public hospital, where the victims—who were still alive—had been taken. The hospital was blocked off with yellow-and-black police tape, and a tall man with black hair and a full mustache, wearing a brown suit, was speaking into a microphone.

"Sunday, July 31," the reporter said. "According to witnesses, at two this morning, shots were fired on Fourteenth Street in Bath Beach, along the Gravesend Bay waterfront. The victims, twenty-year-old Stacy Moskowitz of Midwood and twenty-year-old Robert Violante of Bensonhurst, were found in Violante's 1969 Buick Skylark four-door sedan. Moskowitz and Violante were taken to Coney Island Hospital and transferred here, to the emergency room of Kings County Hospital, where they are undergoing surgery."

"'Hello from the gutters of NYC,'" Max said in a spooky tone, reciting a line from Son of Sam's recent letter, "'which are filled with dog manure, vomit, stale wine, urine, and blood—'"

"You memorized it?" I kicked his foot. "*You're* evil."

Grinning, he continued. "'Hello from the sewers of NYC, which swallow up these delicacies when they are washed away by the sweeper trucks—'"

"I wonder what he looks like?" I asked, hoping to distract him. The police sketches had varied, but the consensus was that he was Caucasian and in his twenties.

"He's probably just some regular guy. Opening a door for some young lady one minute, then shooting her in the face the next."

"What are you smiling about?" I didn't like the expression on Max's face. He'd always been a little strange. But he was seeming weirder all the time, and the look on his face now was outright demented. I had no doubt that our father's abuse was the main cause. I wondered if seeing the old man fall the day before was making him worse. Or maybe living in New York while a serial killer was on the loose was finally taking a toll.

He sat up straight. "There's no such thing as God."

"Why would you say that?" I hadn't said anything about God.

"Nobody cares about anything. Just themselves. Just like that guy at the asylum yesterday—he was upset because he had to clean up that mess in this hundred-degree heat. Not because the old man died. And Son of Sam—I bet he's only killing because of something dumb. Like maybe he doesn't have a girlfriend."

"But he shoots at men, too."

"Collateral damage. They're not his target."

I supposed Max was right about one thing.

People seemed to only care about themselves.

———

Ten days later, I lay on my stomach on the floor of the den, the tops of my feet resting on the sofa behind me.

From the edge of the sofa next to me, Max pointed to the television. "Look, a special report." He adjusted the Yankees cap on his head.

Son of Sam stepped out of a police car in lower Manhattan as bulbs flashed and reporters scurried around him. He had a pudgy face with red lips and curly brown hair. As the detectives guided him through the station parking lot, he smiled a strange grin—lips open, teeth visible beneath rosy cheeks—as though flushed with fame.

"Is he *smiling*?" I asked with disgust.

Max nodded mechanically. "Told you. Doesn't even look like a killer." The truth was, the killer—David Berkowitz— looked simple to me, even a bit dumb.

Max dropped to the floor and crawled over to the television. His eyes were fixated on the grainy screen. He leaned in with his mouth opened slightly. Son of Sam turned toward the camera, and in that moment it was as if his eyes met Max's through the television screen.

"*I see you*," Max whispered.

As I watched him, I felt a sense of dread. I didn't know what it was, but something was changing in Max.

And I had no idea how to help him.

CHAPTER 13

I raced four blocks down Forty-Seventh Street until I came to the corner of Thirteenth Avenue. I was in no mood for an AA meeting, but I knew that going to the Old Park Slope Caton was the smart move and so that's what I was doing. The gruff tone of Dale B., the member Tony had recommended as a sponsor, echoed inside my head: "When you don't want to go, that's when you need it most." Dale was full of "suggestions" like that—suggestions that were, I thought, really subtle commands, but they were also useful spiritual axioms.

I leaned against a streetlamp while the evening rush-hour traffic of vehicles and pedestrians swirled around me. Heavy eyelids and hunger pangs added to my frustration, as did the anger I'd been feeling since ditching Jill at the hospital earlier. I was three-quarters of the way through a classic AA acronym, one that was a warning sign of bad things to come if left untreated: H-A-L-T. Hungry. Angry. Lonely. Tired. Just one of those factors was enough to cause the sufferer to inflict serious damage on his or her fellows. Three was a ticking time bomb. All I was missing was loneliness. Though, when I really thought about it, I realized that I felt alone in my suffering, too.

Multicolored lights popped on outside the small corner shop across Forty-Seventh Street, illuminating the store's awning: The Sweetest Place in the Kosher World. The store was filled with bulk containers of candy—chocolate, gummy, hard, sour, wax, and other. Inside, I filled a small paper bag with sugar-coated fruit slices in a variety of neon-bright colors; I hoped they would boost my energy level. I devoured them outside the shop entrance, then stepped off the curb to cross Thirteenth Avenue.

There was one problem resolved, anyway.

"Hey you," a familiar voice said.

Brie was walking toward me, wearing the same white-and-green-checkered overcoat with a black scarf wrapped around her neck. She had one hand on the strap of her shoulder bag; the other was dragging a wheeled silver canister. As she approached, I noticed a thin clear tube tucked into her nostrils.

Stepping back onto the curb, I tried not to stare. "Hey . . . how . . . how are you?"

"It's just an oxygen tank, Daniel," she said, smiling in the face of my discomfort. "It helps me, that's all." She turned the corner in order to pull the canister up the ramp. Her cheeks and the tip of her nose glowed pink beneath the streetlights. The temperature was dropping as the evening air settled across Brooklyn. "I'm on my way to Maimonides. How's Max?"

I filled her in on the conversation I'd had with Max's doctor, and she listened patiently, even when I raised my voice in frustration. When I grumbled that the psychiatrist was a hard-ass, Brie only nodded, as if it wasn't the first time she'd heard that particular complaint. She even offered to talk with the doctor herself on our family's behalf. Though the woman wasn't a close friend of Brie's, they were well acquainted, and Brie seemed to feel sure that she could help smooth things over.

"Even if he has to stay longer than he'd like," she said, "it's going to be okay. We'll make sure he's comfortable and taken care of. Why don't you let me talk to him about it with you?"

I thanked her and we agreed to meet at Max's room the next morning at ten. I leaned over to look at the oxygen tank. "How long has it been?"

"About a year," she answered. "It helps . . . when I'm out and about. I don't have to use my inhaler as much."

I could tell she was downplaying the reality of the situation. We smiled awkwardly at one another, unsure how to proceed. I wanted to give her a hug but decided against it.

"Check you out . . ." I blurted.

"On the . . ." Brie replied instinctively, before catching herself. Looking directly in my eyes, she smiled. "See you tomorrow, Daniel."

I watched her walk slowly down Forty-Seventh Street. In her long coat and high heels, her blond hair blowing in the wind, she strode with authority, despite her obvious disability. As my eyes followed her into the darkness, I resolved in that moment to do all the Steps of AA's twelve-step program. I'd been procrastinating long enough, and I wasn't going to mess around any longer. I decided that I would finally ask Dale B. to be my sponsor.

Suddenly, a voice cut in from behind me. It was steely and familiar. "You're still in love with her, aren't you?"

I turned and there was Jill, standing with her hands on her hips. She was angry, I could see that. But it was obvious that she was hurt, too. And I couldn't blame her for that.

"Jill," I said with a sigh. "Let's not do this here."

"Answer me," she insisted.

I shook my head. "This can wait. We need to go into the meeting."

"Don't tell me what to do!" Her voice was shaking.

"Fine." I shrugged. "Do what you want. I'm going."

I started up Thirteenth Avenue, assuming she'd be right

behind me. She knew when she needed a meeting, and it was obvious that this was one of those times, even if she didn't want to admit it. When I got to Forty-Eighth Street, I slowly turned around, convinced Jill would be there.

But she wasn't.

I sat patiently in my regular spot at the Old Park Slope Caton, looking and listening for the big man with the throaty voice. The room filled quickly as the clock on the wall ticked off the minutes to 6:00 p.m.

The meeting was standing room only—every chair was taken, including the one in front of me, but for once, it was not occupied by Dale B. The reason became clear when I heard a loud voice echoing behind me.

"Good evening, friends," he called out. "My name is Dale, and I *am* an alcoholic!"

"Dale!" shouted the group.

A smile crept across my face as I watched Dale B. make his way confidently to the front of the room and sit down in the small metal chair behind the table.

To begin, he read from the meeting sheets about house-keeping and other issues associated with AA and the clubhouse—where smoking was permitted, how to sign up for service, how to become a coffee maker and greeter, and, among other things, the "seventh tradition," which stated that each AA group must be funded solely by member contribu-tions. Wicker baskets were passed around and quickly filled with crumpled dollar bills.

"Small price to pay for the gift of physical and emotional sobriety," Dale said. "Cheap help." Then he opened the Big Book and read a short passage on how deep resentments lead to a life of futility and misery.

Dale gently placed the thick tome on the table and looked up at the crowd.

"Carrying resentment is like drinking poison and waiting for the other guy to die." Dale adjusted his massive frame in the small chair. "I want to tell you a story before I open the meeting up to you. Years ago, I worked for a guy in the construction business right here in Brooklyn."

Dale looked out the window as if remembering, then continued with a smile on his face. "Man, this guy was a hard-ass. Constantly riding me, cussing me out, screaming like a loon. And not just me. He was like that to *everybody*." Dale's tone was congenial, despite the content of his words.

"Talk about resentments." He made a small scoffing noise. "I hated him with every fiber of my being. Hell, he was one of the main reasons I drank so much . . . or so I thought."

The group was hanging on every one of the big man's words, just like always. I could relate to what he was saying. *Completely.*

"The funny thing is . . . this guy would end up being the one who saved my life. He was the one who introduced me to AA and took me to my very first meeting, right here at the Caton. I was his heavy-machine operator—a crane. I was also a thirty-five-year-old hopeless alcoholic with three kids from two different women. He knew I couldn't afford to lose my job. He knew I had alimony and child support to pay. Lots of it.

"I was good at what I did . . ." Dale looked down at the open book, then back up again. "But he knew that, on the job, I was a huge liability, a major accident waiting to happen. He said I needed what he called 'cheap help.' He tried for months to get me to go to a meeting—it was better for him if I got sober, honestly. But I wasn't ready." Dale paused. "And then one day, I knew it was time. That man saved my life when he took me to this meeting, nineteen years ago."

I peered down my row at the faces, all full of emotion and

completely focused on Dale, who was looking solemnly back at the group.

"The weird thing was, he didn't go into the meeting himself, although he looked like he could use it. Strangely enough, he recognized that AA could help, but he never accessed the help himself. Still, he got me here. And for that, I'll never forget him. And I'll never forget what you people have done for me. I've got a life now, one second to none. A way to deal with anger, resentment, fear. A Higher Power of my understanding."

He leaned forward, his arms stretched in front of him, his long fingers extending over the edge of the table. "I'll end with this . . . *maybe*." A huge grin spread across his face.

The mood lightened and everyone laughed.

"Three principles in this program changed my life. Number one: there is power in powerlessness. Number two: it is not weakness to rely on others or on a power greater than myself. And number three: to keep something, I have to give it away." Dale nodded, smiling toothily. "Thank you very much."

The crowd applauded enthusiastically.

I wasn't sure if I believed what Dale said, but I believed that *he* believed it, and that was good enough for me. I wanted what Dale had, and I was going to get it.

As the group filed out, I zigzagged my way to the front and waited patiently for the small congratulatory group around him to disperse. I extended my hand. "Hi, Dale. My name is—"

"Daniel," he said with a huge grin. "Nice to see you." He wrapped his bear mitt of a hand around mine and leaned in. Dressed in a black T-shirt and a beat-up pair of green cargo shorts, Dale towered over me, and I briefly felt like a kid again.

"Um . . . I just wanted to say, it was really good to hear you. I could relate—"

"You got time for a cup of coffee?" Dale's voice was congenial and disarming, but still packed quite a punch.

"Uh . . . sure."

We walked a block and a half down Church Avenue to a small coffee shop, where I slid into a booth. Dale pulled up the thick white socks that had fallen into his weathered work boots during our walk, then pushed himself into the booth across from me. The side of the table dug into his stomach, but that didn't seem to bother him one bit.

"So . . . what do you think?" he asked, looking down at the plastic menu.

"Oh, I'm not hungry, thanks—"

He peered up at me. "I meant the meeting."

I thought for a minute. "I liked what you had to say . . . as usual."

Dale nodded. The waitress came over, greeted Dale like a regular, poured us coffee without even asking, then took his order while I sipped from my mug.

"Which part?" Dale asked, slurping from his own steaming mug, a pursed smile on his lips.

"Um . . . all of it, really." I didn't know what to say. Other than Brie, I'd never spoken to anyone about my problem with alcohol before. I didn't share my problems with others.

Dale chuckled. "Come on, man. I don't bite. I'm here to help. Tell me what's on your mind." Dale's demeanor was serene, like a pastor's.

I took a deep breath and glanced out the window. "I've heard you tell that story about the 'boss from hell' once before. Quite ironic."

Dale smiled. "The universe works in mysterious ways."

We sat for a moment in silence. For me, it was an uncomfortable silence. Dale's weightless gaze told a different story. He looked at peace.

Clearing my throat, I finally spoke. "My father started in construction, too." It was the only thing I could think of to say.

"Is that so?"

"Yeah. He started as a builder, then went into buying and selling . . . real estate . . . buildings, mostly, in the five boroughs."

"Must be doing well, then." Dale gulped from his mug. "You work with him?"

"No," I said. "I mean, I used to, but I quit years ago." Encouraged by the sympathetic look he gave me, I blurted out, "He's awful. Working for him is all-encompassing. It means being constantly micromanaged and controlled by him, having no boundaries, no time limitations. And he's not just miserable to family. It's that way for anyone who has the misfortune of joining the company. I'm just glad I got out." I breathed in sharply. I'd said too much.

"Sounds like my old boss," Dale said, laughing.

The air leaked slowly out from between my lips. "Sure sounded like it could have been."

Dale took another slug from his mug and shrugged the possibility off, but I wasn't so sure. "The Zimmer Company," I said, unconcerned that I'd just broken my own anonymity. "Walter Zimmer."

Dale's eyes widened. "You're kidding me."

I shook my head.

Dale rubbed his chin with enormous, timeworn fingers. "Well, I'll be damned." He gripped the sides of the table and shook it for a second, then gazed out the window, as if remembering something. "Carroll Street . . . right?"

I blinked at him. "How do you know that?"

"I came to your house . . . once."

I froze. Neurons fired inside my brain, connecting unconnected dots. A doorbell. A scary man. A running shower. A ferocious beating. A simple name. One word. Began with a "B."

I shifted nervously in the booth. "Benny?"

With his eyes locked on mine, Dale nodded and placed his

massive palms on the table. "My last name's Benson. The guys called me that."

"You wanted me and my brother to tell my father you were *ready*."

"Your father took me to my first meeting that night . . . and that meeting helped me get my life back. Small world, ain't it?"

I gaped at him. *That night . . .* I couldn't believe that anything good had happened that night. And how could the man who didn't care about anyone but himself have saved the life of another man? *This* man? "It's hard for me to swallow," I finally said. "I just can't picture him doing something like that . . . for someone else."

The waitress dropped off Dale's order—a double order of homemade meat loaf and mashed potatoes, a bowl of chili, and a side of onion rings. A meal fit for the giant he was.

His mouth filled with food and his lips covered in orange chili sauce, Dale said, "He was strange that night, I'll tell you that. He came to my home. He looked shaken up, but he didn't talk about it. In the weeks after that, he stuck with me. Made sure I was getting a meeting in every day."

He sat back and looked like he wasn't sure whether to say more. "Maybe he was trying to help me," he said at last. "Maybe he just wanted a worker who would show up and be safe. Doesn't matter. Either way, he saved my life. At times, it almost seemed like in saving me he was trying to save himself.

"I meant what I said back there: I tried to get him to come to those meetings with me, but he refused." Dale slurped his coffee. "Fact is, we don't know people . . . really. What they think, what they do. We like to think we know them, but we don't. People have their reasons, their own histories and behaviors . . . survival techniques." He took another swig from his mug, and then another forkful of food. "The first thing you need to know," he continued, his mouth full, "is this: you don't *know* anything."

He returned to his plate, while my mind wandered back to that morning in 1976.

"You know . . . that morning you came to the house . . . you scared the hell out of me," I admitted. Of course, it was more than that. "Benny's" visit had had tragic consequences—none of which had been his fault. I didn't see the point in bringing it up now.

"Yeah, I used to hear that a lot." He grinned. "Not anymore."

Dale Benson was no longer the brooding, ominous man with the clouded eyes and heavy gait that I remembered. He was clear in thought and spirit. He seemed free. At peace.

"So, how is your dad?" he asked, scooping up the last of the potatoes. "I'd love to catch up with him."

"I really don't know how to answer that, Dale. He's the same hard man I've always known. I don't know the man who helped you." I looked away.

Dale pushed his empty plate toward the center of the table. "I'm sorry, kid."

We sat in silence for a few moments. And then Dale went on to inform me that I was *not* unique, that my situation was *not* complicated, that my problems were of my *own* making, that my drinking was but a symptom of a deeper, more spiritual ailment that afflicted me, and other aphorisms of the program, while my mind drifted in and out of thoughts about Max and the beating he took for me, and the rage Harry must have felt in that moment, before he ran out the front door for the last time. Mostly, though, I thought about Dad and his stupid rules about doorbells and showers. I hadn't killed Harry. *He* had. He was going to be the death of Max, too. And he would be a thorn in my side until the day he left this earth.

Dale sat back and picked at his teeth with a wooden toothpick. He wasn't through proselytizing, and we went on to talk for another few hours at that coffee shop table, about family, life, and Alcoholics Anonymous.

"Thanks for spending this time with me," I finally said. The hands on the wall clock were nearing 10:00 p.m.

"Like I said, kid, I gotta give it away to keep it."

We got up and walked outside. Digging my hands into my pockets, I summoned the courage to ask Dale one last question.

"Hey Dale . . . would you be my sponsor?" There. I'd said it. Our history was complicated, it was true. But I couldn't deny what I'd seen with my own eyes. Benny had been a broken man. Dale was the opposite. I wanted what he had.

He looked down at me with a big teddy bear grin, his brown eyes dancing.

"I thought you'd never ask," he said.

CHAPTER 14

I stood against the back wall of the auditorium, a tenth grader at the end of what would be my last year in public school. Dad had decided that I'd be better off in private school because the so-called "superior" education would enable me to get into the college of my choice—which really meant *his* choice. He didn't care that I was supposed to be first trumpet out of twenty next year or that the John Jay High School orchestra was one of the best in the state or that I was in the pit, jazz, and marching bands, too. He didn't care that playing music was all that mattered to me, or that I had planned to go to Juilliard in two years and then into a professional orchestra. And he especially didn't care that the private school he'd enrolled me in—Berkeley Carroll—had a pathetic music program, if it could even be called a program. The entire troupe consisted of nine players with barely the skill of my elementary school band, which meant that whether I continued playing or not, my dreams of Juilliard and the Philharmonic were dead.

The John Jay High School auditorium stage was dark except for a single light illuminating a large, handmade sign announcing the 1979 Spring Talent Show. Normally, a high school talent show wouldn't draw such a large crowd, but tonight was different. There wasn't an empty seat in the auditorium; the crowd overflowed into the aisles, the pit in front of the stage, and the area along the back wall, where I stood. To address safety concerns, neighborhood firefighters and police officers had been positioned throughout the crowd, which had grown restless. People were chanting for the show to start.

I spotted Max as he navigated his way through the crowd. It had been two years since we'd seen the old man fall to his death. Two years since the summer of Son of Sam. Things had been different ever since. Mom and Max spent a lot of time out of the house after school, leaving me alone as day drifted into night.

Listening in on bits of conversation I wasn't meant to hear, I'd pieced together that she was taking him on numerous trips to see doctors and psychiatrists, though no one ever said anything to me about it. Everything related to Max's mental condition had become one big secret. But no one could hide how Max was doing on the outside. He continued to struggle in school and had begun to harm himself—mostly cuts and bruises in places usually covered by shirtsleeves and other clothing. He had few friends and was terrified of social situations, and his insecurities about himself—mainly his small build and diminishing intellect—were, at times, paralyzing. He'd swing between long bouts of irrational anxiety and feelings of isolation and doom. There was never anything I could do to help. I was sure the doctors had put him on some medication, but it didn't seem to be helping.

Max fell back against the wall next to me, breathing heavily.

"I'm surprised you're here," I said.

"Jerry asked me to come." Max said it like it was no big deal, but I knew it was. Jerry was one of Max's old friends from the neighborhood and now the eighteen-year-old leader of a hot local rock band. Jerry was also the reason so many people were here tonight. Word had spread widely about what he had planned.

Max turned and scanned the room. "Amazing, isn't it?" He sniffed and wiped his nose. "Even they're here." Max pointed toward the front corner of the stage, where four men stood at the bottom of the stairway. Black suits, white shirts, dark ties, and black glasses: men who'd been introduced at a school assembly one day as members of the board of education.

I nodded at the suits. "You really think they're going to kill the performance if he does it?"

"They'll have a riot on their hands if they do." I looked at my brother. It was good to see him outside the house. "I'm glad you're here, Max."

"Me too."

Suddenly the auditorium fell dark, and the crowd went wild. Dry ice machines pumped thick white mist onto the darkened stage, and a band emerged, instruments in hand. A bearded young man took center stage. The crowd thundered, and my pulse beat in sync with its chanting. Students and teachers, all clapping and pounding our feet—we were one.

The crowd cheered as the spotlight followed Jerry to the microphone.

"It's a funny thing," he said, taking in the crowd, "how a student can be threatened with expulsion for playing a song you hear on the radio every goddamn day! What do you think we should do?"

The crowd erupted into screams. Jerry glanced at the men in black, who stood motionless, glaring back at him. My body tingled. We all stood on the precipice of a decision much bigger than the song. Jerry's decision to play it would be an act of pure rebellion. I wanted him to do it. I wanted to rebel, myself.

Jerry stepped out of the spotlight and turned to his

drummer. The other two band members approached with their guitars. Silence fell over the auditorium.

I thought about the new direction my life was being forced to take and the destruction of my lifelong dream. I seethed with contempt for my father and, in fact, for all authority.

"Cocaine!" I yelled at the top of my lungs.

Max's head swung around.

"Co-caine!" I yelled again. "Co-caine . . . co-caine . . ."

Max joined in. "Co-caine . . . co-caine . . . co-caine . . ."

Jerry returned to the mic and shaded his eyes. "Shine a spot back there for me, will ya?"

Max and I ducked our heads under the blinding light, while pumping our fists in the air.

The crowd hammered their fists along with us, shouting, "Co-caine . . . co-caine . . . co-caine . . ."

"Zimmer brothers?" Jerry yelled into the mic. "Well, all right!"

And, with that, Jerry spun around to the drummer and shouted. His hand was already on the neck of his guitar as he crashed down on the strings for the iconic first chords of Eric Clapton's version of J. J. Cale's "Cocaine."

School security had them off the stage within minutes. But it made no difference. The band had rebelled. We'd all rebelled.

And that rebellion was the song I was sure my spirit needed.

———

Afterward, I sprinted to our empty town house on Carroll Street, the sound of "Cocaine" still ringing in my ears. I rushed inside and sped down the hallway and up the stairs into my bedroom, where I lifted the plastic cover from my Onkyo turntable and ran my eyes over the built-in shelves that held my collection of now dozens of albums. I pulled out AC/DC's *If You Want Blood You've Got It*, Judas Priest's *Sad Wings of Destiny*, and Led Zeppelin's *Led Zeppelin IV* and spread them across the rug between my floor speakers.

Reaching beneath my mattress, I grasped the oblong bottle hidden there—this one filled with whiskey—and twisted off the cap and drank. Despite what we'd sung out, I didn't need cocaine. I had no need for drugs at all, in fact. Alcohol gave me all the relief I needed.

I took another drink. I wasn't worried about getting caught. My father was working late, as usual. And my mother had gone into the city to run some errands that day and was finishing out the night by having dinner with Mrs. Olsson—something they did about once a year. It made me angry that somehow they had managed to keep in touch over the past three years and Brie and I hadn't. I still wasn't sure what had gone wrong, and I wasn't mature or emotionally healthy enough to try to understand it better.

I cracked open my bedroom window and lit the cigarette stashed beneath the rail in the gutter of the sill. I placed the AC/DC record on the turntable and fell back onto my bed. As I stared into the overhead light, I lost myself in the lyrics.

Twin guitars burst into a chugging riff beneath a cymbal crash and a guttural wail. Drums followed in step with a rumbling bass line, breaking free, charging forward in odd-meter time, unsettled, unbalanced. Prowling vocals. Lyrical guts and energy. A fist-raising chorus from "Problem Child." The guitars joined in aggressive twin harmonies. The bass stalked, still off step.

When the music finally fell silent, I raised myself up on the bed, exhaling the last hit of the cigarette. Looking around the room, I noticed my *Led Zeppelin IV* album, still on the floor.

Let's get the Led out, I told myself. I pulled the record from its sleeve and placed it on the turntable. A delicate, vulnerable acoustic guitar played with classical precision.

I sat on the edge of my bed, pulled up a leg, and gripped my ankle, the gatefold album cover open on my lap. As the song began, the familiar sound of recorders, with their quaint, medieval tone, layered into a winding hymn. A soothing voice sang plaintively about a spirit crying out to leave.

A layer of electric guitar laid down a relentless but deliberate beat, and the walls in my room trembled. I banged my fists on the bed and sang along in a soprano, then played air drums, my head bobbing forcefully. Tipping my head back, I cried out the lyrics until the song was over and the needle bumped against the label in a blur of static.

Exhausted and now drunk, I slid off the bed onto my knees. My thoughts drifted to Harry, as they often did. I pictured him in his black Led Zeppelin T-shirt and torn jeans, with bare feet. It had been three years since the accident. That seemed like both just yesterday and a lifetime ago. I grabbed the pint of whiskey from the windowsill, put the bottle to my lips, and chugged until it was empty.

The relief I felt was so immediate and so complete, I hardly knew who was in control anymore: me or the booze. I fell back onto the bed and closed my eyes. The answer didn't matter. I needed alcohol to numb the anger and pain I felt inside—to anesthetize the stirring beast.

Within seconds, I had drifted off.

"Daniel—wake up." A pair of hands slapped my mattress. "Wake up!"

"Max?" The whites of his eyes glowed beneath the ceiling light. Disoriented, I lifted up on my elbows and scanned the room, blinking myself awake.

"Fuck, man. I thought you were dead."

I looked down at the bottle on my chest, then back at him. "Not quite."

He looked over his shoulder. "Mom's home," he said, his voice full of warning.

I jumped off the bed, stuffed the flask under my mattress, and unwrapped a piece of gum that I pulled from my bedside drawer. Chewing quickly, I changed my shirt and shook my bushy hair.

Max stepped toward me and sniffed, then gave me a nod of approval.

We turned to leave, but Mom was already at my bedroom door with her hands on her hips. "What are you sniffing him for?"

Chewing furiously, I blurted out, "I asked him to. I thought my shirt smelled funny."

"Uh-huh," she said warily. "And since when do you chew gum?"

I stopped chewing. "I just started," I answered innocently. "It gives my mouth something to do now that I won't be playing trumpet anymore."

"Uh-huh." Mom wasn't buying it, but she looked too tired and preoccupied to pursue the matter further. "I'm going to lie down."

I asked the question on impulse. "How was dinner? Did Mrs. Olsson say anything about . . . anything?" I was dying for news of Brie, even if I couldn't admit it.

Mom gave me a sad look. "I might as well tell you," she said. "Mrs. Olsson is ill, boys." Her tone had softened. "Very ill."

I suddenly felt cold inside. "What's the matter with her?" I asked.

Mom looked uncomfortable, as if she hated to even speak the word. "Cancer. Pancreatic."

My thoughts turned to Brie. I wondered how her "faith" was holding up now. Maybe, I thought bitterly, I would call her and recite the Lord's Prayer, like she'd done with me. The difference was, she'd probably really be comforted by it, whereas the gesture had only enraged me. I instantly felt ashamed of my thoughts.

"Daniel? Everything okay?" asked Mom.

My head was pounding. "Is Mrs. Olsson going to die?"

Mom bit her lip. "I don't know. Maybe. Perhaps you should give Brie a call, Daniel. I'm sure she'd welcome the support." She turned away.

Steadying myself against the bedroom door, I called after her. "We haven't spoken in years." But she kept walking. I wasn't sure if she had heard me.

"You okay?" Max asked. But I was already headed down the hallway. "Where are you going?" he asked, following behind me.

I didn't answer him. All I knew in that moment was that I needed another drink, and the bottle in my room was empty. I stumbled down the stairs and across the foyer to the rec room, where I scanned the liquor bottles on the mirrored shelves of the tiki bar. In the past two years, I had depleted more bottles than I could count. I always drank out of one at a time, eventually replacing the empties with a replacement liquid—water for clear liquors and flat cola for dark ones—before starting a new one. Mom and Dad hadn't entertained since Harry died, and Dad drank Jameson, which he kept in the cupboards of the kitchen and which I didn't touch. The appearance of the tiki bar was my only concern. So long as every bottle remained filled with something, I'd be fine.

I steadied myself against the tikis, then leaned over the bar to examine the shelves. Max had followed me, and he stood at the end of the bar. I pointed to a bottle of bourbon. "Grab that for me, will ya?"

Max glanced at the bottle, then back at me. "You're going to get caught one of these days."

"Probably." I stumbled around the bar. I didn't care about *one of these days*. Right now, I only wanted to unscrew the gold top of a whiskey bottle and drink. I reached under the bar for a cranberry juice—one of the dozens of minicans of fruit juice stocked there—and pulled the ring-tab. With one hand around the bottle and the other around the can of juice, I gulped down the booze, then chased it with the juice. Within seconds, my pounding headache gave way to that familiar and soothing feeling of weightlessness, detachment, and escape.

"How do you do it . . . right out of the bottle like that?" Max's eyes widened, a concerned older brother appearing behind his usual detached expression.

Holding up the cranberry juice, I took another swig of the whiskey and then finished the minican.

"Let me try." Max reached for the bottle, but I pulled my arm away so he couldn't reach it.

"You can't." I returned it to the shelf. "You're on too much medication."

Max's disappointed eyes shifted to the front door as the deadbolt turned.

"Fuck." I dropped to the floor in front of the television and tried to look like I'd been there all along. Max ducked behind the bar.

The door slammed shut, and Dad's heavy footsteps crossed the foyer. "Where's your mother?"

"Upstairs."

"What are you doing?"

"Watching television."

He looked at the blank screen, then back at me. "You are, huh?"

I turned my head. *Fuck.* The television was off.

He glared, then stomped toward the kitchen. "Go to your room."

"Yes, sir," I called after him, wiping my sweaty brow.

Max jumped up from behind the bar and stared after him. "He didn't even wonder where I was." I could see the hurt on his face. "He never asks about me, does he?"

I didn't know how to answer. In fact, my Dad never did ask about Max. But I doubted he asked about me when I wasn't around, either. As I was still considering my response, I heard our father's footsteps and gestured urgently for Max to get back down under the bar.

He did. But then, as Dad reached the foot of the stairs, Max suddenly made a strange cackling noise from behind the bar. Dad slowly turned his head toward me, his eyes narrowed.

"Uh . . ." I cleared my throat as if recovering from a strange cough, exaggerating for effect. "'Scuse me. Night, Dad."

I held my breath, peering up at my parents' bedroom door until Dad went inside and closed the door. The flickering light from the television bled through the small space beneath it.

"Jesus, Max!" I whispered. "You trying to get us killed?"

Max had already popped up from behind the bar, his back facing me. I watched his reflection in the mirror behind the bottle-laden shelves as he leaned forward, straightened the brim of his cap, tucked his fine hair beneath it, then turned around to face me.

I shuddered as his face came into focus. It was that ominous grin again—the same one I'd seen the day he seemingly met the eyes of Son of Sam through the television screen. It was a grin I'd seen a number of times since. In these moments, it was as if Max had stepped away for a moment while something dark took his place. Was it nervous tension that was behind that weird smile? A psychotic break? A demonic possession? I didn't know.

And I didn't want to know, either.

CHAPTER 15

I left Dale at the coffee shop and took my time walking more than three miles back to my apartment in Bay Ridge, in the southwest corner of Brooklyn. I was sweating profusely in the cool evening air. I felt great about finally having a sponsor. I was also hoping that if I took my time, Jill would be asleep when I got home. When I got within ten blocks, I slowed my pace even further. I didn't know what I would say if Jill was still awake when I walked through the door. The doubt I'd felt about our relationship in recent months had turned to something much harsher in the days since Max's suicide attempt—especially since I'd seen Brie again.

What, I wondered, *am I going to do about Jill?*

It had been nineteen years since Frankie Woburn had died. Nineteen years since I rudely ordered him up the street to his death. Why—I wondered now, as I often did—hadn't I just ignored his obnoxious behavior that morning? And why had I opened the door for Benny the day before that? If I hadn't done either of those things, Harry and Frankie would both still be alive. I'd been carrying my guilt over those actions for decades—and that guilt was, most likely, why I was still with

Jill when we obviously weren't good for each other. But did it have to be that way? Or was I only making it that way?

I paused at the stoop of my apartment building and looked up at the windows on the seventh floor. No light, but I still didn't want to go inside. I was too hot, anyway, so I sat.

I owed something to Jill Woburn. It was as simple as that. I really wished I could give her brother back. Barring that, I could at least not be an asshole of a boyfriend. She was upset about Brie, but the two of us would never get back together. Brie and I were simply too different. And I'd blown things completely the last time we'd tried to make it work together. I wasn't certain about a lot of things, but I was definitely certain about *that*.

Jill was also upset that I wanted Max to stay with us for a while, and I needed to listen to her. I had to find a way to convince her that things would work out if Max was there. Because regardless of how I felt, I would stay with her. Jill and I needed one another in order to stay sober. We were bonded by our original pain. It made sense to me that we should stay bonded in our healing. Brie and I were done. We had been for a long time. It would be delusional for me to think that would ever change. I had to stay grounded in reality. Jill was reality.

Feeling that I finally had the strength I needed to face Jill, I climbed up the stoop and went in the building. Our seventh-floor walk-up had gotten old fast, but nothing in this location could beat this price. There were two apartments on the seventh floor, one in the front of the building and one in the rear. Ours was the door on the right, a two-bedroom apartment that overlooked the street.

I put my key in the doorknob, but I could tell instantly that it was already unlocked. When I walked in, the apartment was dark. The strong aroma of incense—spiced and woody—hit me in the face. My heart sank. I recognized this particular incense, called frankincense, as a tool Jill tended to use as a kind of last resort when she was feeling tempted to drink. She used it only during the most precarious of times—when she'd become "stuck," so overwhelmed by anger, anxiety, and loneliness that she became paralyzed in mind and emotion. She swore by its anti-relapse effects. But I knew it had no such powers. Jill was always at her lowest and most unreasonable when that incense was burning. I hated the smell with a passion.

When I turned the corner and flipped the light switch, Jill said in a dull voice, "Turn it off." She was seated at the dinette, pouring wine with one hand. A second, unopened bottle sat on the table beside her glass.

"Are you out of your mind?" I left the light on and approached the dinette.

"Have a sleat." She reached below the table to get something from the floor. "You're just in time." When she lifted her arm, in her grasp was an unopened bottle of Jameson whiskey. She dropped it on the table. "Ta-da!" She said it like she was offering me a present, but I could see in her eyes that she knew she was doing something wrong.

"What are you doing?" I was both shocked and afraid.

"Having a drunk." She lifted the almost-empty bottle of Chardonnay in the air as if giving a toast. "To us." I could hear the bitterness in her voice, and I felt both angry with her for what she was doing and guilty for having caused her so much pain. She glared at me. "I slaw the way you looked at her."

I knew that she was referring to my last encounter with Brie outside the kosher candy store on Forty-Seventh Street, and I understood why she was mad. "It's not what you think, Jill. Brie's a mental health counselor at the hospital now. She's going to help us with Max! I was just filling her in about our meeting with Dr. Rainier."

Swinging her head from one side to the other, she said, "You still love her."

"No, Jill. Now come on. That's enough." I tried to keep my

voice even, but I couldn't keep the anger hidden entirely. "You have a matinee tomorrow, for God's sake."

She fumbled clumsily at the second bottle of Chardonnay, trying to open it.

"Give me that." I reached across the table and knocked over the Jameson bottle.

"That one's yours." Her head wobbled and her arm swayed as she tried to point at the bottle of Jameson, now on its side. "See? I know what you like."

I fell back into the chair. "I'm not drinking that."

"Prove it!" she blurted out. And then, before I could figure out what she meant: "Prove you don't love her." She pushed the knocked-over Jameson bottle toward me, and it spun like a dreidel. I recoiled, as if from a flame.

"If you really don't love her, then drink," Jill continued. She hugged the second wine bottle to her chest. "You know she won't take you back if you're drinking again. If you drink that bottle, I'll know you're over her. I'll know you still love *me*."

It was the unreasonable reasoning of an addict. I recognized it because I'd done it myself before. "Do you hear yourself?" I knew she didn't, because the woman in front of me wasn't Jill Woburn. It was an active alcoholic, unapproachable and incoherent. "I am *not* drinking." I stood, picked up the bottle of Jameson, and dropped it in the plastic kitchen trash can.

Jill stood slowly and steadied herself using the back of her chair. "I *knew* it." She turned and stumbled toward the bedroom.

I followed her and stopped at the door. Despite all of our problems, my heart ached for Jill. There is such a fine line between sobriety and active alcoholism. Her twenty months were gone, just like that. And I was worried for her, too. Alcoholism is a progressive disease. It worsens and becomes more difficult to surmount with each relapse. As much as I wanted to help her—and I did—she was the only one who could help herself.

All I could do was offer my support and be there for her when she became ready. Most importantly, I had to protect myself from the exposure to active alcoholism. This meant that— whatever my intentions, whatever I thought I owed her—my relationship with Jill had to end if I was going to remain sober.

Moments after she'd sprawled herself diagonally across the center of the bed, Jill had completely passed out. The second Chardonnay bottle lay sideways on the carpet. I picked it up and placed it on the nightstand next to the framed picture of twelve-year-old twins Frankie and Jill. In the image, Frankie's big eyes gleamed, as if dancing with life. His wide smile brandished those newly emerged adult teeth, wrapped in a perfect oval by thin red lips.

I took a deep breath. Jill always played tough when it came to remembering her departed twin, as if refusing to accept his death. The loss was, I believed, a resentment that she still hadn't addressed—and Dale said that unaddressed resentments always came back to haunt the addict. In fact, he called unresolved resentments and unmade amends the equivalent of "reserving the right to drink again."

I wondered now, as I had so many times before, why Jill had never blamed me for Frankie's death. She knew I'd pushed him away that day. I wondered, too, why she'd never said anything about Harry. But I had no way of knowing what Jill was thinking or feeling. I only knew that I felt responsible for both of their deaths, and yet I had kept silent about it. I owed Jill an amends for Frankie as much as I owed one to Max and Harry for opening the door that day.

"I'm sorry, Frankie." My gaze shifted to the wine bottle, and I picked it up.

Back in the kitchen, I opened the wine and dumped it down the sink before placing the bottle in the trash, next to the unopened bottle of Jameson. Seeing the Jameson there, I froze for a moment, then pulled the bottle out of the bin. I twisted the tin cap until it snapped and came off. As I held it over the sink, my eyes began to tear from the sweet and smoky aroma. Inside that bottle, I could find home again.

No!

Images of Brie suddenly appeared in my head, and without having to think about it a moment more, I turned the bottle over and poured the whiskey down the drain until it was gone.

CHAPTER 16

I was sitting on a bench in front of the student center and listening to "Unchained" by Van Halen. It was brisk for late summer on Long Island; the sun was bright, illuminating the deep green canopies of the trees around me. A large blue banner hung over the glass doors of the student center, welcoming Hofstra University's class of 1985.

My pulse pounded in sync with the music as the bell tower clock struck ten. I couldn't believe I was finally going to see Brie for the first time in five years.

A week earlier, she had telephoned to say that, like me, she would be attending Hofstra. Apparently, Mom had mentioned my plans to Mr. Olsson when she'd called earlier that summer to check on him, as she'd promised Brie's mom she would do. During our own brief call, Brie had asked to meet outside the student center on orientation day. I'd agreed without hesitation. We'd been living separate lives for the past five years. Now, as the moment drew near, I wondered whether seeing her again would be as awkward as I feared.

Feeling a tap on my shoulder, I spun around.

"Hey you." Brie grinned and sat down next to me. "Even

from behind and all these years later, I could tell it was you!"

I tried not to smile like a twelve-year-old, but I couldn't help it. She looked just as I had imagined she would. Her hair was a little darker now than it had been when we were kids, but it was still long, tucked behind her ears and held back by the sunglasses pushed up on her head. She wore large silver hoop earrings, and her freckles had followed her into adulthood. Her blond eyelashes were black with mascara, her lips kissed with light pink lipstick.

"You look the same, too." I gazed into green eyes that hadn't changed at all.

She dropped her bag between her legs and reached her arms around me. We hugged each other tightly. The gesture felt strange but comfortable. I told her I was really sorry about her mother.

Brie nodded, and her eyes welled up. "She was gone in three months. Can you believe it?" She pulled a tissue from her bag and gently wiped her nose. "Life can be so cruel."

I nodded my agreement. It was good to hear her acknowledge that fact.

She touched a golden cross pendant at her throat. I remembered that she'd worn a similar one when she was a girl. "It's my mother's," she said, noticing that I was looking at it. "It helps me feel closer to her."

I remembered the last time we spoke, when she'd talked about her faith. "I'm sorry I hung up on you that day Harry died. I've been wanting to tell you so for years."

The look on her face told me she understood. "You were hurting."

"Was that why you stopped writing and calling?"

She started to say something, then tried again. "I was so upset after we left. My parents thought it would make things easier if I made a clean break."

It was one of the many possibilities I had considered. "*Was it easier?*"

"No," she admitted. "But it was even harder to hear your voice on the phone and get your letter. I didn't want to be sad anymore. I'm sorry, Daniel."

I looked up through the massive treetops at the cloudless blue sky. I wanted to tell her that everything was fine, that I held no grudge. But I was always stuck in the past, in my memories and my sadness.

I looked back at her and gave what I hoped was a convincing smile. "Ancient history."

We spent a little time catching up. She was surprised that I hadn't gone to Julliard and sympathetic when I explained that my father had made me switch schools. But she wasn't at all impressed by the decision I'd made as a result.

"You really stopped playing?" Her jaw hung open.

"I had no choice. I couldn't be a part of that terrible band at my new school. It was a total embarrassment."

She pressed her lips together. "You could have played at home or taken private lessons."

"My father wasn't going to pay for private lessons and practicing alone was pointless. I moved on." I wouldn't tell her how easy alcohol and drugs had made that choice. It hurt to think about, let alone talk about.

"Well, maybe you can play for me again one day?"

"Maybe." We glanced at one another, avoiding direct eye contact.

I told her I was planning to study finance or business. The fact was, my dad expected me to work for him when I was done. And since he was paying, I wasn't sure how I could avoid it. Even thinking about it made me nervous. But I found myself feeling calmer when I talked about it with Brie.

I asked how she was coping with her asthma.

She shrugged. "Good enough for me to be on my own at

college. I take a lot of medication, though. Steroids. Inhalers."
My face must have fallen, because she added, "It's fine, Daniel.
They keep me going. And when things get bad, I give myself
an epinephrine injection." I stared at her. "Don't look so horrified," she said with a laugh. "It's easy. A self-contained needle
injection. I just stick it in my thigh."

I shook my head. I couldn't believe she had to deal with all
that.

"Hey . . . I'm alive. I'm here. One day at a time."

Deftly, she changed the subject, telling me that she was
planning to study childhood education and become a teacher.
Once we'd caught up on the basics, the two of us glanced
around. I wasn't sure if we would simply walk away from one
another now or if we could actually be friends again. Maybe,
I thought to myself, we could even become something more.

"Look," I said, trying to sound casual, "I'm actually going
down to Jones Beach this afternoon. Wanna come with?"

"Are you kidding?" She grinned. "When are we leaving?"

I felt my heart rise in my chest. We made plans to meet
up in a half hour. Just as we were about to head to our rooms,
she put a hand on my arm. "Um, hey . . . I've got something
for you." She pulled out a brown lunch bag, the paper twisted
closed at the top.

I took the crinkled bag in my hand. The object inside felt
light, but solid.

She swallowed. "Open it."

I reached in and pulled on what felt like the small head of
a doll. "Oh my God!"

The Wolfman figure that Harry had given me for my birthday looked as new as it had the day I got it. "You *did* take it." As
time had passed, I'd begun to doubt she had. Honestly, by then
I had pretty much forgotten about it.

I felt a hint of bitterness rise up in me. "This was a gift
from Harry, you know."

Brie placed her hand on her chest, over her heart. "I am *so* sorry, Daniel. I took it because I wanted something to remember you by, something special, but I had always planned on giving it back to you when we saw each other again." She looked into my eyes. "Then we fell out of touch, and I didn't know what to do. The thought of mailing it back terrified me— there was nothing I could say to justify what I'd done." As she spoke, my bitterness faded. I wrapped my arms around her in a hug.

"It's okay," I whispered. For a moment, I worried that she would smell smoke on me. But she didn't seem to notice.

She let out a long breath she'd been holding, then backed away and smiled. "Thirty minutes?"

I rubbed the figure's head with my thumb. "Thirty minutes," I agreed.

My eyes followed Brie as she walked away. At one point, she stopped and turned around. "Hey Daniel?" she said playfully. "Check you out . . ."

I snorted with surprise. "On the side that's . . . flip-p-t."

For the first time in as long as I could remember, I felt awake inside. I stood there, firmly rooted to the ground, with no desire to run or escape.

Even the pint of whiskey in my backpack had stopped calling my name.

———

The next four years passed almost in a flash. Brie and I were both busy with school, and we soon became busy spending time with each other. College relationships can be hard, but we slipped into ours as if we'd been preparing and waiting for it our whole lives—which perhaps we had. For the most part, I kept my drinking under control—at least when I was around Brie, though I sometimes partied hard with friends. And I never smoked around her. She would have preferred that I not smoke at all, but the compromise—while not ideal—worked for us both. We were too in love to allow it not to.

Now it was more than a year after graduation, the morning of July 4, 1986. Every streetlamp, signpost, and fire hydrant in Brooklyn had been painted red, white, and blue for America's birthday. The local television and radio stations had been giving daily updates on the planned fireworks, block parties, parades, picnics, and barbecues for days. The centerpiece of "Liberty Weekend," as it was called, however, would be Operation Sail, a naval review that would be the largest flotilla of military vessels and tall ships—large, traditionally rigged sailing vessels—to assemble in modern history. This event promised to be even greater than the bicentennial celebration that had taken place in the very same New York harbors ten years earlier.

Brie and I were now living in our own place in Bay Ridge. She was on summer break from the Bayview School, where she taught second grade. I'd been working for Dad in the family business since graduating, at his beck and call day and night: a temporary situation I'd accepted as a way to get us off to a good financial start. My only reprieve came on federal holidays, so when the opportunity arose to view a tall ships parade in the waters surrounding New York City—on horseback, to boot—we'd jumped at it.

"Come on, Brie!" I stood, hands on hips, in the center of the crowded parking lot of the Jamaica Bay Riding Academy, a stable located in the Gateway National Wildlife Preserve along the southeast shore of Brooklyn.

She pointed to a large sign beneath the green entrance awning: No Running.

"Are you kidding me?" I tried to keep my tone light, but there was no doubt that I sounded irritated. "They're going to give our horses away!"

The last year had been hard, and the pressure of working for my dad was taking a toll on me. I'd been drinking secretly all morning and couldn't wait to get to the beach to see the tall ships at anchor in Jamaica Bay. But Brie was having a hard time keeping up with me.

I marched to the front of the line while she waited patiently against the white three-rail wooden horse fence on the side of the building.

I returned with tickets in hand. "You all right?" But I didn't wait for her to answer. I rushed through the open gate and jumped from foot to foot, dodging piles of dried-out horse manure.

"Why are you always in such a rush?" she asked, trying to keep up. "This is supposed to be fun and relaxing."

Why, I wondered, did she need to ask? She knew I hated crowds. "I just want to beat the rush."

"Well, you need to slow down." She was breathing heavily. "If not for yourself, then for me." The air in New York was thick and dirty, and it affected her breathing, even out on the shore.

"Sorry." I stopped and took a deep breath. The intoxicating smell of sea air wafted toward us as we walked past a row of dilapidated barn-style stables. They were old and in disrepair, but clean. The dirt sidewalks and drab buildings washed out the "sugar" white of the sand and the deep blue of the ocean in the distance.

Once we had mounted our horses, Brie and I began our three-mile ride toward the beach of the Rockaway Peninsula, which separated Jamaica Bay from the Atlantic. It was hot and hazy, and a grayish-blue fog covered the sky in every direction. After a while, we stopped to take in the view. A stiff wind blew from the north and white-capped the black bay and ocean waters.

"Check out the boats!" Brie pointed offshore, where hundreds of international vessels were anchored. They were filled with bustling crews that were hosing down decks, burnishing brass, and raising anchors. It was just after 9:00 a.m. and the ships were beginning to fall into formation for the first fleet of the parade, five hundred yards from one another.

A horn blared from the south, and a massive fireboat shot huge streams of water into the sky. People cheered as gigantic sailboats sailed upstream from New Jersey's Sandy Hook Bay and into the Lower Bay of New York.

Brie held her horse's reins with one hand and, with the other, peered through the binoculars we'd brought. "Look! The people are waving."

I looked around the beach at the laughing, cheering, waving, and smiling strangers, young and old, bonding with one another as if we were all one big, happy family—as if we belonged to each other, and also to something so much greater. Like the dehydration I was feeling from the beating sun and the excessive alcohol I'd consumed all morning, it made me ill.

"You know," I said, "they're not always that nice. The holiday just gives people a reason to be nice to one another for once." I checked my words, unsure if I was slurring.

Brie frowned and lowered the binoculars. "Have you been drinking?"

"No," I blurted.

Brie stared into my eyes, waiting for me to flinch. I didn't.

"You're cynical." She tried to hand me the binoculars, but I didn't take them.

"You know I'm right."

Brie ignored me and lifted the binoculars again to scan the piers that extended southeastward from the shore. A sour feeling overtook me. I knew I had ruined the day.

Sensing something, I looked up and saw the Goodyear Blimp over me, there for the celebration. When it passed between us and the sun, a shadow crossed slowly over Brie and me as we looked up to the sky.

That evening, Brie and I met up with my mother at Mr. Olsson's apartment in Sunset Park. Brie had asked her father to come with us to the ship parade, but he'd said he was too busy and had suggested we bring my parents to a barbecue at his place later instead. My father-in-law was an investment banker who worked like a dog, especially lately. The Dow had more than doubled in the past few years, and his client list had grown tenfold. He seemed to know that the economic rally wouldn't last much longer and was determined to squeeze as much, financially speaking, as he could out of it. I didn't blame him one bit. And, as much as Brie didn't want her father to work so hard, she knew he wanted to retire as soon as he could. So she stayed silent.

"Everything was delicious, Brie," said Mom, holding her stomach. Brie's dad had pitched the idea as an "indoor cookout," though Brie had done most of the cooking after the parade of ships, with my mom and I pitching in. My dad had been invited too, but by 6:00 p.m. he still wasn't there. Though he'd worked all weekend, he had promised Mom that morning that he'd come.

Brie smiled at my mom's compliment and placed a homemade unfrosted coconut cake on the table: one of many recipes she'd learned from her late mother. Crusty and stiff on the outside, soft sponge on the inside, it was one of my favorites.

Mom shook her head. "Oh, my. Look at that. I don't know if I have room for dessert."

"I *always* have room for dessert—and for another drink," Mr. Olsson called from the sofa in the den. He tilted his margarita glass until the base was almost vertical and gave a long slurp. "Bartender . . . gimme another!"

I smiled half-heartedly from the love seat and took another slug of my own margarita, emptying the glass without any of Mr. Olsson's drama. Then I rose and went to the bar to make two more.

Mr. Olsson had recently turned fifty, but he looked old for his age. Gone were the bushy sideburns and curly hair, replaced by a clean-shaven face and shiny bald head. In the six years since his wife had died, he'd put on an extra eighty pounds, thanks to countless business dinners with clients, and had begun drinking heavily and smoking cigars not so secretly on the patio.

Mr. Olsson leaned forward. "For someone who's only twenty-three, you sure know how to make 'em. What's your secret? These are the best margaritas I've ever had."

"It's the sweet-and-sour mix, sir," I said as I stirred.

Mr. Olsson gave me a dubious look. His huge belly hung over his khaki shorts, which were held up by a pair of black suspenders over his yellow polo shirt.

"That," I admitted, "and a triple shot of a top-shelf Añejo, like Patrón. You have to taste the tequila; otherwise, what's the point?"

"Really, Daniel?" Brie gave me a stern look that said *Don't encourage him.* "Be careful, Daddy. They sneak up on you. I can't do more than one of those. Right, *Daniel*?" Her eyes were telling me to slow down my drinking. Mr. Olsson and I were going on our third round, and I'd been drinking all morning, too. My tolerance was as high as ever.

"Well, I just can't drink," my mom said. "It doesn't agree with me. Anyway, alcohol has too many calories."

Brie looked between her father and me as if she wanted to say something.

Her father caught the look. "What? A man can't enjoy a little something sweet after all the hard work he does? Anyway, it's not like I'm an alcoholic," Mr. Olsson insisted. "Your man here drinks just as much as me."

I carried the fresh margaritas, limes stuck on their salted rims, back to the sofa and handed one to Mr. Olsson.

"Be careful, Daniel," my mother said, "or you're going to end up looking like your father. That's why they call it a *beer* belly."

I held up my margarita and said, "Sorry, Mom, but this ain't beer." I laughed, too loudly.

Mom looked away. Brie gave me a look that said she disapproved. This only irritated me further. Brie relaxed in the evenings by painting. *She* had a hobby that helped her unwind. Did she really not want me to relax? I could feel the tension rising in the room. Buzzkill city.

"Don't worry," Mr. Olsson said, softening his tone as he sat back in the sofa, "this belly isn't all beer. It's desserts, too!" He clutched the large roll of fat above his waistline and laughed. "Speaking of which . . . bring it on!"

"Daddy! Where are your manners?" With a little frown, Brie got up and disappeared around the corner into the kitchen, with Mom in tow.

Mr. Olsson turned back to me, about to speak, but I stopped him with a raised finger and a nod toward the kitchen. He turned to the kitchen, and we listened to their soft voices.

"I'm sorry, Arlene. Daddy tends to get too relaxed when he drinks. I can't stand it. I worried this would happen."

"Don't be silly. It's a holiday with friends, and he's at home in his own home."

"A little *too* at home." Brie sounded disappointed.

"It's okay," Mom said. After a moment, she added, "We all have different ways of dealing with life and loss."

"He's not usually like this," Brie said. "He's unhappy, always struggling with life without Mom, and the business . . . I don't know what to do."

I turned to Mr. Olsson, who had sunk into the sofa, a sober expression on his face.

Brie continued, "Daniel struggles at times, too."

"He has since he was a child," Mom agreed. "So many things have happened. I suppose he felt like he had no control over anything."

"I think he still feels that way."

Suddenly I felt uncomfortable. I wondered if Mr. Olsson felt as embarrassed as I did to hear them analyzing us in this way. I didn't dare look at him.

"Daniel's more like his father than he'll ever know," I heard my mom say. "They both need to feel control over their worlds, no matter what it costs them."

I swallowed hard. The assessment hit home. Painfully so.

"Those are some smart women in there," I said finally, turning to Mr. Olsson, whose chin was resting on his chest. "Right, Mr. O?"

"Here we come," Brie called, carrying the cake and following Mom back into the den. "Did he fall asleep on us?" She put the cake down and sat next to her father. Gently, she patted his thigh. "Daddy, dessert is served."

Mr. Olsson sat motionless in the same position, legs outstretched, hands at his sides, and head slumped on his chest.

"Daddy?" Brie pushed his thigh. Mr. Olsson didn't respond. "Daddy?" She pushed her father's shoulder hard. "Wake up!"

I jumped out of the love seat and rushed around the coffee table to Mr. Olsson's other side. "Come on, big guy, get up." I lifted his arm and pulled, then dropped it when he only fell over to the side. I threw my mom a desperate look and told her to call 9-1-1.

The moments that followed passed in a haze. With great effort, I pulled Mr. Olsson down to the floor and began to perform chest compressions. I pinched his nose and breathed into his mouth. Behind me, I heard my mother on the phone. I heard her simultaneously comforting Brie and encouraging her to use her inhaler. And still I pushed, again and again, on Mr. Olsson's great chest.

"Slow down, Brie," I heard my mother say. "Take deep breaths."

I renewed my efforts, becoming increasingly desperate, but nothing I was doing was working. Behind me, Brie was wheezing. Her father wasn't breathing.

Finally the paramedics rushed in, and I stood and stumbled backward a few steps as they raced to the sofa. But even as they began their work, I felt certain that none of us would ever breathe the same again.

CHAPTER 17

I left the apartment early the next morning, even though I wasn't meeting Brie at Maimonides Medical Center until 10:00 a.m. It was a beautiful sunny day, the warmth a stark contrast to last night's briskness. Jill was still passed out when I left, practically in the same position on the bed, which was fine with me. She'd miss her Saturday matinee, but I couldn't bring myself to do anything about it, and I wasn't even sure that I should. Jill's choices were her own, and anyway, they didn't affect my life anymore. I'd made up my mind. We were done.

The lobby of Maimonides was outdated and in disrepair. It looked like it hadn't been renovated in decades. The only positive was its cleanliness, which was most important to me anyway. I waited anxiously for Brie in one of the old brown leather chairs facing the entrance. I hoped she could get Dr. Rainier to release Max to me.

After a few minutes, Brie entered the lobby through the double doors with a smile draped beneath her plastic tubing. Her coat was open in the front, exposing a cream-colored blouse and black jeans. She stopped in front of me with the oxygen tank at her side, then took a seat beside me.

She lifted her coat off her shoulders and wiped her brow. "Phew . . . It's warmer than I thought it would be in here."

"Can I get you some water?"

"No, thanks." She fished inside her handbag for her albuterol inhaler, put it to her lips, and inhaled sharply while depressing the small canister, then held the mist inside her lungs. She repeated this two more times. I remembered when she'd only had to do the process twice. She'd also told me that she was now taking high-dose steroids. Between those two things and the oxygen, it was clear that Brie was getting worse. I frowned.

"How often do you have asthma attacks these days?"

She smiled politely. "Daniel, I'm okay." She straightened her posture and sat forward. "We're here for Max, right?"

I nodded.

"Anyway," she continued, "I spoke to Valerie. Like I think I told you, her bark is worse than her bite."

She told me that the psychiatrist would be meeting with Max again on Monday and didn't see any reason why he couldn't be out by the end of the next week. I was surprised. I'd gotten the idea that the doctor wanted to lock him up and throw away the key. I found myself grinning, and Brie beamed back at me.

I cocked my head. "What?"

She gazed at me steadily. "You look good."

"Thanks," I replied. "So do you." And she did. Even sick, Brie was beautiful. I realized that she would always be beautiful to me. An awkward silence followed, and I scooted to the edge of my chair. "Shall we?"

As we made our way toward the elevator, she cleared her throat. "I'm sorry," she said. "That was weird. But you *do* look good. You look . . . I don't know. More in control than before."

I considered her words. It was true—I *was* coping better

with life than I had when she and I were together. Hadn't I, in spite of everything, poured out the Jameson the night before? My sobriety meant a lot to me. But I also felt somehow like I was hanging on to the cliff of self-control by my fingernails.

"I know this is tough with Max," she said as we stepped into the elevator, "but you do seem to be handling it well. Do you go to a meeting every day?"

"I try to, yeah. If I don't have my sobriety, I don't have anything." I meant those words, even though I didn't altogether believe I had the ability to keep that sobriety.

The smile on her face was genuine. "I prayed you'd get sober one day."

I looked at the floor. "You were right. I needed help. I'm sorry for everything I put you through. I hate myself for the way I was . . . how I hurt you. How I messed us up."

She placed her hand on mine and said, "'We will not regret the past nor wish to shut the door on it.'" The quote was an axiom from the Big Book of Alcoholics Anonymous. "You have a disease," she said. "I really get that now—"

"Ugh." I couldn't look at her when she said that. "Honestly, I hate that idea. It's such a cop-out."

She reached for my other hand and, holding both, stepped in front of me. "It's *not* a cop-out, Daniel. It's the truth. I don't mean that accepting that gives you a free pass, because it doesn't. That saying is just a way of understanding that addiction isn't a moral failing, and it's not something a person should be shunned for. It's a condition that needs to be treated. Just like any other disease. And that's what you're doing at these meetings. You're treating your disease. Think of it like your daily dose of medicine."

I thought about Max and the medicine he often refused to take, and I nodded.

The elevator opened, and Brie swung around and led me out by the hand.

I considered her words. She really did understand recovery. "I'm still sorry, though."

"Good. You should be." I gave her a chagrined look, and she smiled warmly, then squeezed both of my hands. "Apology accepted."

CHAPTER 18

The flames from the fireplace of our apartment in Bay Ridge were reflected in Brie's eyes, and her hair shone in the dim light, pale against the brown leather sofa in our den. It was New Year's Eve 1989, more than two years after her father's death, and we were spending a quiet night together.

Brie leaned forward on the sofa. "You are so amazing on that thing."

I smiled around the mouthpiece of my silver Bach trumpet—the same one I'd had in high school—and continued playing "Ragtime" from my spot on the floor. I'd always been able to play better while under the influence, as I was now. As usual, though, I was trying to pretend in front of Brie that I wasn't feeling the alcohol at all.

"You were always a natural."

I pulled the trumpet away from my lips and sat back, almost toppling over. I quickly crawled toward the coffee table, as if doing so had been my original intention. I took a swig from the nearly empty Jameson bottle and almost dropped it on the table.

"I think you're done," she said.

I nodded and tried to focus on her eyes as I placed the trumpet, with perhaps too much emphasis, on the carpet. "Okay. But it's your loss."

Brie sighed. "I'm talking about the bottle, wise guy."

"No, I'm okay." With two hands on the coffee table, I pushed myself up, but the liquor hit me hard and I fell backward on my behind.

She let out a long breath. "I don't get you. We have everything. Careers, our own place . . . each other. Why do you feel the need to drink like this? It's like you can never get enough."

Feeling a moment of panic, I crawled over to the sofa and grasped her hand. "I told you. I'm going to stop."

"When?" Her eyebrows drew together, her face tightening. I could tell what she was thinking. I always said I was going to quit, and sometimes I did, for a day or two. But I was always back at it again in no time—carrying on and feeling sorry for myself, according to Brie. "You're going in circles," she said now. "*We're* going in circles."

The flames danced up the sooty masonry of the fireplace. The wind howled above. I let go of her hand.

"Jesus, Brie. You want me to stop this second? I will. Say the word."

I looked back at the bottle, which glittered invitingly. It could be easy, I imagined—finish it and never open another. I'd gone two months without a drink the year she arrived at Hofstra and then three weeks after her father died in 1986. I was sure I could string a bunch of weeks together, even longer. Couldn't I?

"I can't." She leaned toward me. "Because you won't. You have a problem. You need—"

"All I need is you." I grimaced, interrupting her.

"If that were true, you wouldn't drink so much."

Her words stung. Brie knew what life was like for me in my father's office. The long hours, weekends . . . it was total hell.

Drinking, I was sure, helped me to unwind, and to rinse off the negativity of the day.

"Trust me," I said. "I can stop anytime I want to."

"So, you don't want to? Is that what you're saying?" She coughed into her hands, her body tensing. It sounded like the bark of a sick dog.

"That's not what I'm saying. I mean . . . you *know* what I mean."

"You need to see a therapist," she said sternly, "or go to Alcoholics Anonymous."

I insisted again that I could do it on my own. But Brie only shook her head. "No, you can't. You haven't. And I can't do anything more for you. You're the only one who can work out your past and find peace. What happened to you as a child—"

"I don't want to hear that bullshit!" The words came out louder than I meant them to. I pushed the bottle of whiskey to the far edge of the table. "I'm done. For good this time. Really." I sank into the sofa. I'd never sobered up so quickly in my life.

"How many times are we going to do this? How many more promises are you going to break? You see what drinking does to your father. You *saw* what it did to mine!"

Brie was glaring at me. I was convinced she held me responsible for her father's death, in a "tipping point" kind of way, but she never said so. She wouldn't be wrong if she did, or if she held deep resentment against me, which I was also convinced was the case. The truth was that alcohol had been a significant contributor to Mr. Olsson's poor health and heart attack, and my margaritas that night had done him no favors.

"I'm done, Brie! I swear it." I stood and grabbed the bottle by its neck. Brie jumped up and followed me to the kitchen. She stopped in the doorway and put her hand on the molding.

I set the bottle on the counter next to the stainless steel sink, opened the cabinet above the refrigerator, and reached for the brand-new bottle I had on reserve. There was always a reserve. I yanked off the foil wrapper, crumpled it into a small, jagged ball, and dropped it on the counter. Then I unscrewed the cap and dumped the bottle's contents into the sink. As the woody aroma of the whiskey surrounded me, I breathed in, wishing I didn't have to waste it. When it was empty, I slammed the bottle on the counter and turned around.

Brie nodded toward the first, almost-empty bottle. I wrapped my fingers around it, took a deep breath, and poured the last of my whiskey down the drain.

I turned to her. "For you."

But instead of looking glad, she sighed. "That's my point. You need to stop for yourself, for your *own* sanity. It's not enough to stop for me."

"It's reason enough for me." I ran my hands through my hair, avoiding her gaze.

Brie nodded and blinked. She was skeptical. She had every right to be. After all, I'd already made—and broken—this promise more times than I could remember.

———

Almost a month later, I sat watching the news in the den as Brie got ready for our night out. The report was talking about a tragedy that had happened the night before: after a failed attempt to land at JFK airport, Avianca flight 52 from Bogotá had run out of fuel and crashed into a hillside twenty miles away in Cove Neck, New York. Of the 158 crew and passengers on board, 73 had been killed.

I wondered whether the passengers had been aware of the danger. I wondered what it would be like to sit helpless on a passenger jet, knowing you were going to crash. I imagined the panic would be unbearable. It was, in a way, how I felt all the time.

"Ready to go next door?" Brie asked over the news report.

I glanced at the time. I'd been dreading the get-together with our neighbors; Brie had agreed weeks earlier to attend, and I never would have signed on for it had I known I'd be sober. Still, I'd been on my best behavior since our New Year's Eve fight, willing to do anything to redeem myself in her eyes.

"How long do we have to stay?" I crossed my arms. The thought of making fake conversation with people I barely knew was agonizing. And, with just twenty-six days under my belt, the thought of doing it without a drink left me feeling almost paralyzed.

"Come on, grumpy." She gave me a tender look. I could see it in her face: the playfulness, the affection. Through it all, she still loved me. "You have never once come with me when these people have invited us over. They're starting to wonder if I even have a boyfriend."

I grumbled but reached out and took her hands in mine, stroking her palms with my thumbs. "I'm working on it, Brie. It's not easy being around people who are drinking."

"I'm sure that's true." She patted my hand. "And I appreciate you making the effort. I'll be right there with you."

I looked into Brie's eyes. I wasn't sure I could do it. But it was clear that she needed me to. And so I had to. For her. And anyway, she would be right there, just like she said. How bad could it be?

———

"What can I get you, Daniel?" Cliff was older than me, probably in his early thirties. He had short black hair and a sideways grin and looked preppy in his collared shirt. Moving behind the small bar near the kitchen, he said, "I hear you make a mean margarita." He pointed out the Jose Cuervo, Cointreau, and sour mix next to a tub of salt and a cocktail shaker. I raised my eyebrows at Brie.

"I must have mentioned that to Debbie a while back." Brie blushed. "Daniel is—"

"I'll have a cranberry and club soda." I smiled. "Thanks."

"We have beer, too—Heineken, Beck's, Löwenbräu."

Brie squeezed my fingers, and I dug my nails into the palm of my other hand. "No, thanks. I'm good with the cranberry and soda."

Behind the bar, Cliff poured a small bottle of Schweppes club soda into a plastic cup, then topped it with a splash of Ocean Spray cranberry juice. He pushed the cup with the pink bubbling liquid toward me, then examined the crystal lowball glasses on top of the bar as though searching for a particular one. He used stainless steel tongs to move one ice cube at a time from the ice bucket into his glass. He opened a bottle of Dewar's, poured the caramel-colored liquid until it reached a precise level, and smiled.

My eyes fixed on the glass of scotch as I reached for my cran-soda. Why couldn't I have just one?

Cliff looked up from the bar. "How about a scotch, Arty?" Arty and his wife, Ginny, lived on the other side of Cliff and Debbie, and their son was in Brie's class. She'd assured me that they were all wonderful people.

"Sure," Arty replied from the sofa. "Thanks."

Cliff chose another glass, this time not so selectively, and filled it with ice while I guzzled my soda.

"Whoa . . . slow down there, Daniel." Cliff chuckled. "You're gonna be in bad shape if you keep up that pace."

I pursed my lips and forced a thin smile. "Hit me again, barkeep," I joked. I pushed the empty cup across the bar as, from the sofa, Brie gave me an approving smile.

After getting my new drink, I sat down next to Brie and nodded politely at Arty, now seated in the chair across from us. Wedged between Brie and the arm of the sofa, I listened to the neighbors' conspiracy theories about the downed airliner.

Arty and Cliff also spent the better part of an hour discussing scotch while barely drinking any.

"Oh my God," I mumbled, more loudly than I'd intended. It felt like the boredom was drilling an actual hole through my head.

Brie dug her nails into my knee, the one she'd been holding for the past several minutes. But I couldn't help it. I wanted to leave. I had no connection here. I was incapable of making pleasant but pointless conversation with people I didn't even know. I wished I could, but I just couldn't. That was just one of the many reasons why I drank. And I especially didn't want to sit and listen to a couple of lightweights talk about alcohol while I couldn't have any.

"Don't be rude," she whispered. As she spoke, I could hear a slight wheeze, the soft hum of a tired, congested chest—mild enough, but not normal for a body that was at rest, even a body like hers. Unfortunately, this was quickly becoming the new normal, and I knew, with no small sense of shame, that my childish behavior had to be contributing to her stress.

"Do you need your inhaler?"

Brie nodded and kept her eyes on Debbie, who was saying something to the group.

I lifted myself off the sofa and went to the kitchen for Brie's handbag. When I turned around, Brie stood in front of me, her hand out. I reached in, grabbed the inhaler, and handed it to her.

"Why are you wheezing?" I asked, while she squeezed the canister and inhaled.

Brie expelled the air from her lungs, then took another deep breath. She relaxed her shoulders and leaned against one of the barstools at the kitchen island. "Good question." Her eyes searched the room for something that clearly wasn't there. She tossed me the inhaler, and I returned it to her bag.

When we got back home, Brie kicked off her shoes under the kitchen table, as she always did after a long day.

"Do you have any idea how hard this is?" I didn't need to wait for her answer. I knew she knew.

Her face softened a bit. "You're doing great, Daniel. Twenty-six days. *Real* days. Do you know how amazing that is? I am so happy for you . . . for us!" She was right. It was the largest number of dry days I'd strung together since freshmen year at Hofstra. "I'm proud of you." She stood to kiss me, but my focus was on the cabinet above the refrigerator where I used to keep a bottle. "What are you looking at?" she asked suspiciously.

I froze. "Nothing. Why?"

Brie hesitated for a moment. "I'm going to get changed," she said finally and headed for the stairs. "I'll be *right* back."

I nodded. She was already halfway up the stairs.

As soon as she was out of sight, I opened the kitchen cabinet and searched behind the rarely used blender and Mixmaster. I glanced over my shoulder. There was no sign of Brie. She was still upstairs changing. Standing on tiptoe, I reached in as far as I could, my arm trembling, hoping to find something . . . anything that I could suck down before she returned.

"What are you looking for?" Brie's voice was flat.

"Jesus!" I whirled around, empty-handed. "You scared the hell out of me."

She was wearing a long T-shirt and socks. Her eyes narrowed.

I closed the cabinet door and sat down at the kitchen table. I could feel my cheeks burning with shame. "Do you have any idea how excruciating that was—to watch those guys nurse their drinks all night?"

Brie's face was flushed, and her lips tightened.

"I'm sorry." I was ashamed of myself for looking, and, in a way, I felt relieved that I hadn't found anything.

Brie sat down at the kitchen table. She looked as drained emotionally as she did physically. The look she gave me now was less tender than the one she'd given me before the gathering with the neighbors.

"Look," I said, desperate to defend myself. "I didn't drink—"

"But you wanted to!" She shook her head. "Daniel, this isn't the kind of thing you can figure out on your own." She leaned back in her chair and looked up at the ceiling. "You need help from other people like you." She began to wheeze again.

I snatched her inhaler from the trinket dish on the counter and knelt by her side. She removed the cap and shook it hard. Our eyes met.

"You need help, Daniel—help that I can't give you." She put the inhaler to her lips, pressed down, and inhaled the deepest breath I had ever heard her take. She held the medicine in for as long as she could, her eyes still locked on mine. And then she let the breath go. "Go to AA tomorrow morning," she said at last. "Or I'm leaving."

CHAPTER 19

From the window of my parents' Carroll Gardens apartment, I watched loose newspaper pages flutter in the wind along Carroll Street. It was a cold and quiet Sunday evening. The temperature had swung forty degrees in the past thirty-six hours, from the midseventies to the low thirties. The sun was setting, and the stiff breeze swayed the branches of the trees.

A week earlier—the day before Max's suicide attempt—Max and I had reluctantly agreed to join Mom and Dad the following Sunday for dinner. Sharing a meal wasn't a common occurrence for us, and Mom had refused to give a reason over the phone, other than to say that we were long overdue. Until I arrived, I hadn't had even a clue that something was wrong. They'd filled me in immediately and matter-of-factly.

Behind me, Dad sat grumbling in the distressed leather armchair. I turned and looked at him as he took a swig from the bottle of Jameson he kept on the end table and then took a long drag from his cigarette. All these sights were familiar to me. But now there was something else, too.

An oxygen tank stood beside him, clicking on and off, periodically dispensing gas into his nostrils through plastic tubing that hugged his face. The skin under his jaundiced, black-ringed eyes sagged. His disheveled hair was slightly grayer than his ashen face. It seemed like he'd aged years since the last time I saw him, though it had been only days. The chair he had once dominated now swallowed his body. He looked decades older than his fifty-nine years.

"Liver *and* lung?" I finally asked. "Both? Are you sure?"

"I'm sure, goddamn it," he growled. "How many times I gotta say it?" His entire body heaved.

They'd been told about his bleak diagnosis—late-stage cancer—a few weeks before. It seemed his biggest problem now was that his frail, deteriorating body couldn't support the anger anymore. He could no longer yell his way out of the realities of life.

Hearing the news, I only felt numb. He was my father. And yet, his suffering seemed appropriate. There were good people, like Brie, who suffered despite their goodness. If someone was going to suffer, it seemed better that it would be someone like him: someone who was cruel, who made people suffer. Although Dale's perspective had begun to soften my animosity toward my father, I couldn't help but think that dying peacefully in bed at an old age would be too good for him.

Dad opened his mouth to speak but coughed uncontrollably instead.

Mom ran in from the kitchen, where she was preparing dinner. She appeared startled when she saw my father. "Why are you smoking? You know what the doctor said."

"I'm fine." He wiped his mouth and slumped back into his chair.

Mom gave him a look of uncertainty, like she wasn't sure what to say. She turned to me and rolled her eyes, as if to say that my father was a handful.

Yes, he was that. And more.

"Guess who called me the other day?" she asked. It was

the first time in days that I'd seen her face light up. I smiled. I knew that she'd always loved Brie.

"I know! Can you believe it?"

Dad cleared the phlegm from his throat. "Who are you talking about?"

"Brie Olsson, dear." Mom turned to me and whispered, "I told her where she might find you." Mom knew I frequented meetings at the Old Park Slope Caton, although she rarely acknowledged my alcoholism or sobriety. It had to be a generational thing, because I knew that she cared, even if she didn't know exactly how to show that concern.

I told her that Brie had, indeed, found me, and that she'd visited Max, and we'd all caught up a little bit.

"She's a mental health counselor now," I said. I explained that she was working indirectly for South Beach, for a contractor, in a leased annex near the hospital.

"There's asbestos in those buildings over there," Dad declared gruffly.

I stared at him. "Wait. Which ones?" I asked. "How do you know?"

Dad crossed his arms. "How do you think I know?" He explained that he had, at one point, looked at buying some buildings in the neighborhood of the annex. "Those buildings are all screwed. They should be condemned or abated at the very least."

I wanted to ask him more, but at that point he began to cough uncontrollably again. Mom pulled a paper towel from her pocket and wiped the spit from his chin. He waved her off and leaned forward in the chair, turning the conversation back to what he cared about. "When's your brother getting out anyway? I got a company to run, for Christ's sake."

I glared back at him, resenting the way he always put work above people—including his own son. "I don't know." I looked at Mom, who was sympathetic but silent. "Hopefully in the next couple weeks. I'm taking some time off to help him. The least you can do is give him some time to recover."

"Weeks?" Dad stared at the television, seething.

Suddenly I couldn't take it anymore. "Jesus, what's wrong with you? Your son tried to kill himself six days ago. Have you even asked yourself *why* he attempted suicide? Do you even care?"

His glaring eyes moved from the television to me. I was sure he didn't care. The hard look he gave me didn't exactly prove otherwise.

"Then guess what?" he said smugly. "You're taking some time off? Then you're going to fill in."

My eyes narrowed. "No way. I'm not doing it."

"You ungrateful son of a bitch." He struggled to lift his feeble body off the chair.

Mom jumped up and eased him back into the seat.

"Leave me alone," he said, swatting her away. He glared at me. "After everything I've done for you!"

The anger that rose in me was so strong, I felt like I might choke. "Everything you've done . . . for me?" I managed to spit out. "Like what, Dad? Food on the table and a roof over my head when I was a kid? Paying for college? Is that what you're talking about?" I paced the room like a tiger, glaring at him every few steps, while he stared back blankly. "You did those things because that's what you were *supposed* to do! You never did one single thing you didn't believe you had to, and you've never done anything for one of us out of love. I don't owe you *anything*! None of us do. After all we've put up with over the years, you're the one who owes *us*."

Dad gaped at me. "You hear the way he's talking to me, Arlene? I've got months to live and he's a big shot now?"

Mom's jaw had dropped.

I turned to the window and exhaled. "You have no idea who I am. No idea who Max is . . . you probably don't even know who Mom is anymore." I turned to face him, my voice cracking. "We don't owe you anything. You owe *us*!"

Dad scoffed. "The only one in the family with any brains besides me, and you walked away from the business, from the whole lot of us." He coughed three times into his handkerchief.

It was a backhanded compliment, the only kind he knew how to give.

"You know why I left."

"Oh, here we go again. Big fucking deal. You drink too much. *I* drink too much. We all drink too fucking much—" He hacked into his shirtsleeve. "And so what? If you're an alcoholic, then so am I and so is everyone else I know."

Mom and I looked at each other. Neither of us said a word.

"And what's the big deal if you *are* an alcoholic? Everyone's addicted to something. I'm a workaholic. Your mother's a pill popper." He barked into his hanky. "That's the way of the world. Grow up already."

My eyes burned into his. "First of all, I haven't had a drink for almost a year. Not that you give a shit. But yeah, even so, I'm still an alcoholic. You know why? Because addiction is a *disease*. It's not a moral failing. It's a disease for which there is no cure. Only a daily reprieve. That's all we get . . . if we do the work and manage to stay *alive*." We both knew I was referring to Harry. And to Dad, himself. "And one of the many ways I'm treating *my* disease—my alcoholism—is by working for myself and not for you. I can't be around that way of living—all work, no rest. I can't be around *you*." I couldn't believe the words were coming out of my mouth. Dale really was rubbing off on me already.

Dad looked up at me but didn't say a word. He bobbed his head ever so slightly, waiting for me to finish. I hoped his hardened face would soften, but it didn't, not until he coughed again—a vile, persistent hacking laced with sputum.

I knelt so we were face to face. "It's time to close down the business, Dad. Max and I don't want it."

Dad turned away and gulped the rest of his whiskey.

Mom inched between us and said in a soft voice, "Daniel, I'm glad to hear you're still . . . sober."

"Thanks, Mom." I stood and looked at Dad. "I've even got a sponsor. A real nice guy. His name is Dale . . . Dale *Benson*."

Dad had no reaction. His eyes remained glued to the television. I knelt beside him and looked at his ravaged face. "He used to go by Benny," I said, cocking my head. "Ring any bells?"

"What the hell are you looking at me for?" he growled.

"Who's Dale Benson, Walter?"

Dad kept his eyes on the TV. "Just some drunk that used to work for us. A nobody."

"Yeah, well, that nobody is saving my life one day at a time." I stood and took a seat on the sofa. "So thank you for saving his."

"I don't understand." Mom sat down next to me. I explained how Dad had taken Dale to his first AA meeting nearly two decades earlier.

Dad adjusted his position uncomfortably in his chair.

Mom looked stunned. "Walter . . . you went to AA?"

"Jesus Christ. Not me. The guy just needed some cheap help, and I needed a reliable worker. Do we have to talk about this?"

With my gaze locked on Dad, it suddenly occurred to me that he was an emotionally stunted, spiritually sick man, one I should treat as such.

"You did a good thing, Dad."

"How long did you go for?" Mom asked.

"It didn't work for me, Arlene. Obviously."

"Dale would say it was *you* who didn't work, not the program."

Dad rolled his eyes and seemed to shrink even further into his chair.

I stood and kissed the top of Mom's head; she was still staring at Dad in disbelief.

"Aren't you staying for dinner?" she asked.

"I'm gonna get going. Got a lot of work to catch up on."

She frowned, then stood and hugged me tightly.

"By the way," I said, holding her shoulders, "Dale Benson was the guy who came to the door that morning in 1976 when you were in the shower."

Dad glanced at me, then cleared his throat. Mom's face seemed to crumble. She covered her mouth with her hand, then sat solemnly back down on the sofa.

I reached for the front doorknob. "The very same day that Max got that beating and Harry blasted Dad, Dad took Dale to his first AA meeting."

Dad's face softened, then he spoke in a whisper. "Maybe I should have stayed."

My hand stopped midair. "What?"

His eyes looked wet, maybe because he was sick. But maybe it was something else.

"He wanted me to come in with him, but it was too much. Your brother had just . . ." He stared at his hands. "I couldn't just sit and listen to a bunch of drunks talk while Harry was out there doing God knows what. I took Dale to the meeting because I told him I would. But that's as much as I could do at the time. I had to look for . . ."

He gave me a look that was half-imploring. "I should have stayed out all night looking. And when . . . when what happened, happened . . . I should have gotten myself to that goddamn meeting. I'm sorry, okay? I am. Now I've said it. Is that good enough? Is that what you want from me? Christ."

I just looked at him. It *was* what I wanted—or at least part of what I wanted. An admission. An apology. It was everything.

And it also wasn't enough. Still, it was the most I had ever gotten from him. I told myself to be thankful. I told myself he couldn't do better.

It was important to me that *I* do better.

And I promised myself that I would.

———

My apartment door was slightly ajar when I arrived back home. The hall lamp beside it flickered, sporadically illuminating the dark apartment inside. I pushed open the door.

"Hello? Jill?"

There was no answer. It was quiet inside. I reached in and flipped the switch.

I knew the moment I walked in that Jill was gone. Her framed photos and books were gone from our bookcase. And sitting on the floor was the anniversary gift I'd given her—my silver Bach trumpet, in its case.

Unsure of what to do next, I moved slowly toward the dinette, picked up one of the chairs, and took a seat at the table. While taking long, slow breaths to calm myself, I noticed a white envelope lying on the center of the table. I pulled it toward me and removed the folded piece of loose-leaf paper inside. It was a handwritten note from Jill—block letters in black pen drawn erratically across the lined piece of paper.

DANIEL ZIMMER—YOU ARE THE DEVIL! HOW COULD YOU NEVER TELL ME ABOUT HARRY!? FRANKIE IS DEAD BECAUSE OF EVERYTHING YOU AND YOUR BROTHER DID THAT DAY. WELL, GUESS WHAT. FRANKIE'S NOT THE ONLY ONE WHO'S GONE. AS FAR AS I'M CONCERNED, YOU'RE DEAD NOW TOO.

I jumped up and ran to the bedroom, where the entire contents of my old backpack—the one from college filled with all of my private and personal items—lay scattered across the bedspread. My eyes moved from the empty brown JanSport on the floor to the bedspread and then from one pile to the next. It appeared that Jill had attempted to arrange the contents chronologically. Beside the pillows was the letter Brie had written to me after she moved to Manhattan. Next to them were childhood photos of Brie and me and other photos of me, Harry, and Max. In the center of the bed were piles of letters, notes, and cards—birthdays, anniversaries—that Brie had written and given to me while we were in college and afterward, while we were living together. There was also a pile of photos of Brie and me as adults from that time period.

On the far corner of the bed lay a group of newspaper clippings, meticulously arranged, apparently in order of importance. I moved to the other side of the bed and scanned them. There were two long, single-column clippings, tattered and old—the 1976 obituaries for twelve-year-old Frankie Woburn and eighteen-year-old Harry Zimmer. Neither obituary referred to a cause of death, only that each boy was "taken unexpectedly." Next to them lay two short articles, also weathered and yellowed by age. Each reported on the same accident in Carroll Gardens, where two boys were killed. Neither mentioned the names of the victims, only their ages and the location of the intersection near the school.

I suddenly felt ill. All this time, I'd known deep down that I was keeping an important truth from Jill, even though I pretended otherwise—to myself and to her. She *hadn't* known that Harry was behind the wheel of the car that killed Frankie that day. No doubt, she could have found out who the driver was if she'd wanted to. Clearly she hadn't. Yet I'd acted as though she knew and didn't blame me. Why? Because it was easier for me. I'd never asked myself what was best for Jill.

I held her note in my hand and felt strangely relieved. I felt terrible for how I'd contributed to Frankie's death. I felt terrible for how I'd lied to Jill, and for how I'd treated her. But I also was glad the truth was finally out in the open. Now she knew everything. Now I was free of my lie of omission.

Now I was ready to move forward, and to start again. I hoped Jill was, too.

CHAPTER 20

My attempts at sobriety during the first few months of 1990 didn't last. Within a week of that get-together at Cliff and Debbie's place, I was drinking again. Just not around Brie. I hadn't even gone to an AA meeting as Brie had insisted, but lied that I had.

In March, I decided to break out on my own and start my own brokerage business. It was a huge relief to finally get away from my dad. But the financial stress and uncertainty of starting a new business made me drink even more.

From that point on, I spent a great deal of time concealing my addiction. I was constantly offering to run errands for Brie or to pick up food so that I could stop at the local bar. I drank secretly from bottles hidden in the apartment. Breath freshener, body spray, and other truth-maskers became the ever-present tools of my daily life. I responded to my guilt over the lies, the arguments, the inevitable miscommunications, and my unexplainable cold shoulders by giving her gifts—knickknacks for the house, dinners out, weekends in Manhattan. It wasn't easy, lying to the one person I loved most in the world. But I didn't have a choice. Brie would not stay with me if I drank. And the beast had to be fed.

One late spring evening, I pushed open the door to our apartment and tumbled inside with numerous large and very heavy bags falling at my sides. Outside, the sun was low in the early evening sky beyond the row of apartments on our street in Bay Ridge. Brie was about to finish her fifth year as a second-grade teacher at the Bayview School. In two weeks, the school year would be over, and saying goodbye to students and parents was never easy for her. She made deep connections, and everyone adored her.

The bags at my side were filled with art supplies—paints, canvases, and brushes—that I hoped would keep Brie busy and happy during the summer break.

"You're so dramatic." Brie burst into laughter.

"Dramatic? I just carried all of this eight blocks." I huffed, then smiled. "'Dramatic,' she says."

Brie tied her apron behind her back and flashed a quick smile back at me. She looked studious in her teacher outfit—a long-sleeved floral blouse buttoned to the very top, dark slacks, and closed-toe shoes. Her hair was in a loose bun, her reading glasses on the tip of her nose. She looked down at the three-by-five-inch recipe card in her hand. "Beef kaker okay?"

"If you're not too tired to make it, then I'd love it." It was my favorite home-cooked meal—Scandinavian meatballs topped with fried onions and lemon—and one of the many recipes passed down in her family through generations.

I carried the bags down the hall to Brie's painting studio—formerly my home office. I'd recently rented a space—the first that was my very own—on Eighty-Fifth Street, eight blocks away, so Brie would have a place to paint. Maybe one day it would even become a nursery. Brie's doctor had said that a pregnancy would be high-risk for her, but he hadn't ruled it out. We'd been together since college, and I'd always assumed Brie and I would marry. I'd never felt like I could get married and start a family while I was working for my dad. Now things felt different, and I hoped my business would do well so that I could propose soon. I was more than ready.

I carried the bags into the room that had once been my office. From the doorway, I scanned the room. In the center stood Brie's easel. Beneath the window, a white table with two drawers would hold the new painting supplies I'd brought home. On top of the table lay a King James Bible. Its over-size binding was brittle, the cloth was worn in several places, and the pages were aged and curling. It had belonged to Brie's mother—one of the few items she'd saved after her mother died. I stared at the familiar portrait of Jesus on the cover, then turned to the walls, which were covered with artwork—mostly finger paintings, sketches, and arts and crafts projects made by her students over the past year.

I dropped the bags against the easel and crossed the hall to my new home office—the former storage closet. Behind the bifold doors stood a small wooden desk with a typewriter, a foldable metal chair, and a slim four-drawer vertical filing cab-inet. It was small, but I only used the space when I couldn't be at my actual office.

Clay Bridge Realty Inc. was not even three months old, but business had been good thanks to a tight market and my connections from the family business. As the sole broker and owner of the company, I shared no commissions and set my own schedule.

Unfortunately for Max, the day after I left, Dad had moved him into my old office—the one right next to his own—and the closer proximity was killing Max. It wasn't just the fact that the move made it easier for our dad to pick on him—Max also hated watching our dad harangue others. But the nature of his new location made it unavoidable, and he was suffering.

It was painful for me to watch Max's mental state diminish under our father's abuse. Nevertheless, I moved on as best I could, taking comfort in the fact that I was finally out on my own. Brie supported me every step of the way. She only wanted me to be happy. And I was, mostly. Between my new brokerage company and my plan to propose soon, life was looking good.

Now if I could only control my addiction. Then things would be perfect.

Later that night, I sat at the kitchen table. Our plates were empty, our forks upside down. Only two of the ten beef kaker remained on the serving dish. I was stuffed.

"Your mom would be so impressed with your cooking." It was the truth.

"You're sweet." Brie answered mechanically from the kitchen sink, where she was already washing the dishes. She seemed distracted.

"Everything okay?"

She nodded. "Uh-huh." Her reply wasn't strained, but it wasn't convincing, either. She set the last pan on the dish rack and wiped her hands. "Hey . . . I've got something for you." She looked like she might be suppressing a smile.

I held my stomach. I was full, but never too full for one of Brie's baked desserts. "What is it tonight? Cream cake? Marzipan torte?"

Brie held up a finger and turned to the cabinet that contained her medicine. She fished around inside until her hand emerged, clutching a small, dark rectangular box, black velvet and tied with a white ribbon. She crossed the room and put it on the table in front of me as she took a seat. "Surprise!"

I started to jiggle it, and she stopped me with one hand. "Well, don't shake it!" She shook her head, her expression guarded. "Just open it."

I pulled both ends of the ribbon and carefully lifted the top. Inside lay a yellow rattle and a pregnancy test stick sheathed in plastic wrap.

My mouth hung open. Her eyes, on mine, were wide. "Daniel, I'm pregnant. *We're* pregnant."

I sat there for a while in shock. I was excited, of course. Thrilled even. But now that it was real, and not just a theory, I also felt worry rising in me. Brie's pulmonologist had made it clear that a pregnancy could be a risky affair, and her condition had been growing worse over time. And yet Brie had always insisted that she would have children one day. She wanted that very much, and she trusted that her God would see her through any problems that arose.

I pushed away my worry. This was everything I wanted. Or almost everything.

She told me she'd made an appointment with her doctor for the next week. I promised her that I would go with her. That I would be with her every step of the way. No matter what. And then I jumped up and ran to my tiny office.

"Wait here!" I called over my shoulder.

I ran back a minute later carrying the little box I had hidden in my filing cabinet. "Hey, I've got a surprise for you, too." I reached into my pocket and brought out a small velvet box. I lifted the top, revealing a pear-shaped diamond ring set in platinum, and bent down on one knee.

Brie jumped up, her hands trembling over her open mouth, and slowly backed away from the table.

"I was planning to do this when my business was a tiny bit more stable. But there could never be a better time than this. Will you marry me, Brie Astrid Olsson?" She was glowing in the kitchen doorway, the colors of the sunset bathing the sky through the window behind her.

"Of course I will, Daniel Zimmer!" She burst into tears.

I stood and pulled her trembling hand toward me, lifted the ring, and pushed it onto her finger.

"It fits perfectly," she said.

"So do we, Brie." I held her close.

She stared at the sparkling diamond on her finger, her face stained with tears.

"Hey, hey." I wiped her eyes. "This is supposed to be a celebration, right?"

She rubbed her wet eyes and laughed. "But I didn't make any dessert."

"How 'bout I go get a bottle of Dom Pérignon!" The words just came out.

"What?" Her expression flattened. "Why the hell would we do that?"

Embarrassed, I doubled down instead of apologizing. "Come on, Brie." I tried to keep my tone light. "This is huge. We've gotta celebrate." My tone became pleading. I was desperate and tired of hiding, and this seemed the perfect opportunity to win permission for a drink out in the open.

She got up and searched one cabinet after another. "Did you buy some already?" Breathing heavily, she coughed into her shoulder, then looked back at me. "Where is it?"

"Jesus. I was only kidding." I rubbed the back of my neck. "I didn't buy anything . . . I swear." She nestled her head in her arms on the kitchen table as she struggled to catch her breath. I grabbed the inhaler off the counter and placed it on the table next to her. "I'm sorry, Brie."

"I can't believe you could even joke about it." The muffled words she spoke into her folded arms were stern. "You're such a jerk sometimes."

———

I awoke later that night to Brie crying out my name from the bathroom. She was on the toilet, her body folded forward, her head in her arms.

"What's wrong?" I asked from the doorway.

When she looked up, I rushed inside. Her face was flushed, and her eyes were wet and puffy. I knelt beside her and rubbed her thigh.

"I woke up with horrible cramps and went to the bathroom. Now there's blood in the bowl." The anguish in her face was heartbreaking. She dropped her head into her hands and told me to call her gynecologist. "The number's on my pad on the kitchen table. Tell them what happened and ask what to do."

I ran to the kitchen and did as she'd instructed. When I reached the doctor's answering service, the woman on the other end of the line told me that Brie had likely experienced a spontaneous miscarriage.

"These things happen," she said. "It's nature taking its course. If you think it could be something more serious, you should go to the emergency room immediately. Otherwise, the cramping should subside in an hour or so. She should keep her appointment . . ."

I could hear Brie sobbing in the bathroom down the hall.

I hung up the phone and ran to the bathroom doorway. My face must have said it all, because Brie's breathing grew heavier, her sobs turned to cries, and she buried her head in her arms again.

I knelt beside her and tried to rub her back, but she pulled away. "I'm so sorry, Brie."

She lifted her head. "Yeah, of course. Just like you're *sorry* about everything."

I stared at her. "What's that supposed to mean?"

"I knew this was going to happen. I *knew* it." She glared

at me, and a feeling of woundedness rose up in me. It wasn't fair for Brie to blame me for this—was it? And yet, I'd proven that her worst fears were true: I wanted to drink and I was still haunted by alcohol, even in the most important moments of our life together.

"Get out." I'd never heard her sound so cold.

I said her name, but her face only grew colder.

"*GET OUT!*"

I spun backward, shocked by her reaction. Unsure what to do or where to go, I retreated to my office in the linen closet, closed the bifold doors behind me, and sat down on the metal chair. Brie's wailing reached me through the wall; I stared at the bottom drawer of the filing cabinet, my heart pounding harder and my breath becoming slower and steadier. Bewildered and helpless—and without thinking—I pulled open the drawer, pushed aside the bottle of Dom Pérignon that I'd sworn to Brie I hadn't bought, and clutched the bottle of Jameson that I had hidden behind some file folders. I held it in my hands and stared at the sloshing liquid.

I unscrewed the cap, held the bottle to my lips, and chugged. After two more slugs, I returned the bottle to the drawer and took two mints from the red-and-white tin next to the typewriter. Then I turned to the bifold door, which was now slightly open.

Brie stood in the doorway, shaking her head, her face blotchy and wet with tears. "You are a fucking liar, Daniel," she said calmly, and then she turned away.

Numb inside, I followed her slowly down the hall to our bedroom.

"You wanna know why I miscarried?"

I didn't need her to tell me why. I knew she was going to blame me. I was already blaming myself.

I pulled on my jeans, slipped into my shoes, and walked back into the hallway, where Brie sat on the floor, her back against the wall, her chest heaving spasmodically. Her inhaler lay on the floor next to her, and that comforted me. When I left, she'd be okay.

"God knew we'd be terrible parents." Her voice was weaker now, and she was speaking more slowly. "And by the way, you're not just a liar. You're a *shitty* liar, too. I've known about your drinking for months. I'm not giving you the benefit of the doubt anymore, and I'm not enabling you."

We glared at one another briefly before I turned to leave.

"Wait," she said.

I spun around so fast I almost fell.

"Take your fucking ring!" She threw the diamond band at me. "We're done."

CHAPTER 21

It had been five years since Brie had broken off our engagement and moved out of our Bay Ridge apartment, but in the two months since we'd reconnected, we'd made up for all of that lost time. We'd started dating a month after Jill and I broke up, and things had been going so well that Brie had even agreed to move back into the apartment. That would have been a break-neck relationship speed for some couples. But Brie and I had known each other our whole lives. More than that, her health was declining, and I wanted to be there for her. We both wanted to be there for each other.

"I can't believe this is happening." She wrapped her arms around my neck. It was a holiday—New Year's Day. A whole new year. A whole new life.

"Neither can I." We hugged in the hallway until I noticed Brie straining to breathe. I drew back. "You okay?"

She nodded and smiled.

"Go back to the sofa," I urged. "Use your oxygen." I'd been unpacking her boxes all morning, and just three remained. She could sit and watch me as I worked. We'd set up a kind of makeshift area beside the sofa with two sets of tubing and two different-sized oxygen canisters, depending on whether Brie intended to sit down or move about the apartment.

She grasped my hands. "Don't worry so much." As I led her back into the living room, she turned to survey the progress we'd made, her gaze landing on the picture frame on the coffee table. It was a photo of Harry, Max, and me on the beach at Coney Island—the only picture I had of the three of us. "Are you sure Max doesn't mind me moving in?"

I nodded. I actually hadn't given Max a choice—Brie would live with me, whether he liked it or not. And after all, the plan was that he would move back into his own place once he was stable. He also didn't seem to have any problem with Brie moving in, so long as I left him alone. That was something I didn't have to push myself to do. Max was moody, unpredictable, stubborn, and generally unhappy even when he took his medication, something he did only sporadically.

For years, I had assumed that his mindset and behavior would improve if he were to leave the family business, which is something he'd finally done. A week after his release from Maimonides, he walked straight into our childhood home on Carroll Street and told Dad that he was done being demeaned and chastised. Dad listened without speaking, then said just two words: "Get out." He had managed to tell me he was sorry once. He hadn't mustered the courage to say it to Max—or, as far as I knew, to our mother.

I'm not sure why I ever thought Max would get better after leaving Dad. After all, I hadn't. And Max didn't, either. The reason, for both of us, was probably guilt. Guilt is a shitty emotion, especially a child's guilt over leaving a parent. It was a completely irrational feeling to have. But that didn't stop either of us from feeling it to our core.

"Where is Max anyway?" Brie asked.

"Picking up a prescription. He should be back soon."

I pulled the last canvas from the box—a stunning

multicolor landscape showcasing the aurora borealis floating over a small northern village with a church in the center, its steepled cross reaching into the sky. "This would go perfect here." I held it up against the wall next to the front door.

"That one always reminds me of Mom and Dad." She picked at her fingernail. "I wish they were here to see us back together again. They'd be so happy."

I sat down on the sofa and lay my head on her shoulder. I felt that they were happy to see us together, from wherever they were now, and I told Brie so.

Our eyes locked, and she ran her hand through my wavy hair. "I'm *so* glad we're back together." Our one-month anniversary was a day away. "I've missed you more than you know."

I squeezed her thigh, and we both slouched back into the sofa. "Ditto," I said. But I was distracted. In my new position, I could see a beer bottle partially hidden behind the turntable on the media console. *"For fuck's sake.* I told him *no* alcohol in this apartment."

Brie's eyes widened with surprise.

"I'm sorry . . ." I tried to shake off the sudden rage I felt. "But I've told him a hundred times." I walked over to the turntable and grabbed the beer bottle. When I shook it, it sloshed. "He didn't even finish the damn thing." I walked into the kitchen and dumped the liquid down the sink.

Brie appeared in my periphery, wheeled canister in tow, cradling another two bottles in her other arm.

"Where the hell did you find those?"

"Behind the other speakers."

I plucked the empty bottles from the crook of her arm and dropped all three into the garbage can under the sink. She followed me to the front door, where I yanked my jacket off the hook on the wall.

Brie laid a gentle hand on my arm. "Remember, he's going through something, Daniel. Something you should understand better than anybody. Give him time. He'll come around."

I knew she was right about the first part. But I didn't think Max would come around. And sometimes I wished Brie would give me more of the empathy she extended to him. I supposed it was my fault that she didn't see how much I was struggling. I always acted more in control than I felt. But I couldn't live with alcohol in the house. If I did, I might cave in a moment of weakness, and there was too much at stake to let that happen again.

I shook my head. "I think we should get him back into his own place."

Brie looked troubled, and we agreed to talk about it more later. My mother was going to be coming over soon for a home-cooked meal. Dad was worsening by the day, and Mom was beginning to fall apart at the seams despite having a part-time nurse at the house every day. She needed the break. And I still had a meeting to go to before dinner.

Brie followed me to the front door.

"I'll be back by three thirty." I kissed her on the cheek. "Mom will be here around four. Are you sure you want to cook? We can just order something."

"It's only veal cutlets and brussels sprouts. Max asked—"

I turned back to her. "*Max* asked for . . . ? Are you kidding me?"

Brie cocked her head and said in a soft voice, "He needs our support now more than ever, Daniel."

I'd grown fed up with Max's antics over the past weeks; supporting him was becoming more and more difficult. But in that moment, I quickly lost myself in Brie's gaze. She understood what people needed better than I did. I trusted that as long as I was with her, everything would be all right. She was stronger than I would ever be.

And I was stronger when I was with her.

The smell of pan-fried cutlets and roasted brussels sprouts washed over me as I opened the front door. It was almost four o'clock.

"You're cutting it close, mister," said Brie from the kitchen.

"I'm sorry. Some of the guys insisted I grab coffee with them afterwards." I reached into my pocket and pulled out a bronze-plated coin, which I placed on the kitchen countertop.

"What's that?" She picked it up. "Oh my gosh . . . your one-year medallion?" I smiled and her face lit up.

The doorbell rang. I snatched the medallion from her hand, shoved it into my pocket, and opened the front door. Mom stood on the stoop in a heavy wool shawl, carrying a Louis Vuitton handbag.

I kissed her cheek. "Hey Mom. Come on in."

"Hi, Arlene," Brie called from the kitchen, as Mom disappeared around the corner to use the bathroom. Brie was putting the finishing touches on the miniature buffet, which looked delicious.

"Why didn't you tell me?" she asked from across the kitchen island. "I would have come."

"It was a trap," I said. "That's why Dale had asked me to speak at the meeting. He'd planned to present it to me all along." But the fact was, I never would have asked Brie to come. It was nerve-racking enough for me to chair a meeting. The last thing I needed was to also worry about her reliving those dreadful days as I told my story.

She reached out and held my hands. "I am so proud of you. One year."

"Total miracle."

"It's what happens when you let go and let God."

"Yep." I wasn't going to argue about the definition. If I'd

learned anything, it was that my Higher Power could be whatever I wanted it to be, even G-O-D: a *group of drunks.*

She nodded, smiling slightly. "Just keep doing what you're doing. One day at a time."

"What's one day at a time?" Mom came around the corner into the kitchen.

I gave Brie a quick shake of my head. There was no need to involve Mom.

Ignoring me, Brie said, "Daniel got his one-year medallion today, Arlene." She adjusted the hot plate on the island. "At his AA meeting."

Mom folded a napkin from the holder and placed it between her lips. She patted her lips once, then withdrew the napkin and dropped it into the trash bin. I could tell that she didn't know what to say. She never seemed to know how to talk about my alcoholism with me, or my recovery.

"Come on, Mom," I said. "Let's go sit for a minute before we eat." While Brie straightened out the kitchen, Mom followed me to the den. We sat at opposite ends of the sofa, and I turned to her. "I'm glad you're here." I meant it. I knew it wasn't easy for her to leave Dad at home.

"I am happy for you, you know," Mom said, smiling half-heartedly. I was surprised that she was willing to engage about the subject. "But do you really think you're *still* an alcoholic?" She looked worried, as if admitting the disease was worse than having it.

"Once an alcoholic, always an alcoholic, Mom," I said evenly. "I'm just not *actively* alcoholic."

Mom pulled at the collar of her blouse. "I think my father had a problem with alcohol, too," she admitted. "I was so young, and he . . . died so early. I can't be sure, but he was always angry, always drinking from a flask." She took a deep breath. "I should have been more forceful with your father

about stopping. Just like the cigarettes. And . . . other things."
She sighed. "Instead, I enabled him."

I'd been angry with her for so long for not sticking up for
us more. For not sticking up for *herself* more. But the moment
she became vulnerable, I only felt compassion for her. "It wasn't
your responsibility, Mom, and it's not your fault. Dad made his
choices. We all do." I reached for her hand. "Hey, how did—?"
I hesitated, wondering whether I should ask about Grandpa
Gabe's death. I had hoped it might explain Max's own insta-
bility and suicidal tendencies, but I decided against it. I didn't
want to upset her.

Distracted, she patted my hand and smiled, her thoughts
no doubt still on my father, or perhaps her own.

The grandfather clock tolled the quarter hour. It was 4:15.

"Isn't Max joining us for dinner?" Mom asked.

"That's the plan . . . I'm sure he'll be home soon." Max
tended to keep whatever schedule he wanted to. But I was surprised he was late. Especially since Brie had promised to make
the meal he'd requested.

"Dinner's ready," Brie called.

On the countertop lay a beautiful spread of roasted brussels sprouts, veal cutlets, lingonberry jam, roasted carrots, and
warm dinner rolls. We filled our plates and sat at the round
dinette table.

Mom gazed at the beautiful food on her plate. "Everything's
delicious, Brie. Your cutlets are so crispy."

"It's because I fry them in olive oil, and I always pound
them *extra* thin."

I froze. My eyes wandered toward Mom, then to Brie, who
had no idea about the blunder she'd just made. She'd heard the
stories about Dad's awful reaction to what he'd perceived to be
thick cutlets, but apparently wasn't connecting the dots.

Mom shook her head and waved her hand in the air.

"Relax, Daniel." She smiled. "If there's one thing I learned over the years, it's how to pound a cutlet thin."

The evening passed pleasantly as the three of us reminisced about the old days on Carroll Street. After dinner, Mom nibbled on raspberry-filled delights from the platter of Italian butter cookies while I enjoyed my third cup of espresso. Brie excused herself to the kitchen, only to emerge moments later with a large vanilla-frosted cupcake. A single candle in its center burned brightly as she set it down on the table in front of me. She kissed me on the cheek and said, "Congratulations, my love." Mom raised her glass of diet soda and gestured her own congratulations. I blew out the candle flame, then reached inside my pocket for the medallion. "Check this out, Mom." I pointed to the roman numeral "I" in the center of the triangle.

Mom read the words aloud. "To thine own self be true."

I flipped the medallion over and pointed to the cursive writing. "And that's the Serenity Prayer." *God, grant me the serenity to accept the things I cannot change, courage to change the things I can, and wisdom to know the difference.*

"What a beautiful sentiment," Mom said, reading it. "I'm very proud of you, Daniel."

In the next moment, the doorbell rang. We all looked at each other.

I shrugged. "Well, it can't be Max," I said, getting up to answer it. "He's got a key."

But indeed, there on the stoop, smelling of beer and cigarettes, was Max. He was dressed in a heavy hooded sweatshirt and holding a brown paper bag in the shape of a tall bottle.

"Where's your key?" I forced a smile.

With a stupid grin, Max held up his keychain.

"Why'd you ring the bell?"

He shrugged. "Felt like it."

Pushing down the urge to smack his smug-looking face, I glanced at the paper bag. "What's that?"

But Max only stepped past me, waved blindly at Brie and Mom, and stumbled across the den into the bathroom.

I returned to the dinette table and sat in silence with Brie and Mom. When Max returned moments later, he placed a bottle of Chianti in the center of the table, then staggered into the kitchen, where he rummaged through drawers until he found a corkscrew. Finally, he fell into the empty chair at the table and reached for the bottle. The three of us watched, flabbergasted, as he wrestled with the corkscrew and bottle. After a minute he gave up and proclaimed, "I'm starving. Let's eat!"

Brie snatched the bottle and corkscrew from the table and withdrew into the kitchen.

"Brie," Max called after her, "I need a plate!"

"Dinner's over, you moron!" I snapped. Mom gasped, but I couldn't stop the words that came next. "You're almost two hours late. You're drunk. And you bring alcohol into my place . . . again!"

"Daniel, please calm down," Mom begged.

Brie returned to the table empty-handed and sat down quietly. She began to fiddle nervously with my AA medallion.

"What's that?" Max lunged like a clumsy child across the table for the bronze coin.

I couldn't take it anymore: the alcohol, the demands, the disrespect. And now this. I jumped up and threw myself at him, causing us both to fall over the table edge and onto the floor.

"Enough!" Brie leaped to her feet and held onto the table for support with one hand.

Struggling to stand and mumbling to himself, Max reached for the table and pulled himself up. Mom steadied him and walked him to his bedroom.

Still struggling to catch her breath, Brie plopped down onto the chair.

"You see what I mean," I said. "It's not working." I reached for her hand. "He's got to go back to his own apartment."

Brie looked at me and nodded. I walked over to the counter to retrieve the inhaler and handed it to her.

Her breathing had evened out by the time my mother came out of Max's room. "Come, dear, you should lay down, as well." She gently pulled Brie up by the arms and walked her slowly into the bedroom. Brie stopped herself at the doorframe and turned back to me.

"I'll take care of everything," I said. "I love you."

When Mom returned, she let out a long, low sigh.

"You okay?" I asked.

She looked up and smiled feebly. "Are you? Brie's getting worse. I can tell."

"Everything's going to be fine, Mom." I tried to sound convincing. But the truth was, every day my sense of dread was increasing.

Mom nodded mechanically. "I'm not sure how much longer your father has left, Daniel." Her eyes welled up. "He's not even sixty." She began to weep. "Why does everyone die so young?"

My heart skipped a beat, and the feeling of dread deepened. Not Brie. Brie couldn't be one of those people.

I reached for her hands. "I'm not going anywhere, Mom."

And I hoped with everything in me that Brie wouldn't be going anywhere, either.

———

It took only a week to move Max back into his old third-floor walk-up on Ridge Boulevard. I worried about Max, of course. We all did. There was no way to be sure that he'd be all right on his own again. But he hadn't left us a lot of options. And I reminded myself that he was generally doing better and that he was responsible for his own life and choices. I even imagined that he would in time see the move as an indication of our confidence in him. We trusted that he could successfully live independently. Maybe in time he too would believe it—and do it.

I promised Brie I would visit Max every day on my way home from the AA meeting in Park Slope and, so far, I'd kept my word. Max was still resentful that we had asked him to leave, refusing to accept any blame, insisting instead that it was because Brie and I wanted to be alone. But he welcomed my visits just the same. He'd always viewed us as compadres in the same lifelong struggle—a struggle which he now, with Dad's imminent death, could finally see ending. He began to view each day as one day closer to the freedom he'd sought his entire life. As a result, his state of mind began to slowly improve.

Within a month of us living alone together, Brie had suggested we marry. She'd quickly become convinced of my determination to remain sober—the one missing ingredient from our engagement five years earlier—so it seemed only natural for us to pick things up where we'd left off. I suspected her suggestion also had something to do with her steadily deteriorating health—kids may have been out of the question, but she could still have a marriage. The idea that she was fighting for us to have this both broke my heart and made me more determined than ever to be the man she deserved.

At the time, we were days away from January 30—the date of her parents' wedding anniversary—and Brie wanted to include their memory in our special day. I still had her engagement ring, and neither of us wanted a large, stuffy ceremony, so we didn't need much time to prepare. We decided that a simple courthouse ceremony would do just fine.

It was an intimate affair. Brie looked gorgeous in her off-the-rack wedding gown, which fit her like a glove. I was dapper in my rented black tuxedo with white bow tie and cummer-bund. Mom and Max were our witnesses; Dad stayed home with the recently hired full-time hospice nurse. The justice of the peace performed a secular ceremony, supplemented with Bible verses that Brie had chosen. The whole thing was short and sweet: exactly what we wanted.

After the groom had kissed the bride, we said our goodbyes to Mom and Max and left in a cab with our marriage license, making it home to Bay Ridge by sunset. Slowly we climbed the stoop to our apartment.

"Welcome home, Mrs. Zimmer." I scooped Brie up and carried her over the threshold. She giggled all the way to the sofa.

"Oh, my, Mr. Zimmer, you are so strong!" She tried to laugh as she said it, but when she took a deep breath, she wheezed on the exhale.

I got up and grabbed an inhaler. The first one I tried was empty, so I went to the kitchen and opened the cabinet that was dedicated to Brie's medicine. Filled with dozens of old and new pill bottles—mostly steroids to reduce the inflammation in her lungs—Adrenalin shots, EpiPens, and a myriad of dif-ferently shaped and sized inhalers, the cabinet looked like it belonged in a pharmacy. I snatched an albuterol inhaler and returned to the sofa.

"It's because I've been up for so long." She put the inhaler to her mouth and inhaled. Once the mist inside her lungs had done its job, she exhaled.

"All good?"

She replied with a nod.

Leaning my shoulder into Brie's arm, I whispered, "I have one last surprise for you. I'll be right back."

I returned to the kitchen, opened the refrigerator, and snatched the bottle of sparkling cider that I'd hidden be-hind the milk container before we left. I also pulled from the refrigerator a box of chocolate-covered strawberries I'd stashed in the vegetable drawer the previous morning. I arranged the strawberries in the shape of a heart on a porcelain dish from her mother's collection, then reached into the freezer for two chilled flutes. I filled the glasses with the bubbly liquid and placed all the items on a platter.

"Okay, close your eyes!" I called, making my way into the den.

"What are you doing?" she asked playfully, her eyes squeezed shut.

"Don't open them," I said, carefully placing the platter on the table. "Okay, open your eyes."

Brie opened her eyes; her expression soured when they fell on the flutes.

"What?" I was confused.

She shook her head and her eyes filled with tears. "Are you kidding me?" She stood, her chest rising heavily.

"What? It's sparkling cider . . . to celebrate." I stared at the glasses. It hadn't occurred to me that after all we'd gone through she would think I was actually bringing out champagne. But when I looked at them now, I felt stupid.

She fell back onto the sofa, relieved. "Oh my God . . . you scared the heck out of me."

"I'm sorry." My face burned. "I wanted the romantic gesture of the champagne flutes. I shouldn't have—"

"No . . . oh my gosh . . . it's okay." Brie's tears turned to nervous laughter. "I love you, Daniel."

I sank onto the sofa and lay my hand on her lap. "I'm done with that crap . . . you know that, Brie."

She smiled and we sat silently for a moment staring at the platter while the canister clicked and the oxygen in the tube swished. Brie reached for her flute while I continued to gaze at mine. The dozens of tiny bubbles racing to the surface captivated me. The liquid did look exactly like champagne, and my mind began to romance the idea of drinking the real stuff. Suddenly, I was bombarded by thoughts and schemes on how to gain access to alcohol. I tried to think about something else but couldn't.

"What are you thinking about?" I heard Brie ask, but I couldn't respond. "Daniel?" She leaned into me, and the warmth of her body and voice loosened the grip of my mind. "*Daniel!*"

I came to and took a deep breath.

"Welcome back," Brie said with her head tilted. "What were you thinking about? You were totally lost."

"Um . . . just how much I love you." I reached for my flute.

"To us," she said, clinking my flute with hers.

We sipped simultaneously, and as the liquid spilled down my throat, my body shivered at the realization: like a demon at the controls of a drawbridge, my disease was waiting patiently for my return.

CHAPTER 22

I stood over my father's casket—the simple pine box that is customary in Judaism. It's what he'd wanted, though that desire had nothing to do with our being Jewish. Quite frankly, pine boxes were cheap. "Why spend money on something that's going in the ground?" he'd said. Dad had also insisted that the service not be religious. He said he wasn't about to find religion just because he was dying. It sounded like something I would say, and that realization made me uncomfortable.

"You ready?" Max asked, placing his hand on my shoulder. Ahead of us, friends and family and countless business associates spoke softly among themselves. I saw Dale in one corner, chatting with some men about his age who might have been some former coworkers.

"Why am I doing this?" I grumbled. "You're older."

Max snickered. "Yeah, right. No one wants to hear what I have to say about the old man." He drew a flask from his breast pocket and took a long pull. "Not in a million years."

The smell of liquor wafted over to me. "Nice," I said sarcastically.

"Want a slug?" he asked, tipping it toward me. "Ha ha—just kidding!"

"Hilarious." Max had no idea how hard it was for me to remain sober. Especially now, given the stress of Dad's death and Brie's health problems. The desire for a drink was surging inside of me. I scanned the room for Brie and spotted her talking with some of Mom's friends. Our eyes met, and she smiled suspiciously.

Max nodded in Mom's direction and nudged me. "I wonder if she realizes she can cook those chicken cutlets as fat as she wants now!"

I wanted to laugh but restrained myself. Brie was approaching, and I nudged Max, whispering, "Be cool."

"How's my man?" She kissed my cheek, her lips lingering for a moment as she inhaled through her wrinkled nose. Since Dad's death, she'd been on high alert.

I backed away and patted the small flask in Max's breast pocket. "I *know* you weren't checking *my* breath."

She moved her hands to her hips and blinked innocently. "Don't be insulted. I have good cause." She could tell that the weight of my father's death and its consequences were setting in. I'd become impatient, intolerant, and quick to anger. The future of the family business now fell on me, and the pressure was overwhelming, particularly since my intention was to wind it down rather than take it over—a course Dad would have hated with every fiber of his being. Thankfully, she'd been very understanding and patient with me.

I nodded. "I know you do, but—"

"But nothing, mister. You know the deal." In the days leading up to Dad's death, Brie had implored me to do the AA Step work with Dale. Dale still insisted that not moving forward with the Steps was "reserving the right to drink again." He'd told me that if I wanted to find emotional peace and serenity, I needed to write out and look at my part in my resentments, give up all of my character defects, make amends, and most importantly, find my own "Higher Power," the one to whom I could turn over my will and my life. Brie herself was a living example of the latter, yet real faith still eluded me.

Attributing my obvious unease to my impending eulogy, Brie said, "I told you that you should have written something in advance." She kissed my cheek. "But you'll do fine." Then she walked over and sat down next to Mom in the front row.

The lights flipped off and on several times, and people took their seats. It was standing room only, which kind of disgusted me. I knew Dale was there to show respect. But I couldn't imagine what everyone else was there for. Surely Dad had treated them all horribly at one time or another? I supposed a lot of folks were there because they'd done business with Dad. Maybe attending a business acquaintance's funeral was considered good form. I knew, too, that funerals were about closure. I certainly needed some. Maybe other people did, too.

Max and I made our way to the front. While he introduced me, I smiled and looked at Mom. She looked exhausted.

As Max went to join the audience, I cleared my throat. "Um . . . thank you all again for coming." I scanned the overflowing crowd. "Dad would have been happy to see the turnout. Even though he didn't like people very much."

The crowd erupted with nervous laughter. Mom cracked a smile. I felt lighter.

"So, as you all know, Dad lived life his way, on his own terms. And I think—I think that's probably what made him so successful as a businessman. Well . . . that and working eighteen hours a day." I paused. "But it's also the reason why he never stopped smoking. Or drinking." I looked out into the crowd, my dry eyes burning. "He never admitted it, but I think he wished he had quit both. He was more surprised than anyone to discover he was . . . mortal." I gave the people in the audience a serious look. "Not *fallible*, mind you, but mortal."

There was more laughter then, louder this time. There were no inside jokes here.

"He was always looking for that big score, too. It didn't matter that he'd been closing some of the biggest real estate deals in the city for years. It was never good enough. Sometimes he made me feel like *I* wasn't good enough." I looked down at the podium. "But in a roundabout way, he ended up teaching me that I didn't need his approval." Of course, he'd taught me that lesson by withholding it. Looking out over the crowd, I didn't think I needed to say so. I turned to look at his casket. "Wherever you are, Dad, I hope you find peace." There it was: a no-frills eulogy. Short and to the point.

After I was done, the funeral director told people they were invited to Brie's and my apartment for refreshments.

Now standing off to the side of the coffin at the front of the room, I turned to Max, who'd walked up to me. "I'll see you at my place."

He shook his head and attempted to say with a straight face, "I'm going to Dad's office. There's a ton of work that needs to be done."

I wondered who he thought he was bullshitting. "You need to come to the apartment. It won't look right if you don't."

"You think I give a shit what it looks like?" Max nodded at the casket as Mom approached it. "Good riddance. That's all I got to say."

We watched Mom rest her hand on the pine box and close her eyes. Then, her head bowed, she walked arm in arm with Brie toward the restroom.

Max shook his head. "I don't get it. How can she be so heartbroken?"

"If you're allowed to be glad, then she's allowed to be sad," I said. "She could use your support." When he didn't respond, I tried a different approach. "Please don't leave me alone with all of these people."

"Ah, there it is. The *real* reason you want me to go to your place." His voice was bitter. It seemed perfectly reasonable to me that we both should support Mom, and that he and I should share the burden of politely facing all of Dad's acquaintances one last time. I didn't understand why Max refused. It didn't occur to me until later that the thing I was barely able to cope with was, in fact, too much for him.

He looked away from me, walked over to the casket, and touched the cold pine surface. "Well, father of mine, I guess this is goodbye." He took the flask from his jacket pocket, drank down the last drops, and then slammed it on the wooden box. "I hope karma treats you as shitty as you treated us."

I glanced over my shoulder, embarrassed. But the last of the crowd was still trickling out, and no one seemed to have heard. Max made his way over to the doorway and then stopped. "Later, Blowfish," he said, his voice heavy with meaning. In that moment, I knew he wasn't just saying goodbye, and he wasn't just insulting me. He was saying, *How can you act like you're saying goodbye to a normal human being who didn't make all of our lives miserable?* I didn't really have an answer.

Just then I noticed Dale across the room, keeping an eye on me. He caught my glance and gave me a look. It was a look that might have said *Don't worry about it. Let Max go.* Or maybe it said *Just worry about keeping your own side of the street clean.* The latter was an AA saying that meant, basically, that I was only responsible for my own behavior—no matter what anyone else did and regardless of whether another person had hurt me. It was one of the many shifts in behavior and attitude he had been encouraging me to make.

Once Max had walked out the door, I turned to find Brie and my mother. Max had left me with nothing more than a vacant room, a dead father, and an empty flask. But Brie and my mother and Dale were still waiting for me.

And I was ready to join them.

CHAPTER 23

I held Brie's hand tightly, her wedding ring pressing hard against my palm as we walked toward Fourth Avenue in Bay Ridge. It was a cool and sunny day in April, and Brie had insisted we take advantage of it. Her church—the Lutheran Church of the Good Shepherd, the same one she'd attended when we were kids—was one of the most elegant in Brooklyn, with a gold cross atop a white steeple that stretched heavenward and an even larger cross above the gray shingle roof. The two-story church was surrounded by an iron fence encircling a green lawn. Tall lancet windows with pointed arches lined the facade.

Brie tried to go to church at least twice a week, even though she rarely went to the services anymore. Her asthma symptoms—tightness in her chest, shortness of breath, fatigue, and swollen legs—had gotten sharply worse in the three months since we married. Walking more than a block or two, even with her oxygen tank, now winded her so much that I'd become accustomed to accompanying her pretty much everywhere she went, including to and from work and church. This made life much more complicated. But it was far easier for me than worrying about her being out on her own. Because her coughing episodes had also become more frequent and severe, she always made sure to visit the church before evening services so as not to interrupt them. But she still liked to sit in what she called *God's house* to pray.

Brie's deteriorating health strained everything. I was focused more and more on my worry for her, and as a result my commitment to AA meetings and to my sponsor, Dale, had grown weaker. I was still convinced that I was powerless over alcohol, but that's as far as I went with the program's teachings. How could I possibly believe that God would or could restore me to sanity, or even help me to deal with life on life's terms, when He wouldn't even afford my wife an occasional reprieve from her worsening condition? I was even beginning to fear that Brie might die—and I thought Brie might be considering the same possibility, though we couldn't seem to bring ourselves to talk about it.

As far as Brie knew, I was still going to meetings. But I refused to spend time at the Old Park Slope Caton clubhouse when I could be at the library researching her disease, other doctors, and potential treatments. At thirty-three years old, she should still have her whole life ahead of her, and I refused to accept any other possibility.

I followed Brie through the church gate to the foot of the steps, past the stained-glass window on one side of the door. Brie climbed the steps one by one, pulling the canister she insisted on managing herself, and stopping several times to catch her breath.

When she reached the top, she turned to me. "Are you coming?" She tried to muster a smile but didn't do a very good job.

"Of course." I walked up the steps, head down, and pulled the door open for her.

At the edge of the atrium, I stopped and scanned the empty

church while Brie walked down the carpeted nave, touching each pew as she passed. The center aisle ran between long wooden benches that stood at least twenty rows deep on each side. At the center of the sanctuary was a carved crucifix with a likeness of Jesus—something typically found in Catholic churches, but rarely in Protestant ones.

Brie moved slowly through the church, then stopped and looked back when she realized I wasn't right behind her. She rolled her eyes at my intransigence, and I hurried down the aisle to catch up.

"Get over it, please." Brie clutched my hand and dragged me into her favorite pew.

I played dumb. "There's nothing to get over." I sat down next to her.

She forced a small smile and bent her head forward, closing her eyes. With her forearms rested on her thighs, she put her hands together and moved her lips. Leaning forward like that, she looked docile and serene. But I felt anything but peace. I looked up at the crucifix and, confronted with the image of the God that Brie had been trusting for healing, began to quietly seethe.

I snatched a Bible from the back of the pew in front of me and flipped through the pages, stopping at Psalm 22: *But be not thou far from me, O Lord: O my strength, haste thee to help me.*

Brie smiled, and I realized she'd been watching me with one eye.

I turned the page, stopping at another psalm: *The Lord is my shepherd; I shall not want.* I hesitated. I didn't want much. I didn't want Brie to die, and I didn't want to ever drink again. Those were my only two wishes, the only things that mattered in my life now. Yet I was constantly plagued by the specter of both needs unraveling, not to mention my daily worries about Max and his future. I'd worked hard on my sobriety for almost sixteen months, but what good would sobriety be without Brie beside me? I didn't need a shepherd. I needed Brie.

She gave me a wry grin and nodded at the Bible I was holding. "Anything interesting?"

"Nope." I flipped the book shut and dropped it back into its slot.

We stood. "I didn't think so," she said, but her eyes were smiling. She took my hand and pulled me down the center aisle, her face as joyful as if we were leaving our wedding ceremony.

We were more than halfway to the front doors when Brie shortened her stride and began to wheeze. I dropped her hand to catch the oxygen tank as she let go of it, and she fell against a pew.

"Brie? You okay?" I clutched her arm.

She nodded and started walking again as I steadied her. She leaned on each pew we passed. At one point, she cleared her throat and began to cough violently. She collapsed against another pew.

"Sit down." I settled her into the seat, my hands on her arms. She stared at my legs for a moment. I tucked long strands of golden hair behind her ears.

She looked up and forced a smile before coughing hard into my face. "I'm sorry, Dan—" She looked very pale.

"It's okay, honey." I sat down beside her and rubbed her back. "Better?" I leaned forward to study her face. She was ashen.

It was clear that Brie was getting progressively worse. Her work schedule and client list had been cut back to allow her to recuperate from the days when she did work. Our movie nights and dinners out were a thing of the past. Brie was simply too weak and tired most of the time. But this . . . this was another level of distress, and it frightened me.

I reached into her purse and dug around with one hand while smoothing her hair off her face with the other. As her eyes closed, I turned her bag upside down, emptying its contents onto the pew, and silently cursed the calm face of Jesus looking down at us from the cross.

Brie made a gasping sound and leaned forward. "Outside." She pointed. I sank my hand into the side pocket and finally found what I was looking for.

I shook the inhaler furiously and removed the cap. As she struggled to steady herself, I put it to her mouth and squeezed. She inhaled as deeply as she could and held the medicine in.

"Again, babe." I stroked her wrist. She lifted her head and exhaled, and I squeezed the canister once more while Brie sucked on the inhaler.

As I was attending to her, the door to the church opened and closed. An elderly couple walked past arm in arm, their wrinkled faces radiating concern.

"She's okay," I said with a fake smile. The woman returned my smile, and the man tipped his hat.

I returned everything to the bag except the inhaler, then turned to Brie. "One more?"

"I think I'm okay." She gripped the edge of the seat in front of us and tried to pull herself up.

"Hold your horses, Brie. Relax."

She fell back against the pew and took my hand. As we watched, the couple paused at the chancel, then knelt in unison to pray.

After a moment, Brie stood, clutching her bag. "Let's go."

We walked back toward the entrance. As I dropped her hand to hold open the door, I glanced back at the old couple, still on their knees in silent prayer. I grimaced without thinking. When I turned back, Brie was glaring at me. I immediately felt defensive, and my face tightened even further.

"I don't know what I was thinking, bringing you here again."

Brie thought it was just my old cynicism. But it wasn't just that. I was angry that God was letting her suffer. I was angry that the other couple had gotten to grow old together, and that maybe Brie and I wouldn't.

But all I could say was "I just don't see any results from all this praying."

She turned away. I could see that she didn't want to hear it. Behind us, the heavy door closed with a soft thud.

"I'm sorry," I said. "It's so hard not to say anything. And to watch you put so much into something that's—"

"That's what?" Her eyes were fierce.

I stood frozen as she made her way down the steps, gripping the iron railing. I wanted to tell her to stop wasting time and energy on praying to a God who evidently wasn't bothering to answer her prayers. But I knew that she found comfort in prayer. And how could I begrudge her that peace, when I loved her so much?

"I love you, Brie," I called after her retreating back. "*That's* what."

———

On the third floor of the medical pavilion at Mount Sinai Respiratory Institute, I stood next to a long credenza. A nameplate sat on Dr. Russell's simple hardwood desk: Head of Pulmonary Medicine. The wall behind his desk was covered with diplomas and accreditations.

Brie was sitting in a chair facing her doctor's desk. I stood behind her, massaging her shoulders. I wanted to encourage her.

"You've been stable since the episode in the church," I reminded her.

"That was two days ago. I've had five bad episodes in under a month." She frowned and pulled a tissue from her bag.

It was very difficult to hear her talk like this, since she rarely did. I could see she was nearing her wits' end. This was doubly hard because *she* was always the positive one. I didn't know if I could be that for her, the way she'd always been that for me.

She coughed, a terrible hacking noise, and spat a bit of mucus into the crumpled tissue. "I'm using almost three canisters of Flovent and albuterol every week, I've got this ridiculous tank strapped to me constantly, and I can *still* hardly breathe." She paused and breathed in more oxygen. "I can't believe this is happening to . . . *us*. I know how hard this is for you to watch."

A flicker of shame washed over me. "Brie, don't worry about me—" Just then, the door opened and the doctor, a distinguished man in what looked to be his early sixties, walked in.

"Mr. Zimmer . . . er, Daniel." Dr. Russell turned to Brie. "Good morning, Brie."

He shook our hands politely and took his seat behind the desk. Then he shuffled through the thick folder on his desk and inspected a typed lab report and Brie's latest PET scans.

"How are you feeling today, Brie?" He looked up, his eyes filled with what I was sure was concern.

"Not too good." Brie bit her bottom lip. She was breathing heavily.

Nodding his acknowledgment, Dr. Russell pulled out an enlarged scan and examined it in the light. He swiveled and stuffed the scan back into the folder, then pursed his lips and folded his hands on his desk before dragging them off onto his lap.

"Before we begin," he said at last, "I want to remind you of the importance of remaining calm. As you well know, strong emotions and stress change normal breathing patterns and re-strict air flow."

As Brie assured him she knew this, a feeling of doom fell over me.

"Okay." He paused, then leaned forward. "I'm sorry to tell you that your respiratory system has continued to deteriorate, which is why your symptoms have been getting worse." The look on his face was one of practiced compassion. He explained that Brie's pulmonary function was now less than 30 percent and steadily decreasing, the equivalent of late-stage COPD—chronic obstructive pulmonary disease, which causes airflow blockage and breathing problems. The tests showed evidence of new scarring of the blood vessels to the lungs and chronic inflammation of the airway lumen. The prednisone Brie had been taking was now doing little to reduce the acute thicken-ing of her major airway walls or the abnormal enlargement of the mucous glands and smooth muscles of her lungs.

I didn't know what to think of all this, though the expres-sion on the doctor's face told me the matter was serious. I was suddenly overcome with a burst of rage. "It's that damn as-bestos." I turned from Brie and began to pace the room. "The neighborhood she's been working in for three years—"

"Daniel!" Brie's voice was unusually sharp. "You're not helping."

I glanced at Dr. Russell to see his reaction. He cleared his throat and directed his words at Brie. "The effects of as-bestos exposure typically don't show up for at least ten years. However, given the history of your disease, it wouldn't be un-realistic for such effects to set in much more quickly. It might explain why your condition has deteriorated so significantly, particularly in the past year. But there's no way to know."

I felt momentarily validated, but Dr. Russell's eyes were stern as they caught mine.

"Brie is exactly right. None of this helps clarify her prognosis or treatment. Focusing on cause in this moment is a waste of energy. Her respiratory system is damaged beyond repair, Daniel." He repeated that she was now breathing at less than 30 percent of her lung capacity, as if I hadn't heard him the first time. And in fact, I hadn't. Or rather, I'd heard, but I hadn't understood. But taking in his somber demeanor now, I was beginning to feel clearer. He turned back to Brie, who stared down at the shredded tissue in her hands. "I'm sorry."

I stared at him. "Wait. Are you telling us there's nothing more you can do?"

He glanced at Brie. "I'm really sorry. But no, there isn't."

"What about a ventilator or . . . aren't there any other medications, or technology?" I pressed, sitting down.

Brie laid her hand on my knee and took in a shallow breath. Patiently, the doctor explained her situation in detail again, going over things we'd talked about before. For a minute, I couldn't take in his words at all.

". . . might alleviate some symptoms, but any relief would be only temporary," he was saying when I tried again to focus. "There's nothing left to do that would address the underlying condition. She's beyond pulmonary fibrosis now. The permanent and excessive scar tissue that has developed over the years inside and outside her lungs is—"

"What about organ replacement?" I interrupted.

He said that for some time, Brie had been on a list for both heart and lungs, but she hadn't been ill enough to get them. And now, the damage was too extensive for her to qualify. Her decline had simply been too swift, and the window for qualifying was already closed. The damage extended beyond her lungs and heart now.

He turned back to Brie. "I truly am sorry."

Her lips were shaking, but she managed to stay calm. "How much time?" she asked.

"Brie, no." I sat forward and gave the doctor an imploring look. "We can't be talking about *time*? She's too young for a question like that."

Dr. Russell stood and walked around his desk. "Expectancy varies, Brie. I really can't say because there's just no way to know how quickly things will progress." He put his hand gently on Brie's shoulder. "I'm terribly sorry. I wish there was more we could do."

Brie closed her eyes. Saying that he would give us a moment to process what we'd just learned, Dr. Russell left the room.

I walked over to the window. I was so angry and frightened, I was shaking.

Brie sat with her head bent forward and her hands folded in her lap. After a moment, she lifted the cross pendant from around her neck and stroked it tenderly with her fingers, then tucked it back inside her blouse. She caught me staring at her.

"Daniel, please don't say anything." She looked too tired to fight.

My hands were at my sides, balled into fists. "I'm sorry. Religion just feels like a cruel joke at this point." I wasn't trying to be difficult. I just couldn't see myself turning for comfort toward a God, a Higher Power, that seemed so indifferent to everything that mattered to me.

Brie's eyes were tearing up. She tried to stand. "Really? Is heaven a joke, too?"

I folded my arms. I could hear her chest rattling, and I could see that she was struggling for breath. But she was always struggling for breath. She coughed into the crook of her arm, and then her eyes flashed at me. She was still so beautiful—even sick, even when she was angry with me. "Don't you want heaven to be real, so I can go there? How could you deny me th—?" A cough caught her up short, and she sat back down, gasping.

Instantly, I was ashamed, and alarmed. "Stop, Brie." I moved quickly to her and knelt by her side. "Breathe."

She coughed uncontrollably for a minute, then spat phlegm into her tissue.

"Brie, please," I said. "I'm sorry." And I was. Sorrier than I had ever been or would ever be. I was sorry that she was suffering. Sorry that I couldn't seem to set aside my own pain to comfort her in hers. Sorry that whether sooner or later—and it was beginning to seem like much, much sooner than either of us had feared—I was going to lose her. "None of it is a joke." And it couldn't be. I decided, right there and in that moment, that anything that was real to Brie had to be real, at least at some small level, for me.

"Do you mean it?"

I nodded firmly. "I swear, it's real. All of it. I love you. I *live* for you. There is a heaven. I know there is. There has to be—for you." I stroked her hand with my thumb. "Please—just focus on your breathing."

She slumped in the chair as she worked to breathe. Finally, her coughing subsided.

"That's my girl." I squeezed her hand. "I'm sorry for everything I said. I'm . . . I'm scared." She looked into my eyes, then dropped her head slightly. It was clear that she was exhausted.

I glanced out the window again. The stone cross from a church steeple outside seemed to be suspended in the air, floating in a deep blue sky in front of quickly moving clouds.

"I need . . . my . . ." Brie coughed hard into her fist. She was sweating, and her eyelids were heavy.

I reached into her handbag, pulled out her inhaler, and placed it in her hand. I lifted her hand to her mouth, but she was too weak to take in the medicine. "Open your mouth."

I pushed the mouthpiece between her lips and pressed down on the canister. But Brie only coughed, choking on the inhalant. Quickly, I loosened the collar of her jacket, lifted her arms, and tugged off one sleeve and then the other.

"Come on." I lifted the inhaler to her lips for another attempt. "Try again."

This time, she opened her eyes, put one hand over her chest, and gasped. Her lips, I saw, were tinted blue, and her eyeballs were rolling up under her lids.

"Doctor!" I shouted toward the closed door.

Brie's breathing staggered and then picked up in short, hurried puffs. She now lay slumped in the chair.

"Doctor!" I lifted her onto the ground so that I could get help, laying her down gently. Then I ran to the door and threw it open. "Please!"

A door opened down the hallway, and as the doctor and a nurse ran toward me, I turned back to the room. Lying there, Brie looked almost lifeless. And suddenly I saw what our future was going to be.

CHAPTER 24

I felt as though I'd been standing in front of my kindergarten class for hours, although it was probably only a few seconds.

"These things happen, Daniel." Mrs. Vance squatted next to me and put an arm around my shoulders. "Don't worry."

I glanced up into the shocked faces of my classmates and then down at the yellow puddle beneath my desk in the front row.

"Do you have a change of clothes?"

"No." I began to cry.

"I'll be right back." Mrs. Vance walked out the classroom door, leaving me standing at the front of the room, shaking. There was silence for a moment, and then whispers became snickers. She returned with the school janitor—a giant with a big nose carrying an old pair of overalls—and waved me into the hallway.

After I had changed my clothes in the boys' room, I returned to class, tripping over the rolled ends of the long pants but glad to be out of my wet corduroys.

Mrs. Vance gave me a calm look while the janitor cleaned

the floor, thrashing his mop inside a steel bucket now brimming with yellow-tinged foam.

I stared up at the ceiling, fascinated by the water-stained tiles and the circles around the lights. When I lowered my head, the faces of the other children blended into a mishmash of pink skin and black dots. Their small heads pointed toward Mrs. Vance, whose mouth was moving. I could tell that she was scolding them for laughing, her bony finger extended and waving. But the individual words were all a blur.

I stepped aside for the janitor, who rolled his mop and bucket into the hallway.

"Watch your step," he whispered, motioning to the wet floor behind me. His kindness was comforting, but his huge size still frightened me.

"I'm . . . I'm sorry, sir."

He reached for the doorknob and winked. "Don't worry about it, kid."

I tried to wink back but wound up blinking both my eyes instead. When I turned around, my classmates were gawking at me. I lowered my head and shuffled toward my desk in the first row, but my foot caught in one of the long pant legs. I tripped and made a clattering noise as I fell into the desk next to me and had to right myself.

There was a moment of silence and then the classroom erupted with laughter. I looked at Mrs. Vance, who seemed pained by my embarrassment, one hand over her mouth, the other holding a storybook.

"Hush!" she shouted. "You children quiet yourselves!"

I slid into my desk chair.

"Children!" She clapped her hands loudly. "Stop this minute!" But they kept laughing.

Mrs. Vance's lips trembled. I knew she could feel my pain, but I could no longer take their teasing. I pulled the pant hems up to my knees and sprinted into the hallway and out onto the playground.

———

I stood beneath the tall tree on the hill at the far side of Elsa Ebeling Elementary School. My borrowed overalls had completely unrolled, and now I was out of breath and still just as embarrassed as before. The school's other kindergarten class was at recess, and a bunch of boys and girls I didn't know were running across the blacktop.

The clouds were low, and the air was sticky. I leaned against the tree to roll up the overalls, then sat cross-legged on the thick green grass. Something crawled on my knee—a large black ant. I poked at its front end with my finger and watched its pincers open and close. Then I tilted my head back and looked at the sky. Sunlight was trying to sneak through a small gap between two of the largest clouds.

"Hi," said a girl's voice from behind me.

I ducked my head and focused on the small patch of grass between my crossed legs. I didn't want to be noticed, and definitely not spoken to.

The girl walked around to stand in front of me. With the corner of my eye, I saw her point at the giant overalls. "Those are too big. Why are you wearing them?"

"I don't know." I shrugged and squirmed.

"Silly." She bent and put her hand on my shoulder. "You can tell me."

No, I couldn't.

She squeezed my shoulder. I lifted my head, and our eyes met. Hers were dark green. I'd never seen eyes that color before. Her nose was pointed, and her blond hair reached all the way down her back, covering her blue flower dress.

"You're not in my class." She smiled.

"I know."

She suddenly coughed hard into her hands. The noise sounded like a barking dog that had swallowed a whistle. She bent forward and took a deep breath.

"Are you okay?" I asked.

"Yeah," she said with a smile, wiping her hands on her dress. "I have asthma."

I continued to stare up at her warm smile. "Oh." I didn't know what asthma was.

"It's hard for me to breathe sometimes." She took another deep breath, then pulled out a small plastic pump-looking device. "Just sometimes. This is my medicine."

"I . . . I hope you feel better." I didn't know what else to say.

The girl grinned and returned the inhaler to her pocket. "I can sit like that, too." She sat beside me on the grass under the large tree and folded her legs. "I saw you from over there. You were sitting all bent over, and you looked like Quasimodo."

"Who?"

She laughed. "The hunchback of Notre-Dame. He's from an old movie I watch with my dad." She tilted her head and looked to the sky. "Wow!"

"What?"

"There!" She opened her eyes wide.

I looked up where she was pointing. A sliver of sunlight was peeking through the small space between the two large clouds, and a bright, white ring of light had formed around the entire outer edge of both clouds. I had never seen anything like it. It was beautiful.

"It's heaven," she said, staring at the sky.

"Hmm." I smiled. "Heaven." A place I didn't know much about.

Our eyes met for a second before I returned to the ant. My embarrassment from Mrs. Vance's classroom was still bothering me, and I poked at it, harder this time. Its pincers sank into my thumb, which instantly throbbed.

"Hey—that's one of God's creatures." The girl crinkled her blond eyebrows.

"Uh . . . I guess. Sorry." I pulled my hand back and we watched the ant limp away. A life saved.

"Come on." She stood and wiped the grass from the back of her dress. "It's time for lunch."

I didn't want to get up. I didn't want to be seen in my stupid borrowed outfit. "I'm not hungry."

"That doesn't matter, silly. We *have* to go."

The whole sun appeared from behind the clouds, and I shielded my eyes to gaze up at her.

She reached out a hand and smiled again. "My name's Brie. What's yours?"

"Daniel." I took her hand. It was warm.

She pulled me up and shook my hand. "Nice to meet you, Daniel." She pulled me along with her, but as we approached the dozens of kids who waited restlessly beside the school, I started to drag my feet.

"Don't worry," she insisted. "It'll be okay."

I managed a small smile and we walked, hand in hand, across the lawn and onto the blacktop. We were the last two people outside, and she rushed toward the door.

"Come on!"

I pulled on her arm.

She swung around. "What?" Her voice was soft and kind.

"Thanks, Brie." I squeezed her hand. Suddenly, my overalls felt warm and cozy and dry. She put her hand on the door and opened it. And I followed her inside.

CHAPTER 25

It was an unusually cool and foggy Monday morning in May; the temperature barely reached fifty degrees. Heat pumped out of the floor vents in our Bay Ridge apartment. Brie was sitting on the sofa in her favorite gray sweatpants and a T-shirt, her head resting on my shoulder. I kissed the top of her head.

Brie had not gone back to work after her attack in the doctor's office a few weeks earlier, and I was now working overtime out of the apartment to help cover our medical expenses and take care of her. Another key factor that enabled me to focus on Brie's health was my sobriety, which was still intact even though I hadn't spoken to Dale or been to a meeting in weeks. But my hold on it was tenuous. The stress of Brie's rapidly deteriorating health and of our steadily increasing medical bills was chipping away at the invisible wall that I had built up between myself and the drink. A week earlier, seemingly even without my own permission, I'd stepped into a liquor store that I'd passed every day for over a year without issue and bought two pints of whiskey. Horrified by what I'd done, I had stashed them in the back of my filing cabinet, with no intention whatsoever to drink them—Brie was far more important to me than alcohol was. I still felt clear about that.

Around that same time, Max had essentially gone MIA. He'd accepted a job offer from one of Dad's business associates, saying that he was tired of being a burden and had resolved to pay his own way and stay out of mine. This development was entirely unexpected and confusing to me. Like Dad, Jack Gilchrist was a hard-ass and a difficult man to work for. But I was thrilled to see Max take initiative, both for his own sake and independence and because I had my hands full. His absence and lack of communication still felt upsetting.

I was sitting next to Brie on the couch and had just finished reading through some files for work. As I settled back against the cushions, I happened to notice a collection of VHS tapes we had stored on the bookcase opposite us. The five slipcases of the Universal Monsters Classic Collection were heavily worn from repeated viewings over the years. The artwork was striking: vibrant, colorful headshots of Bela Lugosi's *Dracula*, Boris Karloff's *Frankenstein* and *The Mummy*, Elsa Lanchester's *Bride of Frankenstein*, and, of course, Lon Chaney Jr.'s *The Wolf Man*. Next to the collection stood the eight-inch Wolfman figurine Harry had given me for my birthday.

"Do you remember our monster movie marathons?" I wrapped my arm around Brie and pulled her close.

She nuzzled her head into my shoulder. "Yup. We covered all the classics—but *The Wolf Man* was always our favorite." I thought, as I had so many times in my life, about the character I was still drawn to. Larry Talbot had fallen in love, and so had I. But his story had been heartbreaking. I couldn't bear for Brie's and mine to be.

I pulled her even closer and glanced at a framed photo of us on the mantelpiece: one my mother had taken in front of the apartment on Carroll Street, the week Brie and I had graduated from Hofstra. In it, we both looked so happy and so full of life. We looked like we might live forever.

It was still hard for me to believe that anyone could have stuck with me the way she had. "You always loved me selflessly," I said, playing with a section of her hair. It was flat and limp as a result of her illness but still felt soft under my fingers.

"You need to love yourself, too." Brie turned to face me. "I won't always be here to tell you that."

I looked away. I didn't want to hear that from her now. But she turned my face back toward her with one finger on my chin.

"You need to hear me on this, Daniel." Her voice and expression were solemn. "You need to love yourself. You need to calm that beast inside of you." Gently, she tapped me on the chest. "Your future happiness depends on your ability to do that." I tried to pull away. This conversation was not how I'd hoped we would spend our evening. But Brie only clutched my hand tighter.

"The real story is that Larry Talbot went mad," Brie said. "You know it, and I know it. There was no wolf. There was no bite. He saw only what he wanted to see. His mind got the better of him, like yours always has. The real monsters are *within* you, Daniel. Not somewhere out there." She took a deep breath. "You must live—one day at a time, one moment at a time, if need be. Don't ever forget that tomorrow can always be better than today—with or without me." She looked tired and weak, her eyes heavy, her face swollen and pale.

I sat beside her quietly. For once, I didn't know what to say, and I remained silent.

"I want you to know that you've made me feel more loved and protected than I ever dreamed possible," she said.

It was hard for me to believe this was true, after all I'd put her through. But Brie never lied, so I knew that she meant it. And indeed, this time felt different. I *was* able to be present for her now. I wasn't perfect, not by a longshot. But this time, I was truly *there*. I felt so thankful to have been given a second chance.

In the crook of my arm, Brie's body was relaxing as she grew sleepy. She was dozing more and more these days as her exhausted body sought out rest. I tightened my arm firmly around her. It was impossible for me to imagine that I would ever have to let her go.

I heard her give a little yawn. "You need to go to a meeting."

"I need to be here with you," I insisted, kissing her forehead.

But Brie was right, I thought, as she drifted off. I needed a meeting badly. We both knew it. So did Dale. He'd been leaving messages on my answering machine at work, insisting that I needed to put my sobriety first, or I would eventually lose everything, including Brie. But I couldn't leave her, not even for a meeting. She needed me. And for now, that would keep me sober.

I'd worry about the rest later.

Late that afternoon, Brie lay on the sofa beneath her favorite ivory wool blanket, shivering despite the warmth of the room. The television screen flashed scenes of old black-and-white movies, sporadically illuminating the otherwise dark room.

I reached for the remote and clicked off the television, then begged her to let me carry her upstairs to bed. But Brie wanted to stay put. Her breath rattled in her chest like a pair of heavy chains. "I don't want to . . ." Her words trailed off. Finally, she added: "Not in our bed, okay?"

I could feel my heart hammering in my chest. I didn't ask what she meant. I only sat down beside her and held her close.

She coughed harder. "I feel like I have the entire city on my chest." She breathed heavily and looked up at the living room windows. "Can you open the blinds? I want to feel the sun-light." I propped her up gently against the pillows we had piled onto the couch, and then I pulled the blanket closer around her frail body.

Once I was satisfied that she was secure, I moved to the windows and twisted the rod. The slats flipped open, letting light into the dim room. The coffee table was covered with pill bottles, antihistamines, decongestants, inhalers, and nebuliz-ers. A portable ventilator stood on its wheels at one end of the sofa, the oxygen tank and hosing at the other. On the walls hung photos of our life together—as kids, in college, and from our wedding. She smiled at the sight of them. "We've had a great life, Daniel."

My heart grew cold at her tone. She sounded like she was looking back on something that was over. "Don't talk like that."

She wiped her eyes, and I sat back down on the sofa and pulled her into my arms. "I'm scared," she whispered into my ear.

I told her I was too, and we held each other's gaze. There were no words for what we wanted and needed to say to one another, so our eyes said everything. Then she let me go and leaned backward so she could lie flat against the pillows.

"What do you need?" She pushed me away in a burst of violent coughing. I handed her the inhaler. "What else?"

After a long pause, she said softly, "Can you get my Hofstra sweatshirt? I'm cold."

I stood and searched the room. "Sure."

She trembled and tried to catch her breath.

"Take your inhaler." I bent down and kissed her forehead as I put it in her hand. She closed her eyes.

I climbed the stairway to our bedroom to search Brie's dresser and closet for her favorite blue hooded sweatshirt. When I sat on the edge of the bed, a small envelope on the nightstand caught my eye. My name was on it in Brie's handwriting. I picked it up and slipped it into my pocket so I could take it downstairs and ask her about it.

"I can't find it," I called from the bedroom. "Is it in the laundry room?"

She didn't respond, so I went back downstairs to the laundry room. I couldn't find it there either, so I returned to the den. When I got there, Brie lay still, her eyes closed, the albuterol gripped against her chest. I could no longer hear her wheezing. It was a relief to know that the inhaler was still able to help. She looked so peaceful as she slept.

I kissed her forehead. It was cool under my lips. A feeling of dread crept over me. "Babe?" I caressed her arm and hand. She didn't respond. I lowered my head to her chest and then shook her shoulders. But no matter how many times I called her name, she didn't move.

I grabbed the phone and dialed 9-1-1.

After talking to the operator, I ran back to Brie. Tears ran down my face as I begged her not to leave.

Hearing ambulance sirens in the distance, I jumped up and unlocked the front door. "They're almost here!" I called to Brie. Her body was still motionless on the sofa, her limp arm hanging over the side.

Within minutes, we were in the back of an ambulance on the way to Brooklyn Methodist Hospital. I stared at Brie— the lines on her face, the curve of her jaw beneath the oxygen mask, the softness of her eyelids. She was barely breathing.

———

At the Brooklyn Methodist Hospital ICU, my wife lay under a plastic tent, covered to the waist with blue blankets. Brie looked cold to me. Her eyes were closed, her arms motionless at her sides. Her wedding band, loose on her finger, sparkled beneath the fluorescent bulbs.

Shortly after we had arrived by ambulance, a doctor had informed me that oxygen deprivation had caused irreversible loss of function in Brie's brain. She had fallen into a coma, he told me with great gentleness, and she wouldn't wake up. He said to take my time in deciding how long to keep her hooked up to the machines, reminding me again that they could not restore her to consciousness but would only prolong the inevitable, and then he left me with her.

An accordion hose ran from Brie's throat to a state-of-the-art ventilator that pumped up and down on the other side of the bed. A feeding tube connected her mouth to another machine. A needle in her arm ran to an IV, and another hose ran from her body to a bag hanging on a pole. Her chest expanded and contracted to the rhythm of the ventilator, its loud whoosh echoing inside my head. Her frail body had done all it could for her. I remembered what Brie had said about Karen Ann Quinlan when we were kids—how she'd believed that Karen's parents wanted their daughter to die naturally, on God's time. I remembered all the conversations we'd had about Brie's belief in God, and in a life beyond this one. I knew that she wouldn't want to be kept here like this.

I leaned down and took her in my arms, but in all the ways that mattered, she was already gone. After a long while, I pulled myself away from her and stood. My eyes were wet, and I moved mechanically, doing all the things that I knew I was supposed to do. I slipped off her ring and held it in my palm like a promise—which it was. I picked up the bag with her soft gray sweatpants and T-shirt in it. I kissed her lips one last time. I called the doctor in. It was over in minutes.

Afterward, I called Max from the hospital lobby, but before I could tell him what had happened, he cut me off and said he couldn't talk. I stared at the phone in my hand. He'd already hung up.

I slammed the handset down into its cradle.

Searching for sanctuary on the deserted streets of Brooklyn later that night, I wandered to the corner of Bay Ridge Parkway and Fourth Avenue—the location of Brie's church—a spot where we frequently sat on a bench at night, talking. The terrible events of the night played over and over in my head. In the end, it had been just me and Brie, side-by-side. Deep down, I had known that this is where things were headed. But I still couldn't believe that it had happened.

As I drew closer, my gaze moved up the church's facade, from the tall lancet windows to the steeple and the cross. It occurred to me that Brie's funeral would be held here and I would need to start planning it—a notion that in that moment seemed impossible. I leaned against the black iron fence that surrounded the church grounds, then slid to the sidewalk.

When I stopped by the apartment earlier, I had grabbed one of the bottles of whiskey on instinct and shoved it in my sweatshirt pocket. I could feel it resting against my stomach now: a weight of possibility. Sitting on the cold ground, I pulled the hood of my sweatshirt over my head and closed my eyes as a feeling of emptiness engulfed me. The minutes felt like hours. I was still in shock. It didn't occur to me yet to drink the whiskey. All I could think was *Brie is gone.*

"Daniel?"

The toe of a black leather wingtip tapped the underside of my sneaker, startling me. I glanced up, wiping my eyes. My brother was standing there in a tailored pinstripe suit over a white shirt. A tie hung loose around his neck; he looked as though he had just left the office. His dress shoes gleamed in the light of the streetlamp. I'd never seen him dressed this way.

"I've been looking for you all night." He glanced up at the church. "When you and Brie weren't at your place I tried the hospital, but they wouldn't—"

"Brie's dead," I said coldly.

His face grew pale. "Oh my God . . . Daniel . . . What happened—?" His voice was shaking.

I lowered my head and pulled my hood down over my face. I didn't owe him anything. I didn't want him now.

Bending down, he grabbed my arm. "Hey . . . I'm sorry. I should have—"

I wrangled my arm away and stood up. "You blew me off."

He shook his head. "That's not fair—"

I didn't know why I was so angry. Max looked like he was doing well. I should have been happy for him. But in that moment, I couldn't think of anyone but myself.

He held out his arm and stepped toward me. I pushed him away. The neck of the bottle of whiskey slid out of my sweatshirt pocket. I caught it before it fell and shoved it back in.

Max grimaced. "You're drinking again?"

"What do you care?"

"Christ . . . I've been searching for you all night, worried sick because I care!"

I wasn't ready to give him that. "You just felt guilty," I said.

He took a deep breath. "The point is, I'm here now."

"Too late."

"Oh, that's right." He looked at the pocket that held the bottle. "I see you got what you need."

That was rich. Max was lecturing *me* about drinking? "You're one to talk."

Max gave me a dark look. "I haven't had a drink in two months, actually. I'm seeing more clearly than ever." I stared at him. "It's true," he insisted. "I was going to tell you, but I wanted to get a little more solid. Make sure it was real before I said anything." He was only trying to explain. But the fact that he was standing there talking about himself—*defending* himself—when I'd just lost Brie filled me with rage.

"Don't worry about me. You've got yourself to think of,

don't you? You're all grown up now." I threw myself at him, but he stopped me with a hand at my neck and shoved me back into the fence.

"Don't say that again," he said through gritted teeth.

I swung my arms down on his, knocking them away, and he backed off, breathing hard. "Leave me the fuck alone." I turned away from him but didn't get far.

"That's right," he called after me. "Run back to the drink. Just what Brie would have wanted."

I turned and sprinted straight at him, catching him on the chin with a right hook. The bottle flew from my pocket again, falling to the grass next to the pavement, miraculously intact. Max staggered to the fence, his lip cut and his nose bleeding, and leaned against it. He tested his swollen lip with his fingers.

As boys, and even as adults, we'd wrestled and gone after one another, as I'd done the night of the veal cutlets dinner at Brie's and my place. But I'd never punched Max before. My hands were shaking as I picked up the bottle and waved it at him. "It's unopened, asshole."

He spat blood. "You still bought it."

I threw the bottle at his feet, where it landed with a thud, and then stormed away.

I found that I was shaking. Max was right, and we both knew it. This was not how Brie would have wanted me to cope. But it didn't matter which of us was right. Max had not been there for me when I called in the worst moment of my life. He'd made his choice.

And in buying the two bottles of whiskey, I suddenly realized, so had I.

CHAPTER 26

I stood in the middle of our bedroom, staring at Brie's closet door. The voice of the radio newscaster traveled through the early morning airwaves from the top of the Empire State Building and down the Belt Parkway to emerge from the speaker of the old clock radio on our nightstand. The clock read 8:00 a.m.

Beyond the partially open window, a moving van shifted gears, and I glanced down at the vehicle double-parking on my quiet street. The thought of moving had crossed my mind more than once since Brie's funeral two days before, but it was only fleeting. This was where Brie had spent her last months. I could never leave this place.

The funeral had been lovely, just like Brie. It had been a bright, sunny morning, the air crisp and cool. The sun shone through the stained-glass windows of Brie's church, casting a kaleidoscope of colors over the white silk blanket that covered her casket. A spray of milky white gardenias flowed over its edges, their fragrance filling the church with an intoxicating, sweet perfume. Floral arrangements—orchids, roses, tulips, and carnations—choked the aisles.

Looking out into the church from the front, I saw that the pews were crowded. My mother, old neighbors and college friends, and even Dale Benson were all seated toward the front. There was an empty seat beside Mom. Max hadn't come. I couldn't believe his selfishness. Though, the truth was, I had been avoiding him. I didn't know whether it would have been better for him to come or stay away. He probably didn't know either.

The eulogy I gave was a simple one. "I'm a lucky man," I told the gathered crowd. "I met my best friend, my wife, when I was five years old. Brie taught me things about myself, and the world, the very first time we met. She shared everything in my world: the good and the bad. She showered me with selfless love. Even when we were apart, she was always near to my heart. Brie was my soulmate." Solemn faces stared back at me.

I talked about how much she loved people, including those who were present, and I thanked them for bringing joy into her life, and for loving her. Tears streamed down my cheeks while I walked over to Brie's casket. I placed a single red rose on the spray of gardenias. I bent down on one knee, rested my forehead against the fiberglass casket, and whispered, "I love you, Brie. Always."

Now, in our bedroom, the newscaster droned on while I scanned the framed photographs and bright-colored canvases that covered the walls. My gaze quickly returned to the door of her big walk-in closet, and I took a deep breath. It was the only space in the apartment that I hadn't entered since her passing.

The hinges creaked as I pulled the door open an inch at a time. A small pile of Brie's treasures lay on the floor in the corner: family photos, her mom's King James Bible, and a wooden step stool with multicolored removable letters spelling her name—my family's gift for her sixth birthday. And next to it was her old Holly Hobbie lunchbox, plastered with monster trading cards and Wacky packs. I knew she'd kept dozens of our love letters and homemade cards in it. I could still make out the name *Olsson*, scrawled in smudged black marker on the side. The rest of the closet was filled with her clothes, shoes, and handbags. Everything was in its place, just as she'd left it.

I reached for the oversize Bible with its brittle binding and faded cloth and stared at the image of the bearded man with pale skin, dark eyes, and long, reddish-brown hair. I ran my finger across the phrase embroidered below the portrait: "King of Kings." My body tensed around a clenched jaw until the sound of a car horn in the distance jolted me back to the present.

Unable to bear the sight of her things any longer, I stumbled back into our bedroom, then out into the hallway and my tiny office. Without thinking, I dug into my filing cabinet, unscrewed the cap of the remaining whiskey bottle, and took a gulp. Instantly, I felt the barrier between myself and the drink disintegrate. I took another and then kept drinking. The liquid burned as it ran down my throat. Blood rushed to my head, and my eyes watered. It was everything I remembered.

Within minutes, I'd downed the whole bottle, reveling in the feeling of instant relief. But my body wasn't used to drinking anymore. Cold sweat dripped down my face, and I scrambled into the bathroom, where I leaned over the toilet. Once my stomach was empty, the spinning in my head stopped and I made my way to the sink and guzzled cool water from the faucet. Standing up, I caught my reflection in the mirror: unshaven, eyes glazed over, wearing a wrinkled hoodie. I looked like shit but felt like I had come home.

And all I wanted to do was drink again.

Although I'd been "in recovery" for almost seventeen months, my half measures had finally come home to roost. Who had I been kidding? I'd been a "dry drunk" all this time, retaining my alcoholic tendencies without a permanent change in mindset, without real peace of mind. And now the one thing that *had* given me purpose—my Brie—was gone.

I needed a drink. I jumped up and ran back into the living room. My trumpet case, brown leather weathered by age, lay on the floor next to the television. For one moment, I wondered if going to Juilliard and playing in an orchestra would have changed anything. Maybe it would have. Maybe not.

I checked my pocket to make sure I had my wallet, then threw open the front door and jumped off the stoop onto the sidewalk. It was cool outside. A young girl across the street was staring at me. Her long hair and innocent smile reminded me of Brie. She raised her arm to wave, and I waved back.

I made my way up Fifth Avenue into Sunset Park, with no clear idea where I was going. In the distance, I saw the word *Liquor* on a sign and moved toward it. Once I got there, I stared through the window of Fifth Liquors at the dozens of bottles lining the shelves behind the counter. The skinny man at the register glanced up and nodded.

Minutes later, with a new pint of whiskey in a bag under my arm, I stepped out of the liquor store and froze. Across the street stood a new sporting goods store in the building that had once housed the five-and-dime emporium of my childhood: Woolworth's. I crossed the street and stepped onto the old store's weathered bronze marker, which remained on the sidewalk. As I stood there, a reflection in the store window caught my attention. A dark figure, taller than me, was standing across the street directly behind me. Every nerve ending in my body seemed to flare. Was that Dale? I whipped around, but the figure was gone.

I unscrewed the cap of my bottle, lifted it in its bag, and drank.

Was Dale watching me—following me? Or was I like Larry Talbot, imagining things that weren't true, as Brie had claimed? I took another swig from my bottle, then stopped and leaned against a rusted blue mailbox, scanning the street around me, trying to collect myself.

"Excuse me, sir," said a woman, startling me. A mail carrier, dressed in a gray uniform, stood next to me. "I need to get in there." She pointed to the mailbox.

"I—I'm sorry," I mumbled, backing away. I could smell the stink of liquor on my breath; it permeated the air. Our eyes met, and I froze. Her eyes were striking and green—like Brie's. My knees buckled as my shame intensified. Was Brie watching me too? Was she disappointed in me?

"Are you okay, sir?" The woman leaned in to help me but recoiled as the stink of whiskey hit her.

I spun away from her and stumbled down the sidewalk. Dale-isms like "Nothing is so bad a drink won't make it worse," "It's the first drink that gets you drunk," and "God never gives us more than we can handle" flooded my mind. I shook them out of my head and told myself I couldn't have seen Dale. I only felt guilty because I'd been avoiding him since the funeral. I took another slug of whiskey.

A little farther up Fifth Avenue, I spied a dark silhouette against the sky. As I approached, shielding my eyes with my hand and squinting into the bright sunlight, I saw an old, nearly forgotten figure, an old man in a white gown, standing on the ledge. He took a swig from a bottle like mine.

A hush fell over a crowd of people that had gathered below as the man stood up on the ledge, took a last gulp from the bottle, and stepped off. I cried out and threw my hands over my eyes. But when I opened them, people were walking by as usual—some of them throwing me looks of concern, some of them ignoring me. There was no man lying on the ground, and there was no man standing on the building's roof.

I looked around. I felt like I was going crazy.

Suddenly, a familiar voice spoke from behind me.

"Is this how you want to end up?"

I spun around, my vision adjusting as the big man with the bulbous nose and determined eyes came into focus. Dale's large nostrils were flaring, and the bags beneath his dark brown eyes were unusually large. He was looking at the bag in my hand. I wondered if he was really there. He looked real to me. But in my drunken state, I couldn't be sure.

"Follow me." He turned and walked away. "You've got an apology to make."

"An apology?" I shouted. "To who?" But of course I knew.

"Your brother."

The memory of my last encounter with Max swam back to me, and I felt a wave of shame. But it was immediately swallowed by the ocean of resentment I felt toward Max. He'd stood me up when I needed him most—first at the hospital, then at Brie's funeral.

"Me . . . apologize to him? *Fuck that*," I mumbled. And then I ducked down Fifty-Ninth Street to Fourth Avenue, where I hurried down the steps and into the subway station.

———

I'd had no plan of where I wanted to go, but when I stepped from the subway platform onto the Coney Island–bound N train, the action felt right. I used the chrome pole to swing myself into the first empty seat. I was filled with anger over Dale's words, over Max's betrayal of me. Feeling anger came easy. I did my best to ignore what was beneath it. I was willing to feel everything except what I was feeling the most—grief over my loss of Brie.

"Stand clear of the closing doors, please," came a disembodied voice from the subway's speakers. The bell chimed two short tones as the doors slid shut. The train hurtled through the tunnel, and the half-empty car fell silent. I took the bottle from where I was holding it between my legs and lifted it to my lips. Looking up, I met the wide brown eyes of a sweet-looking young boy sitting across from me. His buckteeth and freckles reminded me of Max. With the bottle still at my mouth, I forced a smile. The small child stared at me blankly. I lowered the bottle and replaced the cap, turning it slowly, my eyes still locked on his.

"Don't stare." A skinny older boy with a square chin and disheveled hair nudged the younger child. My eyes darted to him, and he glanced away. I leaned forward, squinting. He looked like Harry. It was uncanny.

A young woman on his other side turned toward the boys. "Don't hit your brother."

"It's okay, Mom," said the younger boy. "It didn't hurt."

The older boy leaned into his brother and wrapped his arm around the younger boy's neck. I couldn't tell if he was trying to hug his brother or hurt him.

Maybe Dale is right, I thought. I had to apologize to Max.

"Next stop, Coney Island," the mechanical voice announced. I found that I was having trouble breathing the stale air in the subway car, and I stumbled to my feet.

The station at Stillwell Avenue in Coney Island—the largest aboveground terminal in the world—was falling apart. Built in the early 1920s, it served as the entry point to the historic neighborhood that locals and tourists from all over the world visited regularly. When I set foot on the platform at the station, it was unusually quiet for a Saturday morning.

I looked at the liquor bottle in my hand, twisted the cap off, and chugged the remainder of the whiskey. A new train barreled into the station. A few people disembarked and walked past me on the platform. When the train pulled away, I tossed the empty bottle onto the track.

Caught between drunkenness and exhaustion, I wandered out of the vast terminal in search of something else to drink. The warm, stagnant air was tinged with the scent of salt water. I stopped to take in the beautiful unobstructed view of the shoreline, then scanned the nearby cafés and newsstands fruitlessly for liquor signs. I tried to relax, but blood pulsed relentlessly in my right temple.

A loud thump sounded behind me against the wall outside the terminal entrance. A young woman with long, bleached-blond hair knelt beside a tattered brown rectangular case on the sidewalk. Wearing torn jeans and a long black sweatshirt, she opened the case, revealing a worn gold-plated trumpet inside. She tied back her tousled hair with a red bandanna and began softly playing an ethereal version of the Beatles classic "Hey Jude."

I reached into my pocket for some loose change and dropped it into her open trumpet case. Continuing to play, she nodded and turned away. But I had already recognized her.

"*Jill*? Is that you?" I stepped directly in front of her.

She lowered her head farther and continued to play. It had only been six months since she'd left, and she looked terrible. But it was definitely her. I studied her tired face and sad eyes. Her oversize sweatshirt engulfed her frame, which seemed frail. She looked a decade older and as destroyed as I felt.

I crouched down next to her. "Are you okay?" Abruptly, she broke off playing and gave me a hard look. After a moment of thought, she placed her trumpet—the one she'd used before we reconnected at AA—in its case. Then she slammed it shut and glared at me. "I'm outside at Coney Island playing my horn for quarters, so what do you think?" But the problem was worse than that. As she'd put her trumpet away, I'd seen marks on her arm: needle tracks.

I stood up fast and nearly stumbled. She didn't seem to notice. "I didn't mean . . ."

She shook her head. "Go fuck yourself . . . *Daniel Zimmer*."

She grabbed her trumpet case and pushed past me. When

I called after her, I remembered how Max had called after me outside of Brie's church on the night she died. But this time, I was the one who was being denied forgiveness.

Stunned, I watched Jill Woburn walk away, then closed my eyes. The sun beat down on me, penetrating the blackness behind my thin eyelids while thoughts of Frankie, Harry, and the accident swarmed inside my head.

————

From the Coney Island station, I walked down Stillwell Avenue until I reached Nathan's Famous, where the smell of grilling hot dogs nauseated me. With eerie organ music ringing in my ears, I turned onto Surf Avenue, desperately searching for a liquor store. I dodged throngs of tourists marveling at the nearby historic buildings and the thrill rides in the distance until I arrived at the Coney Island Circus Sideshow on the corner of West Twelfth Street. Plastered with bright-colored posters featuring human freaks of nature, the old building was famous for its peculiar attractions and eccentric live shows. A group of police officers was huddled on the sidewalk in front of the ticket booth, and I kept my head down, hoping to avoid a citation for public intoxication. There was no liquor store in sight.

I turned the corner onto Jones Walk, the historic alleyway that connected Surf Avenue to Bowery Street, and sat down on the grimy sidewalk beneath an abandoned cotton candy and taffy stand. The alley was empty and shady, and I pulled my knees to my chest and glanced over at the crowded old B&B Carousell from the early 1900s.

I watched as children and adults moved up and down on their wooden horses, each of the colorful, dramatically posed mounts rising and falling via a drop rod that descended from the bottom of the carousel's canopy. The sight—around and around, up and down—made me queasy. I hated merry-go-rounds, which seemed to me the most pointless of all carnival attractions. Never advancing, never retreating; there was no escape, and no arrival.

Sitting in the alley, I closed my eyes and leaned my head against the wall behind me. I focused my attention on the rinky-tink music blasting from the carousel's eighty-year-old pipe organ. Simple and repetitive, the rhythm was obnoxious but somehow comforting in its familiarity, like the soundtrack to an old cartoon. As I became drowsier with each beat, I slipped into a river of distorted memories as fractured as dreams.

When I opened my eyes, Surf Avenue was empty, and I was surrounded by an eerie silence. I stood and stumbled over to the carousel, which had been transformed. The old rotating platform now held dozens of angry gray horses, brows furrowed and eyes blazing, their manes tangled and their hooves wickedly sharp.

A bright white light snapped on, blinding me. I squinted over my shoulder and saw my own silhouette projected behind me onto the carousel's panels. I turned around and watched as images flashed before me in nonsensical order—shapes and colors, people and places, faces. Faces. *Faces.* Max's. My mother's. My father's. Harry. Jill. Frankie. Dale. And Brie, her emerald eyes shining, her pink lips mouthing words I could not understand.

The horses started to gallop, their hooves against the platform, my head pounding in time with their step. Their eyes smoldered, and acrid smoke blew from their nostrils as they passed on either side of me. My vision clouded, and I went limp, the echo of their hooves reverberating inside my head. I shut my eyes against them and tried to breathe.

The carousel shook wildly as the bolts began to jiggle

loose from the steel plates attaching each rod to the ceiling. Hardware fell around me; the drop rods collapsed, and the horses rose. The speakers crackled and hissed, and the organ music grew higher until it became a voice that shrieked "All aboard!" I heard a sinister laugh. A bass guitar thumped, shaking the canopy in time to my heartbeat. One side of the carousel rattled, and then the other. The bass strutted along. A guitar screamed and exploded into a noise-melting riff, and the tiny bulbs along the perimeter of the canopy flashed on and off with dizzying speed. The horses accelerated into a trot and then erupted into a full gallop. The guitar riff echoed the beat of their sharp hooves on the carousel floor.

As I watched, the horses leaped from the platform two by two, then sprinted toward the chain-link fence that surrounded the park. I leaned against a drop rod. Once the horses reached the fence, they split off to the left and right before turning back toward me in a full gallop. Their yellow eyes blazed, their nostrils flared, and their black manes tangled in the wind; I closed my eyes to ease the dizziness that overwhelmed me. I curled my body into a ball, sure that I would be crushed, but silence fell upon me instead. When I opened my eyes, the horses were back in place on the carousel platform, once again bolted to the floor.

I looked around and found that I was on Jones Walk, my head resting against the shuttered food stand. I had no idea how long I'd been sitting there. I sat up. Surf Avenue was bustling with tourists, and the B&B Carousell was full of color and happy families.

My lips were parched, my stomach growled. I felt like shit. The guilt—self-loathing, really—of my relapse was finally kicking in. I knew of only one way to cope, so I hurried up West Twelfth Street. When I found a liquor store at the corner of Neptune Avenue, I pushed hard on the smudged glass door.

It didn't move. Using both hands, I pushed harder. Nothing. The lights were on, and I saw someone standing inside. *What the hell is going on?*

A rush of adrenaline shot through me, and I leaned into the door with my shoulder, shoving as hard as I could. The more I pushed, the harder the door pushed back. On the street behind me, someone snickered. When I turned, a toothless vagrant in a dirty trench coat with a grimy Yankees cap on his head was shuffling by, a paper-bagged bottle in one hand. His bloodshot eyes were trained on me as he passed. That is how I would look if I kept on the road I was on. He turned a corner. And then he was gone.

I crouched against the side of the building and thought about what I'd just seen. I thought about Brie's God, about my own Higher Power. "Please." At first, I didn't know who I was speaking to. And then, I did. "God . . . Help me. I can't go on this way."

I tried to stand, but a wave of dizziness sent me back down to the sidewalk. Then, just as I was about to try again, something fell out of my pocket. A wrinkled envelope. I smoothed it out and ran my thumb across my name in Brie's perfect handwriting. My eyes flooded with tears.

With trembling hands, I removed the single sheet of thick paper torn from Brie's sketchbook. I had been carrying it around with me since the day I found it on Brie's nightstand—the day she had died. It had been unfolded, crumpled, smoothed, stained with my tears, and carefully folded again more times than I could count.

My dearest Daniel,

Although it may be hard for you to see this right now, we've both been lucky. We've had a best friend and soulmate in one another, and you've been my strength when I needed it the most. You've always made me feel like the most special and beautiful person in the entire world, and I am so grateful for the wonderful life we had together. I know you must feel bitter, but I pray that the pain will soon be replaced by joy over the experiences we shared.

Please don't blame God, Daniel. He answered my earliest prayer—that I would have a best friend. When we met on the grass behind the school in kindergarten, you were the answer to that prayer. I think we ended up on the same block in Brooklyn because God knew we each needed someone special to help us fight our demons. Mine were physical, yours emotional. Ever since college, my prayers have been for you, Daniel, not for myself. All those times I prayed in church, I was praying for you to overcome your addictions and your trauma. You don't need to drink. You never did. You deserve to be sober. Never forget that. Be grateful. Anger and resentment only feed our fears and the monsters that live within us.

Stay strong and healthy. Not for me anymore, but for yourself. Play your trumpet and pursue your dream. It's never too late. Love your mother and brother. Most importantly, love yourself as I have loved you every day. As I will always love you.

Brie

I wiped my eyes and slowly stood.
Inside the liquor store, the cashier walked up to the door.

He bent down and pulled a long metal doorstop out from beneath the base of the door, then smiled and turned away.

Immediately, someone bumped past me, and I watched the man in the trench coat with the Yankees cap hurry inside. A rush of warm air engulfed me, and I watched him stumble to the shelf and then to the register, bottle in hand.

I carefully returned Brie's letter to its envelope and tucked it into my pocket. Suddenly, I knew—I was not alone anymore. I never really had been.

And I knew something else, too. I could do this. I *deserved* to do this.

I turned away from the door. *It's never too late,* Brie had said.

I hoped that she was right.

CHAPTER 27

When I reached my apartment in Bay Ridge, Dale was there, circling back and forth in front of the stoop like a plane in a holding pattern.

"Where've you been?" he asked.

I gave him a funny look and asked him if he'd been following me, but he only shook his head as if I had been imagining things.

I climbed the stoop, unlocked the front door, and made my way inside, avoiding eye contact. He stood in my doorway as I plopped down on the sofa.

"You wanna talk about it?" Dale stepped inside and closed the door behind him.

I looked away, embarrassed by my weakness. "Not really." I knew that I had to. But that didn't mean it would be easy.

"It's okay, kid. These things happen. Look at the bright side: relapse can be progress. It's all in how you look at it."

"I knew what would happen once I took that first drink," I finally admitted. It felt horrible to say, but it was true. "I knew I wouldn't stop." Dale sat down beside me, and I peered at him out of the corner of my eye. He was watching me carefully. "But I didn't care."

"You didn't care," he said, "because, all this time, you've been reserving the right to drink. You haven't cleaned house and made amends. This is what happens when you don't do that necessary work."

I knew he was telling the truth, and I hated it.

I was sobering up quickly, though.

"You're not the only one I've been avoiding," I admitted. I told him about my fight with Max.

When I was done, Dale leaned forward, his eyes trained on me. "You've got to make things right."

"But he's the one—!"

"It doesn't matter what he did. What did *you* do?"

He didn't make me say it out loud, but I knew. I had been selfish and unforgiving. I had blamed Max for all the things I believed he'd done wrong while ignoring my own offenses and letting myself off the hook.

"We can't control other people," Dale reminded me. "If Max decides to choose work over you, then he's entitled. If he wants to miss the funeral, he's entitled. Nobody owes you anything. You're lying to yourself if you say otherwise. And that resentment will . . . *is* eating you alive. But you're acting this way because you're afraid of something. The question is, what is it?"

"I need to get some aspirin." I leaned forward but Dale grabbed my shoulder and pulled me back down.

He went on as if I hadn't tried to escape. "Usually, our fears boil down to one of two things: fear of losing something we already have, or of not getting something we believe we're owed." He stood. "Now where's that aspirin?"

"Kitchen cupboard, next to the sink." I pulled at a loose thread on the sofa.

Dale returned with two aspirin and a glass of water. "Look," he said gently. "We all tend to believe that a parent, or maybe a sibling, owes us something just because they're our parent or sibling. The truth is, they don't. People are people. Your father had his own childhood, his own trials and tribulations. The same thing's true of your brother. And you, too. Most people think only about themselves. That is the dis-ease we are trying to combat with the Twelve Steps—the disease of self."

I nodded, finally looking him in the eyes.

"Until you accept those facts, nothing inside of you will change. And even once you do, if you don't have that Higher Power to rely on to help relieve those fears, you'll still be hopeless and helpless in the end. Your way of doing things, of dealing with things, doesn't work. Your best thinking got you to this moment, kid. You need a new way. That's what I'm offering."

I took a deep breath and stared straight ahead. Dale was right. It's what I'd been hearing in meetings for over a year now. Finally, I understood. *I am the maker of my own problems.* "I get it, Dale."

After that, I told him about what had happened to me at Coney Island: about going to buy another bottle, about Jill, about the liquor store whose door wouldn't open, about the drunk in the Yankees cap.

"I tell you, I saw my future . . ." I stared at the blurred colors and shapes of Brie's paintings on the den wall, almost as if I was in a trance.

"Did you buy that bottle?" Dale's question brought me back to the moment.

"No." I felt myself shaking my head.

Dale sat back and chuckled. "Good for you, kid." He slapped his huge palm on my thigh and grinned.

"It's so strange, Dale. I've never been in a darker place. And yet, I've never felt more hope than I do right now."

"Surrender is the way forward," he told me. "It's ironic, I know. But, strangely, there's great power in admitting defeat."

I let out a long breath. "I don't get why you care so much. How can you spend so much time . . . ?"

But Dale just wrinkled his distinctive nose and winked at me. "In order to keep it, I gotta give it away." He nudged me. "You know that."

I nodded and stood. I knew what I had to do next. "Let's go find Max."

CHAPTER 28

I passed through the red doors of the Lutheran Church of the Good Shepherd—it was empty and quiet, like the last days when Brie and I had come in to pray—and sat in a pew at the rear of the sanctuary. Dale and I had called Max a number of times, but he hadn't answered. We'd separated and looked for Max at his workplace and at his apartment in Fort Hamilton before returning to Bay Ridge. I'd even tried my mom's house. But Max was nowhere to be found. Finally, Dale and I agreed to meet in the Lutheran church basement for an AA meeting. I got there early. My drunken excursion through Brooklyn had exhausted me, but I would not use that as an excuse.

I stared at the carved Jesus hanging at the front of the sanctuary. The sunlight shone through the church's stained-glass windows, refracting color everywhere. I pulled a Bible from the back of the pew in front of me, placed it on my lap, folded my hands on top of it, and closed my eyes.

After a while, I felt a hand on my shoulder. My instinct was to pull away. I looked up. "Oh—sorry, Pastor. I didn't know—"

"It's okay, Daniel." Pastor Kircher was a thin older man

with an oval head, bald on top. He gestured at the pew. "May I sit?"

"Of course." I slid over.

We sat in silence for a few moments. I knew my breath stank of whiskey—in fact, my entire body was saturated with it—but Pastor Kircher didn't say a word.

"I miss her," I said, staring forward.

"I know."

"I'm angry, Pastor—so angry." I looked up at the wooden Jesus and shook my head. "How . . . how can anyone *truly* believe? It makes no sense."

"Sense isn't what faith is about, Daniel," he said. "Faith is about trusting in God."

"You mean the same God that let Brie die?"

He turned to me. "Maybe God doesn't allow or disallow anything. Maybe things just happen, and that is the way of this world." His expression was thoughtful. "I've found that for me," he said, "it's best to view God as an inner resource, a foundation of strength to tap into, rather than an external being to question or blame."

I shook my head. "I'm sorry, but I don't follow."

He considered for a moment. "Do you remember the Son of Sam murders?" he said at last.

Man, did I.

"Well, did you know that the Guardian Angels were founded here in Brooklyn during those dark days?"

I nodded. I remembered the volunteer group very well.

"The founders originally called themselves the Magnificent Thirteen," he said. "They stood guard at various store entrances across the borough."

"I remember," I said. "But they didn't do anything. They just stood there in their red berets and white T-shirts, unarmed. They refused to carry weapons." I'd barely noticed at the time. But, looking back now, it seemed quite strange to me.

"That's right. But do you remember how you felt when you saw them, even knowing that they were unarmed?"

I thought for a moment, recalling their rigid bodies and stern faces, their crossed arms and focused eyes. It had been obvious to anyone who saw them that they meant business. "Safer, I guess, but I was a little kid."

He shook his head. "Everyone felt that way. It didn't matter that they were unarmed." He looked into the distance. "It defies logic, doesn't it? They were there to serve as a presence, a symbol of comfort, hope, and protection to help us combat our fears." He stood up and put a hand on my shoulder. "Perhaps that's how we might think of God."

My eyes filled with tears. "You sound like Brie."

He grinned and removed his hand from my shoulder. And then he walked away. Suddenly I didn't want him to go.

"Wait," I called.

Pastor Kircher stopped and turned.

I swallowed hard. "What do I do now?"

He came back toward me, placed his arm around my shoulders, and pointed me toward the door. "You *know* what to do." He looked at his watch. "There's an AA meeting in the basement in a half hour. You'll find all the help you need right there."

———

The sun was setting, and the quiet church was growing dark inside. A pair of sconces threw dim light on a vestibule doorway that led to the basement. The meeting wouldn't start for another twenty minutes, but I plodded down the poorly lit stairwell to the Sunday school classroom that moonlighted as an AA meeting room.

"Hey," said Dale, startling me. He already stood next to the coffee maker across the room, a large push broom in his hands.

"What's with the broom?" I said, chuckling. "You the janitor?"

"Used to be," he said, walking toward me. "Years ago, at an elementary school here in Brooklyn . . . before I got into construction." He grinned, then whispered: "*Elsa Ebeling.*" Before I could even process the words, he pointed at the door and bellowed, "Look who's here!"

I turned and saw Max standing on the other side of the room, his blue tie loose around the neck of his creased dress shirt. He raised a hand tentatively.

"I'll be back for the meeting in a few," Dale said, closing the door behind him. His heavy footsteps echoed from the stairwell.

Max and I looked at one another, neither saying a word. I approached him slowly.

"Nice guy," said Max. "I saw him upstairs while you were talking to the pastor."

"Dale's my sponsor . . . Do you recognize him?"

"No . . . should I?"

I told him about Dale being Benny. For a moment, Max looked at me blankly, and then it hit him. "Oh my God . . . I thought I recognized that voice." He stood in silence for a moment while I pulled two chairs off the stack and unfolded them. "Small fucking world," he said at last.

"Small fucking world," I agreed. We sat down across from one another.

"I got your messages, Daniel," he said after a moment. "I know you used to come here with Brie, and I figured you might be here."

I almost laughed. I never would have thought that anyone would look for me in what Brie used to call *God's house.* But Max had. And strangely, I had been here. I imagined that wherever she was now, Brie was smiling.

"I'm sorry about everything I said," I told him. There was

no point in beating around the bush. Dale had made clear what I needed to do, and I was going to do it. Both for Max, who deserved to get an amends from me, and for myself. No more going through the motions. "And for hitting you. And for . . . well, everything. Opening the door that day. Letting you take the blame."

Max sat quietly. Maybe he couldn't believe what he was hearing. "I should have been there for you," he said finally. "The night Brie died."

He looked so miserable, I reached out with my toe and kicked his shoe. "Hey," I said, "I forgive you." I was surprised to recognize, as I said the words, that I meant it. "I'm tired of holding grudges. I want to let them all go. I *need* to."

He made a snorting noise. "Not all of them, I hope."

I told him that I meant all of them. He gave me a horrified look and I nodded. "Yeah," I said. "Even Dad."

Max shuddered. "That guy caused so much fucking damage," he said. "Sickening. And now I'm working for a guy just like him. It's like I can't ever get away from it."

I tried to tell him about Brie's letter, about my conversation with Dale, about what I'd experienced at Coney Island. I tried to talk to him about leaving his job and starting fresh somewhere new. But he was too caught up in his own anger to hear me. I watched as he became increasingly upset, winding himself up as he listed all of Dad's offenses. Finally he stopped. "And do you know what happened to me at Hofstra? Why I left?"

"No."

The look Max gave me was so hard, I almost imagined that he was picturing Dad. Slowly, he gave me the answer to the question I'd been asking myself for so many years.

It turned out that he'd made a suicide attempt while at Hofstra—taking all of his antidepressants and sedatives at once. Another student had found him, and he'd been rushed to the hospital, where his stomach was pumped. Afterward, the college had asked him to leave.

"Jesus, Max. Why?"

He told me that our dad had forced him to rush a fraternity during his sophomore year, insisting that fraternity brothers would turn into lifelong "networking" partners for business. Anyone who knew Max should have known he wasn't cut out for Greek life and its social pressures. But Dad had insisted—once again, putting his own interests first. In the end, none of the fraternities had asked Max to join, and his embarrassment—and our father's subsequent insults—had proved too much for Max to take.

I reached for his shoulder, but Max just shook his head and wiped away tears. "I never thought the day would come when you'd forgive him for all the shit he did."

"You have to, Max. Or it'll eventually kill you. It's the only way to free yourself."

He stared straight ahead, unblinking. "I'll find my own way to be free," he said in a low, steady pitch.

"What do you mean?"

"Don't worry about me," he snapped. "I'm going to be just fine."

I didn't understand what he meant but was glad to hear him sound somewhat positive.

By that point, Dale and a few other people were walking into the room. I eyed the clock and stood up. We had a few minutes until the start of the meeting. "Seriously, why don't you stay, Max?"

"Why would I?" He chuckled. "I'm not an alcoholic."

"Okay . . ." I didn't want to push it. Max had told me he hadn't had a drink for two months. Maybe he thought he had it all under control. I remembered what that was like. "But there's a lot more to AA than just putting down the drink. It's really a program for living life on life's terms. You don't have to be an addict to be helped by it."

"Nah." He scanned the growing crowd of AA members. "It's not for me, Daniel." They were familiar words. I knew I couldn't force things.

"Come on, then. I'll walk you out." I followed Max up the stairs.

As we walked outside, an incredible sight greeted us: two enormous cumulus clouds overlapped the setting sun. Radiant light burst through the opening between them, causing them to shine in that bright white otherworldly way. I stared at the sky, bathed in the warm light. It felt like being in Brie's presence.

I smiled. "Doesn't that just look like heaven?" I hopped down the steps to the sidewalk.

"Hmm," Max said hesitantly.

I reached my arms around him, squeezing him as tightly as I could. "Max," I whispered. "I'm so sorry. I'm so, so sorry." Now that I'd said the words, I didn't think I could ever say them enough.

His arms were limp around me; he stood there, as stiff as a mannequin. Hugging was new territory for us. After a moment, I began to pull away, but then Max tightened his arms around me, and for a good, long minute, he wouldn't let go. It felt strange—but good.

I pulled my head back and studied his damp eyes.

"I know you are," he said, and then he turned away and let me go.

CHAPTER 29

I woke up early the next morning feeling energized, so I decided to head over to Owl's Head Park. Known for its meandering paths, rolling hills, and spectacular sunsets, the twenty-four-acre park also provided unforgettable sunrises to those who knew the right spot. I had about fifteen minutes to make it there.

It felt good to have the city practically to myself. As I walked through the lush green grass to the top of the hill, the sun was just beginning to peek through the sparse trees. It burned an orange red while the sky gradually turned from blackish blue to a deep royal blue. It was a beautiful sight, and I suddenly felt overwhelmed by an awareness that I would be okay. The weight on my shoulders had finally let up. I knew now that I was a servant to life, not its master. And as I bathed in the soaking rays of the rising sun, I made plans for the day. First, I'd visit Max and take him out to breakfast. He was an early riser, too, so he was surely awake by now. After that, I'd take the ninety-minute ride out to Mount Lebanon Cemetery to visit Harry and Dad. I'd invite Max to join me, although I doubted he would come.

As I was leaving the park, I dialed Max on a pay phone but got no answer. Figuring he was probably in the shower, I continued on foot down Ridge Boulevard toward his apartment in Fort Hamilton. Ten minutes later, I stopped at another pay phone. Still no answer. I began to walk faster, partly convinced that nothing was wrong, even while terrible thoughts crossed my mind. But things were good now—*we* were good. We had finally cleared the air between us last night. *Stop worrying,* I told myself.

As I approached Max's apartment building, I saw a police car parked outside, its lights flashing. I raced toward the building and ran inside. An officer was speaking with a tenant in front of the resident mailboxes.

"How many shots did you hear?" asked the officer.

"Just one," said the elderly woman. "Sounded like the third floor."

My chest tightened and I ran up the stairs. When I reached the door to Max's apartment, it was locked. I banged with both fists on the solid wood. "Max! Open up!" I put my ear against the door, but I heard nothing inside. My heart was racing. "Max! Open the door!"

The officer from the lobby came up behind me and motioned me to the side. He rapped on the door and announced a welfare check.

A minute later, the super arrived and unlocked the door. The policeman and I followed him in.

"Aw, fuck," the officer mumbled as I pushed past him.

Max lay still on the white tile floor, next to the kitchen chair he must have been sitting on when he pulled the trigger. A pile of blood pooled beneath his head. A .22-caliber revolver lay beside his right hand. There was no need to check for a pulse.

I dropped to the floor beside his body and touched his sleeve. Under my palm, his body still felt warm. I wondered if

I was imagining it. Words rose in my mind, remembered from the day I'd sat with Brie at her church: *But be not thou far from me, O Lord: O my strength, haste thee to help me.*

As if in a daze, I watched more police come in the front door. One of them was talking to the super. Another was headed my way. I could hear what sounded like neighbors talking in hushed voices in the hallway. This was not like the last time. There would be no cradling of my brother, no comforting him. I wanted to hold Max, and I also could not bear to look at his face.

Looking up instead, I saw something yellow on the counter. I looked more closely—it was a bunch of bananas. They were yellow and perfect, unmarred by bruise or pen.

Max had been hopeful enough to buy them. But that was as far as his hope had taken him.

———

Mount Lebanon Cemetery was covered with headstones and monuments as far as my eyes could see. It had been two months since Max's death. The bright midday sun penetrated the granite stones, causing their fine crystalized surfaces to glitter in the warm summer air.

"I'm going to jump over to Harry, while you're here with Dad," I said to my mother.

Dressed in beige slacks and a pastel green blouse, Mom stood over Dad's grave without responding. Her long, dyed-black hair ruffled in the warm breeze; her vacant stare concealed the hurt she felt. It was no secret that she felt cheated by life. Why wouldn't she?

I had promised myself I would be there for her, and I was doing my best to keep that promise. But I couldn't force her to cope with her pain in any particular way, just as no one had been able to force me. I hoped she would find her way, just as I was trying to find mine.

Harry's stone was one row over and five graves down from Dad's. The barren plot next to Dad's was reserved for Mom. At the time Dad had purchased their plots, he had also purchased plots for my brothers and me. Harry, sixteen at the time, had told Dad he didn't want his. He would be buried with his own family when the time came, he'd said. But that wasn't what had happened.

I read the words on Harry's stone aloud: "Harry Nathan Zimmer—March 7, 1958 – May 23, 1976—Cherished son and brother—Gone too soon—Forever in our hearts."

I searched the patchy grass for a small rock, then knelt and placed it on the top edge of the granite gravestone—a tradition symbolizing remembrance of the dead.

"I'm sorry, Harry," I said softly.

There, I'd finally said it. I'd talked to everyone I could think of to whom I owed an apology. I had raged at my father's grave, and I had told him I was sorry. Apologizing to Harry was harder, perhaps because it hurt more. But other than Jill, whom I'd been unable to locate, this was my final amends. It was a necessary step for me to take, even though by now I had stopped blaming myself for Harry's death. If I'd learned anything from Dale, it was that I could no longer allow my mind to generate fictitious scenarios and imaginary problems. Doing so was only a waste of valuable energy.

Here was the truth: I could not have known that Harry would not come home that night. Nor could I have foreseen that he would skip school the next morning, get blind drunk while driving his Gremlin, and crash in that intersection. That complicated result was just one far-flung possibility out of an endless number of possibilities—and one I would never have been able to imagine before it happened.

Why was I sorry, then? Because, like Frankie, Harry was dearly missed. And yet, in death had come life. Dale had gotten the help he needed from Dad and had gone on to save countless other lives, including my own, through AA. I hoped that the deaths in my life would open up opportunities for me to help people, too. Though that, like everything else in my life, was something I could not control. All I could do was show up. The rest was up to a force beyond me.

I stood up and moved away as Mom approached so that she could have time alone with Harry.

Standing at my father's plot, I peered at her as she stood in front of Harry's grave, her head lowered, eyes closed. Nineteen-ninety-six had been a shitty year for us. Three deaths in as many months, and we were only in July. When we were done here, we would walk across Middle Village cemetery to All Faiths and visit Brie.

I reached down for a small rock and placed it next to a pebble on the top edge of Dad's gravestone, then backed away and read the engraving. "In Loving Memory of Walter Matthew Zimmer—Nov. 1, 1936 – Feb. 16, 1996—Beloved Husband and Father." That was it. Nothing long or fancy. Probably more than he deserved.

Even as I had that thought, I reminded myself to move into acceptance. Acceptance of what had been. Acceptance of my life as it now was. I thought about the AA principle of willingness and what it meant to me. It was a concept that was indispensable to my recovery. Without willingness, all the words and knowledge meant nothing. I had to be *willing* to put them into action—to love and pray for my fellows, to improve my conscious contact with a power greater than myself, to understand that acceptance was the answer to almost everything.

"I only wish you'd had willingness," I said to the gravestone. Dad had been convinced he couldn't change even if he wanted to. Perhaps Max had felt the same. I knew now that

that was bullshit. If things get bad enough, if life hurts enough, if a person cares enough, they can change. If I could, anyone could. Of that I was convinced. I wished Max could have understood that. I wished he could have known how much losing him would hurt us.

Once again, I urged myself to move into acceptance.

I stood and glanced again at Mom, who was now looking back at me. She smiled, and something inside of me shifted, as if my heart had been unlocked.

My eyes welling up, I walked over to her, and together we stood in front of Max's gravestone. I was still trying to make sense of what Max had done. I supposed she was, too. It occurred to me that maybe wanting to die was in some ways like addiction; what would have once felt irrational to Max had somehow become, for him, the most rational-seeming option. I wished he had lived long enough for that calculus to have shifted once again in his mind.

"A mother is not supposed to outlive her children," she said softly. She pulled a tissue from her pocket and patted the corners of her eyes.

"Come on," I said, "give me a hug." We held each other tightly.

As she pulled away, Mom glanced at Max's gravestone. "I like what you did." She nodded at the engraving, which had finally been completed a week earlier.

"Max Evan Zimmer—June 16, 1961 – May 11, 1996—Cherished Son and Brother."

"I'll be in the shade." She walked off toward a row of tall trees.

I knelt and put my hand on the stone. "I love you, you know that?" I hoped that he did. I thought that he did. At least, that's what I thought the evidence indicated.

It turned out that Max had left a suicide note. When the police told me about it on the day he died, I'd felt something leap up inside me, like hope. But when I opened the note, all it said was "I'm sorry, too."

For a moment, I had thought the note might give me answers. Why had Max done it, especially after all we'd been through? After he had finally started to address his drinking?

But in the end, I knew there was no reason that would make sense. Drinking was the deceiver that had pursued me nearly my whole life. Max had been pursued by both drinking and thoughts of suicide. I couldn't understand why he'd done what he'd done. Maybe he hadn't even understood it himself. There was really only one thing I understood clearly anymore, and that was that I couldn't do anything on my own.

I patted the headstone one last time.

"Well, brother, I'm off to Brie, and then to a meeting." I stood and wiped my jeans. "After all, I gotta use it, or I'll lose it."

CHAPTER 30

It was a blustery autumn morning, and the sun was rising over the line of buildings on Church Street. AA members began gathering outside the tall entrance door of the Old Park Slope Caton clubhouse. An elderly woman with rosy cheeks and curly blond hair hugged me at the door.

"Hi, Joan. How are you?"

"Great, Daniel. How about you?"

"Excellent," I replied with a smile. "I'll see you inside, okay?"

Joan stepped aside and Tony G. reached out his hand.

"How's it going, Tony?"

Still wearing that same plaid wool ivy cap, Tony's face had thinned, and his handshake was growing gentler as he aged. "Great, Danny boy. How *you* doing?" It was the same caring reply he'd always given me.

"Good, Tony. Thanks."

Tony tipped his cap, and I followed him inside. The clubhouse was still fairly empty, but in fifteen minutes it would be packed, standing room only. I'd been coming to this meeting for almost three years now, and it hadn't changed a bit. The walls were still covered with the same slogans and banners and the core membership returned day after day, along with a constant flow of newcomers. I took a seat at the front table and thought about what I planned to share. It was the second Saturday in October, seventeen months to the day since Max had taken his life. It felt like seventeen years.

After Max had passed, I made the decision to "deal myself in" to the fellowship and the program. Like the smart buffalo in the herd, I had learned that it was safer on the inside than on the periphery, where I might get picked off by the drink. In the process, I had turned from a socially awkward recluse to a fearless and useful member of not only Alcoholics Anonymous but also humanity. I owed it all to Dale, but he would accept none of the credit. "Pay it forward" is all he asked. Nothing more.

I watched an unfamiliar face glance nervously at the clock, a young man who took a seat in the back row. I had a minute before it was time to open the meeting, so I raced to the back of the room to greet the obvious newcomer. He smiled uncomfortably while I told him he was in the right place. Then I returned to the front of the room and opened the meeting.

"It works if you work it," I said, beginning my share. "So clichéd . . ." I smiled at Dale, who was sitting in the front row with a huge grin on his face, like a proud papa. "But *so* true."

I proceeded to discuss my battle with Master Alcohol, from my first drink at thirteen until my most recent relapse seventeen months before. I declared that alcohol was but a symptom of a deeper, more insidious disease, a disease of self and control, of endless attempts to wrestle satisfaction from a world that wouldn't cooperate. Such behavior was insane and completely ineffective, whether I was drinking or not.

I spoke of resentment and fear, the two things that had blocked me from the sunlight of the spirit. I spoke of my work with the Twelve Steps and of a power greater than myself: one of *my* understanding, not anyone else's.

I concluded by saying that my problems had always been of my own making and that my mission, today and every day, was to get out of my own way. To turn my life over. To let the universe unfold the way it wants to, and not the way I want it to. I explained that I was no longer paying lip service, and I meant every word.

The crowd applauded, and I was heartened by the response. It felt amazing to be part of something that asked for nothing in return but that worked better if a person gave rather than just took.

"This meeting gives out chips to commemorate various lengths of continuous sobriety within the first year," I said at last, standing and reaching for the chip case. It was filled with different colored plastic chips that denoted different spans of sobriety, as well as bronze-plated medallions for members celebrating multiple years. "If you're celebrating an anniversary, please come up and get a chip when called." I reached inside the case for the purple eleven-month chip and held it high. "Is anyone celebrating eleven months?" The crowd erupted as a young woman, Erica, made her way to the front of the room. I handed her the chip and said, "Congratulations," then we hugged. "Erica!" I shouted as she returned to her seat, receiving congratulations along the way.

I proceeded month by month, congratulating and hugging members as they came and went, until we finished with the one-month anniversaries.

"Okay, now for the most important person in the room . . ." I reached for a white twenty-four-hour chip and held it high. "Anyone new or coming back?" I glanced at the young man I'd greeted before the meeting started. "No shame."

"No shame," the voices throughout the room responded in agreement.

The man kept his head lowered and didn't move. But another man, who was standing in the back of the room, raised his hand and came forward. Two other figures followed behind him.

Wearing jeans and a blue blazer, the first of them, a man with gray hair, took the white chip from me with a grin. I reached out and hugged him awkwardly, then asked him his name.

"Bill," he whispered. "This is my first meeting."

"This is Bill, everybody."

"Welcome, Bill," the group shouted in unison with cheers and smiles.

The next person stepped forward as I reached for another white chip. Unshaven and unkempt, the portly man reached in for a hug and breathed his name into my ear.

"I know your name, Earl," I said teasingly. Earl was a chronic relapser who was homeless but always welcome. He took the white chip and raised it triumphantly.

"Earl!" responded the crowd.

When Earl stepped away, I reached for another white chip. Light chatter and whispers flowed throughout the room as a woman wearing a baseball cap pulled down over her eyes hesitantly stepped forward. When I looked up, I was speechless.

Jill Woburn stood in front of me with her hand out and her face blank. "Coming back," she said in a monotone. I handed her the chip, then leaned forward and hugged her. Her arms stayed limp at her side, but she didn't shy away. With black circles around her eyes and red rashes on her cheeks, she looked half a heartbeat from death's door.

"Jill, everybody." I plucked at her sleeve as she turned to leave, and she stopped. It was precisely 10:00 a.m.

The crowd repeated Jill's name, and I closed the meeting with the Lord's Prayer.

Turning to face Jill, I asked her how she was while other members milled about, waiting to say hello.

"I'm here," she replied, forcing smiles at the faces around us.

"I'm glad. Can we talk? Want to get a cup of coffee?"

"Um . . . I don't think—"

"Jill, I'm so sorry," I blurted. "For Frankie. For never telling you about Harry—"

"It's okay, Daniel," she interrupted. "It's okay." She spoke with a sincerity I'd rarely heard from her, and I exhaled with relief. "I mean . . . that doesn't mean you're not on my resentment list," she remarked in a sharp voice. She reached inside her bag and pulled out a small loose-leaf notebook. "You're number one, actually." She opened the notebook, and I glanced at the black ink blanketing the pages as they turned. "Ten pages so far." Her glare weakened, then turned to a feeble smile. "It's good to see you, Daniel."

"It's nice to see *you*, Jill." I meant it. I was determined to play my part in her recovery. Because I had finally understood what it meant to surrender.

Surrender, I now knew, isn't about giving up at all. It's about swimming with the current, instead of against it. It's about fitting myself into the world *as it is*, rather than fitting the world into me, as I wanted it to be. To surrender is to stop fighting. To give up control. That's what the phrase "Thy will, not mine, be done" means to me. And in this surrender, one day at a time, I had found victory—a victory I could hang onto only so long as I understood that in order to keep it, I had to give it away.

And I was determined to keep it.

ABOUT THE AUTHOR

Michael Eon earned a BA in psychology from the University of Michigan and an MA in international affairs from Columbia University. A former board member of the Audio Publishers Association and a former producer of major motion pictures and television productions, Michael worked in the publishing and entertainment industries for more than twenty years. Michael discovered the core of this story through the cathartic processing of autobiographical memories, following its evolution into this novel of redemption and recovery. *These Things Happen* is his first novel. Originally from the New York area, he currently lives in New Hampshire with his family.

DANIEL ZIMMER WILL DO ALMOST ANYTHING TO END HIS PAIN—EXCEPT FOR THE ONE THING THAT MIGHT WORK.

Growing up in 1970s Brooklyn under the shadow of his tyrannical father and against the backdrop of the Son of Sam murders, the Karen Ann Quinlan tragedy, and the New York Yankees' back-to-back championship seasons, Daniel Zimmer struggles to find a sense of safety and belonging. Daniel and his brother Max find moments of solace in the rebellious rhythms of early punk and metal bands like the Ramones and Judas Priest. But when faced with an unexpected family tragedy—for which he feels responsible—Daniel discovers the magical escape that alcohol can provide, numbing his pain and guilt.

Carrying the trauma of his youth into adulthood, Daniel falls deeper into alcoholism as he fights to face life on life's terms. Then, just as he finally begins to embrace sobriety, Max attempts suicide and Daniel's ex-fiancée makes an unexpected reappearance. Forced to face his demons head-on, Daniel struggles to take things one day at a time.

Flashing through Daniel's life, past and present, this nostalgic ode to Brooklyn is an unflinching account of the inevitable ups and downs of recovery and coming of age. Ultimately, it is a story of the ravages of generational abuse and the power of recognizing addiction and opening the door to the possibilities of redemption.

U.S. $17.95

ISBN 978-1-959411-16-1

51795>

9 781959 411161

GFB **GIRL FRIDAY BOOKS**

www.girlfridaybooks.com